GW00507772

Spider's First Catch

Robin Kempe

Best wishes
for Maria

Robin Kempe
x

Oakenshield Publishing

Published in the United Kingdom in 2017 by
Oakenshield Publishing

Oakenshield Publishing
47 Brook Street
Polegate
E Sussex
BN26 6BH

www.robinkempe.uk
e-mail: oakenshieldpublishing@gmail.com

ISBN 978-1-9997794-0-5

ACKNOWLEDGEMENTS

The author wishes to thank the following people without whose help and encouragement this book would not have been possible.

jay Dixon, Terry Hall, Kym Jarvis, Sophie McGarel

PROLOGUE

From his bed in the emergency ward Jon Webb's father looked up at his only son and said 'Look at me, Jon, nothing to look forward to now, but don't do what I've done and don't look back. Enjoy the present. Whatever you do, lad, don't wish your life away. Plan exciting or ordinary things, but don't rush time, it goes too quickly by itself. I couldn't wait till the holidays, or that new car, to where nothing else mattered.

I never had much money as you know, but I never appreciated the things that I had. I didn't realise how much your mother mattered to me, but then she died and my life fell apart. So if you get that new job, well done, but if you don't, so what? I know your divorce is a disappointment to you, but such things happen, and you'll get by. Count your blessings, as they say, come and see me tomorrow and we'll talk some more.'

CHAPTER ONE

On the last working day of the year Jon Webb's mobile phone rang to bring news that would change his life.

His divorce was final, so he hadn't spent Christmas with his ghastly in-laws. He and his ex-wife had sold their house, and his share of the net cash was in his bank. He gladly let her take their car and household effects, which had no sentimental value for him, leaving him content with just his personal possessions.

He was well aware of the effect upon him of his father's death, and his memorable advice at their final meeting. He kept repeating to himself that if only he'd seen his father more often, or learnt to understand him, what good friends they could have become, but taking his father's advice, he put aside his regrets for a disappointing past and plunged with determination into a new life.

Known to his friends from school as 'Spider', and full of confidence that he'd get another job, he'd resigned from a company which he detested, and taken stock of himself. He was ambitious, aged mid-thirties, not bad looking, short brown hair, brown eyes, average height, slim, reliable, conscientious, an experienced engineer looking for a new challenge. He now had enough money to buy a car and to pay for several years' rent for his flat in Eastbourne owned by landlords he liked. He'd applied for a job in a company named TLC Ltd making mining machinery, and had been interviewed by Henry Catchmore the CEO. All in all, he was pleased with himself, and hoped that his father would have agreed.

He answered his phone with his usual greeting, 'Hello, Jon Webb speaking.'

'Good morning, Mr Webb, this is Alice MacInnes, Mr Catchmore's secretary. He's instructed me to tell you that the company would like to offer you the position of Chief Designer, to start as soon as you're able. I'll email the formal offer now, to be followed by hard copy. He wanted you to have this news today, rather than having to wait over the holiday. We hope that you'll take the offer, and your acceptance by email will suffice until after the New Year festivities.'

Throughout the Christmas holiday Jon had been unsettled by the possibility that he wouldn't get this challenging job, so with this news he had difficulty in restraining his pleasure.

'Thank you, Mrs MacInnes, that's good news, but just one question if I may. At my interviews there was no mention of "Chief Designer" just "Designer", so what has changed, please?'

'During your first visit here you asked if TLC could make factory conveyors other than our heavy conveyor belts for moving stone and so on. There's now a policy decision to diversify and your job will also be to research possibilities. Mr Catchmore will explain later.'

'Thank you, I've no more questions, and look forward to meeting you again. I wish you and the company success in the New Year. Goodbye.'

Jon was delighted, and wanted to tell someone. His friends would be pleased, but who else would care? Of course, if he had a partner, no doubt she'd be interested, but he hadn't, and that was that. For a moment he felt a stab of loneliness, vaguely missing even Jane, his ex-wife, but he shook his head. Not likely! In all the adventures that his father had told him to look for, he'd surely somewhere come across a woman who'd become his partner, but there was no rush. He decided to tell the landlords of his flat, Sybil and Eric Abbott, who had no children, and seemed to regard him as the son they'd never had. Easily a generation older than Jon they weren't old-fashioned, and despite Eric's disability they had a spirited outlook on life. Jon phoned them.

'Hello, Sybil, it's Jon here, I have some good news. May I pop up for a while?'

'Sure, if it's that good, we'll open a bottle.'

The Abbotts had bought a large semi-detached Victorian house in Eastbourne already converted into two flats. For some reason they preferred to live in the upstairs flat, which to Jon was curious as the quality of their clothes, furniture and the stairlift indicated that they weren't short of money. Surely they could buy a house for their sole use? But that was no business of his. Jon's ground-floor flat shared the front door to the house and its small entrance lobby at the foot of the stairs to the Abbotts' flat.

A ground-floor passage alongside the staircase was divided by a door, making Jon's flat self-contained. He had a galley kitchen, a bathroom, a bedroom big enough for his bed and clothes storage, and a large front room he used as lounge and office. He had rented it for six months until after the expected date of his divorce, intending then to decide where to live or what to buy. From force of habit he locked his flat, climbed the stairs and found the Abbotts' door open. He simply knocked and went in.

'Well now,' greeted Sybil with her customary warmth, 'come in, and tell us all. Eric's gone to get the sherry.'

Dutiful as ever, Eric trundled into their living room in his wheelchair. 'Hi, Jon, I must say that this bracket you've made for my chair works a treat. A bottle of sherry or spirits fits in well, but Sybil's threatening to get a milometer fitted so she can check my visits to the drinks cupboard!'

Good moods prevailed when these three were together. They'd hit it off within weeks of Jon moving in, and had a convivial relationship in which they helped each other by taking in parcels, lending each other items forgotten on shopping lists and so on. Jon planned to renew his tenancy for a further year.

'Come on now, Jon,' Eric encouraged as he opened the sherry bottle and poured three glasses, 'don't leave us in suspense.'

'Well, it's quite simple really. I've been offered that job with TLC that I told you about, but I seem to have been promoted before I start. Instead of just Designer, I'll now be Chief Designer.'

With one voice the Abbotts said, 'Well done Jon! When do you start?' But Sybil demanded, very much tongue-in-cheek, 'Promoted, eh? Will you get more pay so we can increase your rent?'

'Regrettably, I don't think so, Sybil,' Jon retorted, trying to look smug. Raising his glass he said, 'But here's to your good health, and thanks for your interest.'

Eric was curious. 'Tell me about this firm, Jon. We've lived in and around Eastbourne for years, but I'd never heard of TLC before, and it doesn't have a web site.'

'Well, it's an old company originally started in the Midlands by a man named Thomas Leonard Catchmore, hence the initials TLC, to make conveyor belts for quarries and mines. It flourished, but in his will Catchmore made the classic mistake of leaving his shares equally to his two sons. Upon his death, the elder wanted to run the business, but the younger wanted to sell up and enjoy the money. While they argued, the business slowly went downhill, and virtually went bust.'

'Henry Catchmore, the present CEO, is the grandson of Thomas, and bought the wreckage of the company from the administrator for one pound sterling, but he had to take over its liabilities. He sold the firm's freehold site for development to help pay off its debts, and moved it to Eastbourne where he preferred to live. The assets were few, but he just didn't want the family business to vanish ignominiously, which was purely sentimental, and he underestimated the liabilities and suffered pressure from the bank. I'm sure that he still does.

I first met him months ago at an engineering seminar when we'd both skipped a boring lecture on employment law, and escaped to the hotel lounge along with several other delegates. He didn't "dress to impress" as he said, just a tweed jacket, check shirt, and corduroy trousers. He looked the image of someone's favourite uncle, and I liked him on sight. I asked if I could join him at his small table for company, and was welcomed. We introduced ourselves and shook hands. 'I asked if employment law bored him. "Bloody hell, yes! I've got advisers for that. What about you?" he asked.

'I'm here to learn about Graphene, but the speaker's ill, so the lawyer's a sub. If I wasn't booked in for two days, I'd have left.'

'It was soon "Henry" and "Jon" as you'd expect. His firm interested me for disparate reasons – its small size, its daft trading name suggesting "tender loving care" which isn't synonymous with tough engineering, and a curious company structure top heavy with directors. I didn't pursue my curiosity, and was happier for him to quiz me about me and my job. I let it slip that I didn't like the firm I worked for because it was part of a huge conglomerate, where staff felt like nonentities, but he didn't take the bait and offer me a job.

'However, I was curious about Henry Catchmore the man. We chatted for hours with him doing most of the talking, and I sensed that something was troubling him about his company. He gave nothing away, but he openly discussed difficulties with me which I was certain he wouldn't have shared with his subordinates. I realised that men in his position could be lonely without anyone at the same hierarchical level to bounce ideas off, so I felt mildly privileged to be his trusted listener, and he actually said that "it was good to have someone new to talk to". At one point I asked him point blank if because of the economic circumstances of the time he had a cash flow problem, and to my astonishment he agreed quite openly. I liked him, and given the chance I would be glad to work for him, but as I just said, that wasn't discussed. We swapped business cards, hoping to meet again, but when the seminar eventually broke up we went our separate ways, and after a while I forgot about the meeting. After some months I saw their ad in the local paper for a designer, so remembering Catchmore, I applied.'

'So what's left of the business now, Jon?' Eric interrupted.

'Virtually all manufacturing is sub-contracted now, and they work from old designs that came with it when Henry took over. They've been relying on repeat orders from existing customers, and I was astounded when Catchmore divulged that to me at our first meeting. There is on-going profit from repairs and spare parts sales, but they definitely need new business.'

'Did he remember you when you went for your interview?'

'When his secretary, Mrs MacInnes, ushered me into his office he looked at me quizzically, asked me to sit, and then made us coffee from a small machine. For the next couple of minutes he simply sat back in his chair, and just looked at me, saying nothing, sipping his coffee. It was the most weird beginning to any interview and I felt like leaving, but he suddenly relaxed and smiled. It was a transformation, and obvious that a momentous decision had been made. He said, "Mr Webb, or I will call you Jon? Okay? Good. I remember you now, when we met at that awful seminar. I see from your CV that you are now a free agent, with no family ties, and able to start work here tomorrow, so to speak, if I asked. Is that so?" and I said, "Yes, Mr Catchmore" instead of Henry. He then said, "As a matter of principle and courtesy to the other directors I need to consult them before proceeding, and although you are being seriously considered for the post I must follow that procedure. We'll write to you shortly, and in the meantime I thank you for your interest in the company."'

'They must have a factory of some sort with a works manager?'

'Yes, an agreeable man named Roger Martin who showed me round the factory before my interview. He has a staff of three, I think, but he can call in temps as required. He's responsible for organising the subcontractors, supervising sub-assemblies, packing and shipment of machines, and also organises installations of conveyors in quarries, and so on. Quite an interesting job, I should think. I liked him, and think we'll get on okay, but I sensed that he's worried about the future because the works wasn't very busy.'

'But, Jon, with respect, it could be months before one of your designs could turn into cash.'

'Exactly. The situation is so fragmented that I'm keen to get involved with improvements although I've no obligation to the company structure. There are five directors, three being non-exec, and the structure's modest, but as I said earlier, top heavy. Accounting, including payroll and billing, is all out-sourced. Day-to-day operations are managed by Catchmore, his wife who's also a director, the secretary Alice MacInnes and the works manager. One of the non-execs is O'Flynn who's the Finance Director, whom I haven't met. Roger Martin respects the other directors, but was evasive when I asked about O'Flynn, and seemed to want to warn me about something.'

'Jon, I can't help thinking that this company is very fragile, and you couldn't have taken the risk to join if you had family commitments, could you?'

'Good Lord, no! The thing is, Eric, I'm curious about TLC's revenue and how it pays for five directors' dividends. Talking of risk, will you two please relax about my ability to keep paying the rent, because my ex and I have sold our house and the money's banked. Of course, a rent reduction is always welcome!'

At this point, Jon sensed that Eric and Sybil were unsettled, as glances between them confirmed. Eric came straight out with what was on their minds.

'Jon,' he began, 'if you'll excuse me being blunt, your tenancy expires on the last day of December, which is today, and we'd like to know, or indeed need to know, if you are now settled in your work hereabouts and wish to renew it.'

Jon couldn't be more adamant. 'Yes, I do indeed, and for twelve months, although I think that I'd like to be here for longer than that. Is there a problem?'

Eric still looked apprehensive. 'Jon, when we bought this house we decided to live in the upstairs flat because there's a good view over the town, and we'd be away from the traffic noise, or most of it. However, my condition has deteriorated and despite the stairlift it's now a chore to leave the house, and what I'm getting at is, before you renew, would you consider swapping flats?'

Jon was surprised, although the logic was obvious. Instinctively he glanced around the room. 'No, I've no problem with that at all, Eric. But isn't my flat smaller than this?'

It was now Sybil's turn to get involved. 'To be candid, Jon, we've been thinking about this change for weeks now, but it's never been the right time to raise the question with you. We'd no idea if you wanted to stay here, although we enjoy your company and hoped you wouldn't leave. You're right about the difference in the size of the flats and we concluded that we could have a conservatory type of extension to give us the size we'd need, and some modern designs offer comfort as good as any living rooms. French windows would give Eric much easier access to his buggy in the shelter that you've made for it. You know that the ground floor partitioning is only stud work and plasterboard which could be rearranged to give more suitable accommodation for us, and without going into too many details we've been looking forward to the change. Or the possibility of it.'

Jon's next question settled the matter. 'Leaving aside any changes in my rent and exactly how we'd go about the physical changeover, when do you want to make the change?'

Eric answered immediately. 'How about tomorrow, so to speak? We've had permission for the conservatory extension, and a price for its construction. There's no "change of use" permission needed, and the builder's pencilled in next week to start work. Obviously he'll need access to your flat eventually, but not in the first few weeks. Then smiling, he said. 'I have another question, Jon. Would you like to share another celebratory sherry with us?'

'Yes, please, and I have a question too. Would you please not sell the stairlift but leave it there so that I can invite you up to my flat to return your hospitality?'

Before that question could be answered, Jon's mobile squeaked, and from the caller display, he said, 'It's my new firm, will you excuse me if I take the call?'

'Go ahead.'

'Hello, Jon Webb here.'

'Oh, Mr Webb, it's Alice MacInnes again. The ds always have an informal drinks get-together with senior staff and others such as our accountants or lawyers at this time of year and Mr Catchmore invites you to come over to join them. Could you be at the offices in about half an hour?'

'Yes, thank you, I'll be there. What's the dress code, please?'

'Oh, good heavens, come as you are, there's no ceremony today, and Roger Martin will probably be in his factory overalls.'

'Fine, thanks Mrs MacInnes, I'll see you soon,' Jon said and ended the call.

To the Abbotts, he said, 'Well now, I'm invited to the directors' New Year's Eve drinks party, to be there in thirty minutes. Will you please excuse me, and can we discuss our plans again later?'

'Of course, Jon,' Sybil reassured him, 'but as you haven't a car now would you like a lift? Yes? Be at the front door in ten minutes then.'

***

As they arrived at the TLC works in the outskirts of Eastbourne and she saw the

12

buildings, Sybil asked, 'Are you sure about joining this firm, Jon? It looks rather run down, and if the business is short of money, why are the directors having drinks when they should be working?'

'I can't answer that, but the job's a gamble I'm prepared to take. Thanks very much for the lift, Sybil.'

TLC's factory and office building were in an industrial estate which, judging by the boring appearance of all the identical buildings, was built in the 1950s when building design was stagnant. The main front door led to the original reception area, now used only to receive VIPs by appointment, and not by staff who entered by another door off the car park to the side of the building, as Jon had done when coming for his interviews.

He used that door and the staircase leading up to the first-floor offices. Voices could be heard coming from the other end of the corridor serving several offices on that level. The far end office was Henry Catchmore's, doubling up as the Board room, which had internal windows overlooking the workshops below. As he walked along, a lady whom he hadn't met emerged from an office, seeing Jon as she did.

'Oh, hello, are you Jonathan Webb? I'm Millicent Catchmore.'

'Yes, good morning, Mrs Catchmore. Thank you for this invitation.'

'You're welcome. Come and meet the others.' She ushered Jon into Henry Catchmore's large office where his desk, which doubled as a Board-room table, had been moved to one side to carry a modest array of wine and sherry. Enough to lubricate speech, thought Jon, but not unseemly so. A small group of men stood around chatting.

'Henry,' she addressed her husband in a commanding manner, 'Jonathan Webb is here, are you going to introduce him?'

'Of course! Hello, Jon,' Henry Catchmore greeted him. 'This is Alan Bryant, and this is David Phillips who are non-executive directors. Gentlemen, Jonathan is to join us as Chief Designer, as you know, but I'll leave you to get to know each other because Frank O'Flynn's just arrived.'

Jon knew nothing about these men and their experience relevant to TLC, but they appeared to be genuine in their welcome as they shook hands. Bryant said 'Hello, Jon, what have you been doing until now?'

'I was chief draughtsman for a subsidiary of a conglomerate. It made indoor conveyors for a variety of industries, and most of my work concerned bespoke designs. I enjoyed solving the problems of one-off products, but not working for a large organisation.'

'What was wrong with it?'

'We were never sure who really owned the company unless we read the financial news because its ownership was traded too much within the group. I seemed to spend more time trying to keep up morale among my staff than in designing, therefore from what I learnt about TLC, and its size, I was naturally attracted to it.'

David Phillips said, 'I learnt this morning from Alice MacInnes that you'd accepted the offer to join us. Welcome to the company. Henry consulted us about your position and we'll be interested to hear your ideas.'

'Thank you, Mr Phillips. It's a good time to begin a new job, and I look forward to working with you all.' Having just said that, he wasn't so sure that he meant it, for in the doorway to his office Henry Catchmore was in a heated exchange with an aggressive newcomer who once or twice stabbed a finger in Jon's direction. Catchmore actively pushed the man across the corridor into another office and shut the door behind them.

The sound of raised voices went on for several minutes until Catchmore opened the door again, and called out, 'David and Alan, would you join us please?' then quickly shut the door until the others pushed it open to join him and the other man. Bryant and Phillips had spun round to watch the new man's arrival, ignoring Jon, who noticed that Mrs Catchmore was looking fussed and apprehensive.

He had turned away from the sight of this contretemps and purported not to notice it by studying various photos of TLC machines pinned to the walls. They featured conveyor belts moving all manner of materials like rocks, ores and coal, and even enormous quantities of sugar beet.

After five or so minutes the door of the office opposite crashed open, and the stranger glared again at Jon before striding away muttering under his breath. It was obvious that this man O'Flynn objected to Jon's employment, and also didn't mix socially with his fellow directors, and Jon wondered how this firm could possibly function and stay in business. Perhaps O'Flynn didn't care if it failed, but if so why didn't the other directors vote him off the Board?

Bryant, Phillips and Catchmore emerged looking angry and embarrassed, but relieved when Roger Martin came to join them in the gathering. 'Hello, gentlemen, and it's good to see you again, Jon. I'm pleased that you're joining us. What was going on just now? I heard an argument as I came up the stairs.'

An awkward silence was broken by Mrs Catchmore. 'Hello, Roger, is all well in the works?'

'Yes, fine thanks Mrs C, the Guv gave everyone the rest of the day off as he didn't think it fair on them to stay at work when we were up here. We're quiet at present and up to date with our annual maintenance. They've all left, and asked me to wish you all a Happy New Year.'

Jon enquired, 'Excuse me, Roger, but who is "the Guv"?'

'Sorry, Jon, it's Henry Catchmore's popular nickname. We lesser mortals all use it. Alice MacInnes never does, perhaps thinking it's presumptuous, or too familiar. Without preamble, another voice spoke on entering the room. 'I heard that, Mr Roger Martin, I trust that you don't find my manners too old-fashioned?' It was Alice MacInnes, a middle-aged lady wearing slightly dated clothes on an ample body but a beaming smile. She joined the group, and said to Jon, 'I'm pleased to meet you again, Jon, and don't forget your email to accept your position. Welcome aboard, as they say.'

'Hello, Mrs MacInnes, thanks for your reminder, but it seems that I've come at an eventful time. I'll quite understand if you'd prefer me, as a newcomer, to leave you to resolve what appeared to be a difficulty just now.'

'Oh, don't worry about that,' she reassured him, 'that was Mr O'Flynn who disagrees with alcohol on company premises. He's reluctant to accept a tradition which the founder started and whose principles Mr Catchmore follows in everything.' Giving nothing away, Jon didn't believe a word of that excuse.

'Shall I get you a glass of something?' he offered, seeing the drinks table behind Phillips and Bryant, who were now in a huddle apparently talking about the recent argument.

'Yes, thank you that would be nice. Dry sherry, please.'

Jon's offer to leave concerned more about the Guv's argument than courtesy to a lady. Eavesdropping carefully on the other directors' conversation as he poured the sherry, he heard slanderous words muttered about Mr O'Flynn that should not have been heard by a new employee. Or any employee. 'Your sherry, Mrs MacInnes.' As he offered it, he became aware that the room had gone quiet and the others were gazing thoughtfully at him, no doubt wondering what he'd heard.

He felt compelled to say something, so to camouflage what he had actually heard clearly he said, 'Ladies and gentlemen, it seems that perhaps Mr O'Flynn objects to a new employee sharing in your tradition of drinks together at this time of year, and if so I'm quite prepared to withdraw now if you wish.' He had no intention of leaving this gathering until he found out the real reason for O'Flynn's outburst, but he picked up his coat from the back of a chair as a sign that he might leave, until Henry Catchmore said, 'No, Jon, stay with us, it'd be better if you did.'

The insistence that he should stay confirmed Jon's assessment of Henry Catchmore. He appeared to be a quiet man who cared for his employees, wishing to be liked by all, but lacking the get-up-and-go determination of an entrepreneur. Signs of a 'laissez faire' approach were abundant. Jon was reminded of his crude report to Eric Abbot that the company needed a kick up its backside.

CHAPTER TWO

Jon hung his coat over a chair again, took a sip of his sherry, and waited politely, all the while remembering elements of his long first meeting with Catchmore several months ago.

'Right, everybody,' Henry Catchmore began anxiously, 'I need to explain Mr O'Flynn's approach, and as we're all here, we'll have an informal meeting.'

He resumed, 'Jon, events have moved quickly recently, partly because you asked if we could diversify into other markets, which prompted us to give the UK market more attention because perhaps we've been too complacent. Also, having sold a machine a few years ago to a semi third-world country in Africa called Lngusha – if you can pronounce or spell it – we thought to look again at that market but Mr O'Flynn predicts a world mineral price slump, just as the price of oil is collapsing. He thinks that an export market for TLC machines is not worth pursuing, but I disagree with him. That disagreement was obvious in our heated exchange just now. So whether we agree with Mr O'Flynn or not, Jon, in the last weeks we have been considering every aspect of the business. We appreciate that you have been pitchforked into this discussion now, but after the long discussions when we first met and at your interview I'd value your reaction to what I've said. You may speak quite freely.'

While Catchmore had been talking, Jon was thinking that the Board must have run out of ideas if they had to rely on a totally new employee for stimulus. He had never heard of a CEO of any sized company speaking with such candour, and Catchmore's admission that "perhaps we've been too complacent" was a serious revelation. Was that a sign of weakness? Perhaps these people were going to rely upon Jon more than they would admit. If, and it was a big 'if', he could make the difference that they needed, his job could become very interesting indeed.

Well, he asked for my reaction even if he won't like it. 'You asked for my spontaneous reaction, Mr Catchmore, and please don't take offence, but why haven't you given the UK market more attention? Also, has anyone from TLC kept in touch with past customers on a regular basis, including the one in Africa?'

Catchmore was quite candid. 'Fair questions, Jon, and the reason is a manpower shortage. We haven't had the people to spare, and to date our orders have come from recommendations or arisen from magazine features, or from existing customers.'

To Jon, TLC's problems were obvious, but not wanting to seem precocious he asked, 'May I perhaps make some suggestions?'

'Of course,' Henry Catchmore quickly agreed, confirming their paucity of ideas.

'Thank you, ladies and gentlemen. You engaged me to devise new and diversified designs, but from what I've learnt today that isn't a priority because a new design would need months through development to convert to revenue. My first suggestion is to put new designs on hold until a more appropriate time.'

That idea caused raised eyebrows and some murmuring among the directors, who were obviously wondering why Jon had been employed at all. Was he going to do himself out of a job?

Alan Bryant stepped in immediately 'What do you call "a more appropriate time"?'

'I was coming to that, Mr Bryant. If nobody has followed up previous contacts with existing customers, for all we know some of them may be about to order new machinery, if not from us, from someone else. My first suggestion is to write to them all in the UK, with a pleasant and courteous letter from me as the Chief Designer enquiring how their machine or machines are working, and asking if they have ideas which we could incorporate into new designs.'

Another challenge came from Bryant. 'Jon, why do you want new ideas if you're not going to use them?'

'Mr Bryant, with respect, if the customers haven't heard from TLC for some time, maybe years, they may have forgotten who made their machines, or worse still are miffed with TLC for seeming to have forgotten them. We neither need nor want their ideas at present, but they should believe that we take an interest in them. My second suggestion is to find out what's happened to the machine in Africa by sending a letter similar to the others. With respect to Mr O'Flynn there is still a market in Africa for manufacturers of TLC's size, although I agree with his prediction about a slump, or at least a slowing down in the market. Before writing to any of the customers I'd research all that we can discover about them from published information. That will tell us who's still in business, who's in trouble and who's growing and in which markets. If you agree with these suggestions, I could start work on them immediately.'

He realised that everyone was gazing thoughtfully at him, with the exception of Roger Martin who stood modestly and unobserved in the background, raising his refilled glass in a symbolic toast to Jon, offering a 'thumbs up' and a huge grin. Well done mate, sock it to them! How the hell, mused Jon, am I supposed to look serious with Roger behaving like this? A silence descended on the group for a short while, then it was Phillips who spoke first. He was another man whom Jon liked at face value. Short in height, stocky, short bristly grey hair, smartly dressed, with a vice-like handshake. About sixty years old, similar to the Guv.

'I propose that we accept all of Jon Webb's suggestions. We should postpone new developments and exploit our existing market. He'll need help with admin, so perhaps Alice could help with that. The cost of the scheme would only be paperwork, postage and phone calls, but if Jon needs to make visits then he should be authorised to do so, but only in the UK.'

Phillips had really taken the lead away from Catchmore, who, judging by his smile, had no objections, but Jon thought he's acting as a follower, not the leader that he should be, and was disappointed with him.

'Well, do we all agree with David in principle?' Catchmore asked.

There were nods and smiles all round, and Catchmore continued, 'Okay, Jon, there you have it. Talk to Alice now about the help you need, and start work as soon as we return from the bank holiday. Make notes as you go along, and if you need to travel please tell me but keep receipts of all expenses. Frequent reports would help.'

A pleasant ambience pervaded as the group resumed their various conversations. Roger Martin sidled up to Jon and reported, 'That's got to be the quickest decision I've ever seen in this firm, Jon, and I hope they don't have second thoughts. Regardless of that, you've already made a huge impact here. Well done! But let's talk quietly in the corner there.' They moved away.

'Thanks, Roger, but it struck me as Mr Catchmore was talking that I had nothing to lose. The lack of contact with customers is incredible, and I expect some sarcastic replies to my letters, but as I said, someone may be ordering something soon and we must know which customer. Who was it who used to deal with customers?'

'Mostly it was the Guv, or I got involved with any problems, but we've never had anyone charged with actually looking for business.'

'Bloody hell, Roger, think of the lost opportunities that there may've been. But just suppose for a moment more business came in, could you increase production?'

'Easily. The subcontractors have spare capacity, and there are others always looking for work. Mrs MacInnes had been listening, and joined them. 'When will you be back to work, Roger?'

'Tomorrow's a bank holiday, and the Guv's given everyone Friday off, but I could be here if needed.'

Then, 'Jon,' she asked, 'what about you? When are you prepared to start on your proposals?'

'I'm happy to come in on Friday. There's nothing urgent at home and I'd be thinking all the time about what I could do here, so I might as well be here and get on with it. But I'd need a key to get in.'

'Mmm,' mused Mrs MacInnes. 'I'm also happy to be here. Suppose we three work for just the morning, then go out for a pub lunch afterwards? By the end of the morning we could have all the letters sent. What do you two say?' Jon and Roger nodded happily as she took charge of the plan and said with authority, 'Right, we'll start at eight thirty. Roger and I will ferret out past customer records while Jon drafts the letter, which we'll all review. We'll then decide who gets the letter, and I'll type their addresses and fax them off. Don't worry about a key, Jon, I'll be here first.'

Jon's enthusiasm was unstoppable. 'Mrs MacInnes, or may I call you Alice? Yes? Good. Look I'm not doing anything tomorrow, but if you could give me the names of, say, the last ten customers now, I could do a lot of Internet research at home ready for Friday. I'd be looking at general information, at the very least whether they are still in business!'

'My, you are keen Jon!' she said. 'I can give you their company names, contacts, and addresses in ten minutes, but such other details as what they bought will have to wait until Friday. We'll take a chance that the contact names aren't out of date. Come with me to my office, I'll dig out the files, and you can copy the basic stuff that you need.'

Before leaving the room with Alice MacInnes, Jon asked the Guv, 'Will you please excuse us for a short while? I have time to spare at home, so Alice is giving me the names of the last ten customers so that I can do some research to save us time on Friday.'

'What's happening on Friday?'

'The three of us are coming here to get the mail shot faxed off.'

'Good Lord, it's going to be hard to keep up with you, Mr Webb if you carry on like this!'

Gradually the meeting broke up, with exchanges of New Year wishes, and the temporary reappearance of a smiling Alice MacInnes, with Jon carrying a bundle of papers. He phoned Sybil for a lift home, which Roger overheard and interrupted by offering to take Jon back to his flat. Alice MacInnes confirmed their plans to Henry Catchmore, resulting to her evident astonishment in receiving a kiss on her cheek, and a 'Well done, Alice!' For his part Jon was dumbfounded by the excitement he'd caused by simple suggestions, and was torn between optimism for the future, and puzzlement about why the firm hadn't acted before. It was all very amateurish.

As they climbed into Roger's car, he asked Jon, 'I've just realised that I don't know where you live. Where d'you want to go?'

'Central Eastbourne please, Roger, and what do you think of that meeting?'

'It was amazing. You don't know them at all well, yet you came charging out with all those ideas with such confidence that I reckon they didn't want to challenge you. They've probably all gone home wondering what the hell happened, and who is this Jon Webb, and where did he come from? I think it's brilliant, Jon, but what do you say?'

'I can't understand how TLC is still in business. For example, what are you working on in the factory?'

'It's an extension of a customer's existing conveyor belt, the sort of modification which we've done before. If someone's digging away in a quarry removing rocks to shift to a crusher, eventually the crusher becomes further away from the work face and it's sometimes better to extend the conveyor rather than buy trucks to do the moving. There's another one to follow next month.'

'Is there enough money in such orders to support the firm?'

'Yes-ish, obviously depending upon the size of the order, but don't forget that we have some revenue from spare part sales, and from repairs when the customer has no suitable staff.'

'Thanks, but changing the subject, I don't entirely accept Mr Catchmore's explanation of Mr O'Flynn's outburst. Has that happened before?'

'You bet! And it'll happen again, Jon, so don't get involved with the man, he's poison! He argues against any novel ideas, and I don't know why. He seems to have some hold on the Guv, otherwise surely he and the others would have voted him off the Board by now. Sorry to give you bad news, but as I said, I really don't get involved. Here we are. This is a good area of Eastbourne, Jon, the houses look pleasantly old-fashioned and well established. A good place to live.'

'Yes, thanks, Roger, and I'll see you on Friday. I'll ask my landlady to bring me in if the buses aren't back to their normal routine.'

CHAPTER THREE

The wine had flowed freely at their party as Spider and his friends celebrated the New Year and his new job. With the inevitable hangover behind him he launched into his work with vigour, realising that it was years since he'd last worked with enthusiasm on a public holiday. By the end of the Thursday he'd completed his customer research and learnt more about TLC itself from the files. Mrs MacInnes' trio worked well as a team the next day, and the celebratory ploughman's lunch was a success, to be repeated when justified.

During the weekend Jon continued his review of the TLC customers' details. On average, TLC sold just two of their heavy machines each year, but according to Roger it had the capacity to supply more. By Jon's reckoning, TLC was heading towards a financial crisis, because sales revenue against his estimate of overheads simply didn't stack up. Maybe O'Flynn was frustrated, but then thinking about Roger's remarks before the weekend, did O'Flynn want TLC to progress, or didn't he care if it didn't? If so, why?

He also spent some time with the Abbotts that weekend preoccupied with working out the logistics of their moves, and adjustments to the financial arrangements which were simplified in the end by no changes being made to Jon's rent. Sybil, however, suggested that Jon should make a token gesture in the form of supplying some bubbly because he'd allegedly drunk so much of their sherry.

Back at work on the Monday, Alice brought Jon his mail and he found that some replies to his enquiries had come back very quickly, which surprised him in view of the deluge of unwanted faxes and emails suffered by businesses. Perhaps those who'd replied preferred to be at work instead of at home with family relatives lingering since Christmas, or hopefully these prompt responses were signs of TLC's good PR.

He took a phone call from one of them. 'Good morning, Mr Webb. My name is Tindall, and I'm CEO here at Oxonstone Ltd. It's odd that you should write just as we're thinking of expanding the quarry because our market for reconstituted stone is growing. Could you come to see us to discuss it?'

Taken by surprise, Jon stuttered, 'Um, er, certainly, when would you prefer?'

'Let's see, could you manage tomorrow, say, ten thirty? By the way use your satnav because we're a bit out in the sticks. Tomorrow isn't vitally necessary, but it's quiet now until we get back into full production and the machines start pounding away, so I'd appreciate tomorrow.'

'Yes that's fine, I look forward to meeting you then. Goodbye'. Then after the customer had hung up he remembered to his horror that he didn't have transport. Oh, bloody hell! He couldn't borrow the car back from Jane because she was away. Did TLC have a pool car somewhere? Or the van he'd seen in the factory car park? He went down to the factory floor to Roger Martin, who with a sardonic grin asked, 'Hello, hello, what brings the Chief Designer down to our level?'

'Actually, Roger, I've just given myself a problem and you might be able to help.'

'You want a favour, eh?'

'Not exactly. I need wheels for tomorrow. I arranged to go up to Oxfordshire to visit a customer quite forgetting that my ex-wife now has our car, and I can't borrow it back.'

'Burnt your boats, eh? Or should I say punctured your wheels, ha ha?'

'It's not funny, dear handsome, helpful, and intelligent friend.'

'Cor blimey, what a creep! But since you said that so well maybe I can help.'

'Thanks, could I use the van that I've seen here?'

'No, it's out of action. One of the men overloaded it and buggered the suspension going into a pothole. The Guv's trying for compensation from the council, but I don't think he'll get it because he's so honest he'll tell them what it was carrying. I can't let you borrow my car because it's not insured for business purposes for someone else to drive, but shall I come with you and do the driving? What do you think? I'd have to get the Guv's okay.'

Jon didn't think twice. 'Brilliant! I'd enjoy your company, and you probably know the customer. I'll go and check with him if two visitors will be okay.'

'Who's the customer?'

'Oxonstone Ltd.'

'Oh, that would be Les Tindall, yes? He's okay, is Les, but don't call him Les until he tells you. If I remember correctly, their yard gets wet, so take your wellies and I'll lend you a hard hat.'

'Right, I'll go and phone. Be back in ten.'

Tindall was available to take Jon's call, and was quite happy with two visitors. 'I need your colleague's name, for a visitor's badge. Health and Safety regs you know, but promise me you will absolutely not bring Mr O'Flynn.'

'It's Mr R Martin, nobody else.'

'Roger Martin? *The* Roger Martin?'

'Yes, is there a problem?'

'Not at all, except that he owes me a pint. When your lot installed the last conveyor here, and after my surprise that it worked – if you'll excuse my sarcasm - I took Rog off to the pub for a beer. So he owes me. In truth he's okay, and knows what he's doing. By the way, what's your first name?'

'Jonathan, preferably Jon.'

'Thanks, I'm Les, please use that, and I'll see you tomorrow. Cheers for now,' and he hung up.

Back in the works Jon found Roger. 'Well?' he asked. 'No problem, Roger. According to *"Les"* you owe him a pint so he seems to be happy with the prospect of getting it. If so, that means we'll still be there around lunchtime, so we won't be back before late in the afternoon. By the way, he said that on no account was I to take Mr O'Flynn. I'll leave a note for the Guv to tell him what's going on, because I'm sure he wouldn't disagree with us going. And thanks again for your help.'

'No probs. You're up to "Les" already, eh?'

'His idea, I didn't ask him. By the way, get a chauffeur's cap will you?'

'Get lost! I'll pick you up at seven.'

***

The following day dawned wet and miserable. Typical English weather, it had to rain just when it should be fine and sunny for putting everyone in a good mood for tramping about in a quarry and doing business. True to his promise, dead on seven Roger banged on the outer door of Jon's flat.

'Your door bell doesn't work', he greeted Jon, 'and I nearly trod on that patch of oil on the driveway! Are you going to do something about all that?'

'You're quite right, the bell doesn't work, and I'm going to do something about the oil,' and then with a smile Jon went on, 'but unlike yours, my good manners tell me to greet you. So good morning, Roger, and thank you for giving me a lift.'

'Yes, okay, but you know me, I'm usually only polite to people I don't like. Typical of many Englishmen.' They piled Jon's hard hat, wellies and waterproofs into Roger's car and set off.

'This is a posh area, isn't it?' observed Roger, glancing at the large houses of the area, 'expensive rents, eh?'

'Well, Meads is said to be expensive but I don't rent the whole house just the ground floor, and the rent's reasonable. I've been here for much less than a year and it's convenient. My landlord and his wife live upstairs, and they're good company, and we've now planned to swap flats because he's partially disabled.'

'Are you settled here for the long term?'

'Who knows? My divorce is over, as I've told you, and I've no other commitments. I was adjusting to that new situation when now I find myself charging off to do business for TLC, and I haven't thought too much about my home situation. I can't predict what my job will bring, especially as it's already changed since my first interview. Les Tindall hinted about buying something and if by some amazing decision he does, it'll prove the value of the mailing we did the other day. He was polite, but my best approach to him, or indeed any other customers, is to be up-front and candid with him if I'm asked about my experience of TLC type products.'

'Quite so,' Roger agreed. 'He'd soon trip you up if he thought you were bullshitting. Have you been out on many new business visits?'

'Yes, but not to this type of company. Usually problem solving when customers' existing machines are unsuitable for moving a new product within a factory, an inevitable result of an airy-fairy designer failing to ask the works manager if he actually can make the bloody thing. It happens often, and I've wasted hours in useless site meetings waiting for the two sides to stop arguing. I walked out of a meeting once, leaving them to it. When I returned a half hour later they'd come to their senses and were all smiles as I was welcomed back. Pathetic, I thought, but I get Christmas cards from a few of them. Just did, actually.'

After half an hour they reached the outskirts of Brighton, then headed north for the M23 and M25, agreeing as they went along that it was good luck that neither motorway was blocked by accidents or just volume of traffic. Well, not yet. Having left an hour early to provide for delays they agreed to stop at the new M25 service area for a break, and over coffee they exchanged notes about TLC, because as colleagues they hadn't had many chances to do so before. Jon didn't want the subject of O'Flynn to crop up, but Roger thought otherwise.

'Jon,' Roger asked, 'why do you think O'Flynn disliked you at that party?'

'I've absolutely no idea, and can only speculate. He's no reason to dislike me so I'm wondering if he just objects to me on the grounds of the cost of my salary. There's no secret about the firm's precarious finances, Roger, is there?'

'Of course not, it's obvious to all the staff that orders have dropped away, and that some machinery is old and should've been replaced. No, there's no secret, and the men trust that the

Guv will sort it all out. None of them are planning to leave, or if they are they haven't told me. But what's that got to do with you and O'Flynn?'

'The Guv took me on to improve our designs and innovations, which is an investment. Perhaps O'Flynn thinks that it would have been more relevant at present to employ someone to get new orders instead. Perhaps he might be happier if Les Tindall places an order.'

'What did Les want to talk about?'

'He didn't say. He just said that they're thinking about expanding their quarry, and could someone go and see them.'

'How did he know your name?'

'He didn't before I wrote to the customers introducing myself. Changing the subject, though, if you've finished your coffee we'd better get a move on.'

The motorways still being clear for once, an hour or so later Roger announced, 'As you can see from all this mud in the road, Jon, we're arriving at Oxonstone's plant.' Right on cue, a hefty road sweeper truck emerged from the quarry gates and attacked the mud with a vengeance, leaving a clean surface and a good first impression of Oxonstone for Jon, who liked public-spirited companies. This visit is going to be okay, he thought. A notice on the entrance gate instructed, 'Please park in the yard and go to the building marked Reception, pick up the phone and press O.'

The short walk to Reception showed Jon that here was an efficient business, for the yard was tidy and cleaned of mud. Over the phone a pleasant female voice enquired, 'Who do you want to see?' Roger answered, 'Two visitors for Mr Tindall, please, names of Webb and Martin.'

After a pause the voice came back. 'Mr Tindall is somewhere in the yard at present, but will be with you shortly. Please take a seat.'

This was all typical stuff at any reception, but neither man needed to sit after their drive, preferring to inspect a wall display of Oxonstone photos of the firm's history going back decades. Looking at several group photos, Jon asked Roger, 'Is this a family firm, and is Les Tindall a family member?'

'It is, and I am,' came a voice through an open door to one side. 'You must be Jonathan Webb, and I'm Les Tindall,' said a rugged man, obviously the owner of the voice, 'and it's good to see you again, Roger. Good morning, gentlemen.'

Les Tindall was thickset, six feet tall, aged about sixty, wearing tough-looking jeans and a sweater under a vis jacket, and muddy safety boots. His huge hands were hard and calloused, giving the impression as they shook that he'd spent years heaving lumps of stone around, but were dexterous when it came to tying fish flies in his fishing hobby featured in some of the photos. Jon assumed that's one reason why Les and Roger get on so well – a common interest in fishing.

Les Tindall continued, 'Shall we have a chat over a coffee while waiting for this god-awful weather to clear?' Not waiting for an answer, he went back through the open door with Jon and Roger obediently following to what was obviously his office. He shook the rain from his jacket, and pressed a button on his desk, causing a young lady to materialise with a tray of coffee and biscuits as the three men took their seats. 'Thank you, Lucy,' he said.

'So, Roger, how've you been? I haven't seen you for ages. Are they biting?'

'Well, Les, it's the off-season anyway, and we really have been busy at work, so I couldn't take the odd days off. But believe me, sitting on a bank even in this weather has its appeal.'

Les Tindall turned his attention to Jon, who was acutely aware of the man's direct, assessing gaze. 'And you, Jon, pardon me for asking, but do you know what we've been referring to?'

'Oh, yes, indeed I do,' said Jon with a laugh. 'I don't have a car at present, so Roger has given me a lift here. I quite fancy having a Land Rover because I was persuaded by his suggestion that in my job for TLC if I arrived in quarries or mines in a Land Rover, I'd have better credibility than if I'd turned up in some shiny hatchback. However, he wasn't entirely honest because he had, or has, a vested interest in me having a Land Rover which he could borrow for his fishing expeditions.'

'Clever of him! Do you fish?' asked Tindall.

'No, shoot.

'Rough?'

'Clays.'

'Browning?'

'Perazzi.'

'Hmm,' murmured Tindall with raised eyebrows, guessing at the cost of Jon's shotgun. By that exchange between three men of few words, each knew where they stood in direct conversations.

'Right,' announced Les Tindall with authority, 'now that we know each other, let's talk about why you're both here. First of all, apart from what your letter said, what's your job in TLC, Jon, you didn't say and I didn't ask.'

'I was taken on by Henry Catchmore to create new designs, and improve the existing range of conveyors. There's no possibility of dramatic innovations because all belts in heavy service do much the same as you know, and nothing's really changed for decades apart from new materials, but I'm looking for ways to reduce costs without loss of quality. I'm very grateful for the opportunity to see one of our older machines in use, if I may, and to look for areas of improvement. Actually, Les, should the need arise, could I consult with you about new ideas? It's all very well me sitting in my drawing office visualising machines in use, but your on-site experience would be helpful. To be honest, I've only worked in this industry for less than a year, so you can see my need.'

'You're very welcome, Jon, I'd be glad to help. When this rain leaves off I'll show you around then leave you and Roger to make your preliminary survey, which will take an hour or so, then come back to the office and we'll shoot off to the village and Roger can buy me that pint he owes me! Incidentally, thinking of money, after you've sent me your quotation and we start to negotiate terms and so on, I'm happy to talk to you two chaps and Henry Catchmore, but just keep that awful Frank O'Flynn away from me.'

Jon was troubled. 'Excuse me for asking, Les, but did you have some difficulty with Mr O'Flynn? After all he is a Director of the firm.'

'Difficulty? Not really,' Les replied reluctantly, 'but he was obnoxious, and rude. When one of our stage payments for the last machine wasn't processed by the bank by the due date, he phoned me the following day pointing out that it was overdue, and that penalty charges would now be levied. I reminded him of the bank's massive IT glitch reported in the media affecting millions of accounts, but he gave no apology, and said that he'd check later that day that we'd paid. Please don't let him near me, and if I may suggest, not near any other customers for that matter.'

'We are sorry about that,' offered Jon with Roger nodding agreement. 'It's not usual for TLC to act that way.' Jon just presumed that was the case, and was being tactful.

'I'm sure that it isn't, Jon, for if it was, you wouldn't be here!' said Tindall with a wry smile.

A hazy sun had by now struggled through the clouds, so they left the offices for Tindall to show them round the quarry, and to indicate

39

where additional stone had to be shifted. Jon's impression of the quarry indicated good management. It was as tidy as a working quarry could be, with no rubbish or old scrap lying about. Safety notices proliferated. They discussed a specification to enable TLC to prepare a supply-and-install quotation, and after an hour Roger and Jon were left to themselves to get on with it.

They all reconvened in Tindall's office, then left for a simple and convivial lunch in the local pub, which Les insisted on paying for under protest from the others. 'You're both very welcome gentlemen, but Roger still owes me a pint!' Back at the quarry offices, farewell wishes were exchanged, and the TLC men left. Roger was obviously pleased with this first meeting between Jon and an existing TLC customer. It augured well for their future working together.

CHAPTER FOUR

Back in the car and on their way home, Roger asked Jon, 'Well, what do you think? And by the way, I liked your remark that you'd been in this industry for "less than a year". Less than a year? Less than a week would have been nearer the truth! I nearly choked.'

'Well, I wasn't lying, was I? And if Les finds out how long I'd actually worked for TLC he'd probably have a chuckle, and if he'd been in my place he'd do the same. I like him. I think he's straight and honest, and I imagine that he doesn't "pussyfoot around", but his opinion of O'Flynn worries me, and that's twice now he's told me to keep O'Flynn away from his business. Why would a director of a company behave as he did over that late bank payment? Was he desperate to get the cash to pay one of TLC's due debts? Surely the firm hasn't been sailing that close to the wind, has it?'

'To be honest, Jon, I don't know, but around that time we'd supplied the belt to a mine in that country somewhere in Africa which was late in paying. I know the Guv was worried, but I wasn't involved at all. We assembled the machine here, tested, dismantled and packed it, some other firm shipped it and installed it, and that was the last I heard of it.'

'Where did it go?'

'I can't remember, except that it's been absorbed into another country apparently. You know how state borders are forever shifting there. Was the customer one of those you've written to recently asking how their machines are doing?'

'I don't remember, but we only wrote to the last ten customers. Alice typed the letters and I signed them as you know, then she faxed them, personally addressed where we had known contacts. I'll look tomorrow, but I think the country was Lngusha or something else equally unpronounceable. I'll call it Zed, for simplicity.'

Roger glanced at his watch. 'I'm interested to know, but meanwhile it's too late to go back to the works. Would you like to meet my wife Pam? We live west of Eastbourne and it's not out of our way back to your flat.'

'Yes, that'd be great, thank you!'

'Good. My mobile's in the dash pocket there, phone her and introduce yourself and say we'll be there in about an hour. She's on speed dial two.' Jon struggled for a moment with the unaccustomed phone, but it was answered quickly.

'Hello, it's Jon Webb from TLC here, Mrs Martin. I'm travelling with Roger back towards your house and he's invited me to meet you. Will that be okay? It will? Thank you. Roger says we'll be there in about an hour … Oh! and you too. Bye for now.' He ended the call. 'That's okay, Roger. When I gave my name she said that she's looking forward to meeting me.'

'I bet she didn't, I bet she really said that she was merely *curious* to meet you.'

'No she *didn't*, she said "looking forward", but she said nothing about looking forward to you coming home!'

They continued in a companionable silence, and the hour passed quickly. Roger turned off the main A27 road into a lane and pulled up in front of an end-of-terrace cottage, probably once an artisan's home, and cut the engine. Even for the bleak time of year the house was attractive. It was built of red brick under a slate roof, with white painted woodwork, and a modest front garden with neatly pruned roses round the front doorway. A wisp of smoke drifted from one of its chimneys.

Jon stayed in the car for a moment gazing at the cottage with envy. 'Roger, your house and garden look delightful. I bet that you two enjoy sitting on that old bench under the tree on a summer's evening, and watching the world walk by?'

'We certainly do. We decided to leave the car on the road instead of having a driveway so's to make more space for scented shrubs and flowers, and often just sit there thinking how lucky we are. Anyway, come on and meet Pam.'

To the side of an old wooden front door Roger's tug on a rusty chain almost hidden in the roses produced a distant jangling in the house, and a smiling petite lady emerging from it.

'Hello,' she said, 'you must be Jon, and you're very welcome. I should explain that I do permit

Roger to have a front door key, but he likes to ring for me to come and open it to give the impression that he is master here. I'm Pam, do come in. Have you two had a good day?'

'Hi, love, yes, it's been good,' offered Roger, with a hug for his wife. 'I've offered Jon a sherry as a minor celebration of it.'

The inside of the house was as promising as the outside. It was neat, clean and tidy. As Pam went for the sherry the tempting fragrance of a casserole came from the kitchen, combined with a gentle smell of wood smoke escaping from a stove in the front room.

'This is lovely,' complimented Jon glancing round the room, sinking into a comfortable settee, and accepting the sherry. 'Here's a toast to your good health, and thanks for your hospitality.'

'And to you,' Roger replied, obviously pleased with his wife's welcome and how Jon felt at ease. 'We've been to see Les Tindall, Pam, do you remember him?'

'Oh, yes, up in Oxfordshire isn't he? You took me there when you'd finished installing a conveyor in his quarry, and he insisted on buying us lunch. A real gentleman if I remember, very polite to me, but no nonsense in business I bet. If I'd known you were going there I would have liked to come along.'

'Pam, it was all business I assure you, and it was Jon's first customer visit with me, and it went well except for a few moments when O'Flynn's name came into the conversation.'

'Why on earth did you talk about that dreadful man? He's a property developer, isn't he? Not accustomed to dealing with business customers. And not good at that either, it seems. I met him once at a TLC social event, Jon, and his wife was supercilious and unpleasant towards the staff.'

'We didn't raise the subject of O'Flynn, why would we? But Tindall told us that he had a brush with him over payments for their last machine when O'Flynn was tactless, and he instructed us to keep O'Flynn away from his business. I was worried that Jon would wonder what sort of firm he'd joined where one of its directors was so crass.' Turning to Jon he said, can you forget O'Flynn, because I'm sure that you and I will work well together, and I'm confident about the future now.'

'I quite agree with all that, but thinking of time, I really ought to leave you soon to your evening. Roger, could you take me when it's convenient to you?'

Pam had other ideas. 'Jon, why don't you stay for supper? When I knew you'd be coming I added to the casserole, so there's plenty for us all. What do you say?'

'That would be great, Pam, thank you, but I hope you don't mind if we talk about business?'

'I don't mind at all, and I'm pleased for Roger. He likes his job, but he's been worried and gloomy about the future, which rubs off on me sometimes. We were both pleased to hear that a new person was to join the firm, whoever it was going to be, because we took that to be a result of the directors' own self confidence.'

Jon watched through an arched opening to the kitchen as his hosts busied themselves with food, and laying cutlery and condiments on an old pine kitchen table surrounded by four mis-matched wooden chairs, all clearly bought at random times. Jon's envy at first sight of the cottage returned, as did his father's words, "Don't look back, Jon, forget what went wrong, look to the future."

Pam disturbed his reverie. 'Are you alright, Jon, you're looking pensive and sad?'

'You're an observant woman, Pam. Yes, I was sad over the memory of my late father. No, no, please don't look gloomy. I'm not, because when he was brooding over failures in his own life, he was telling me not to let past mistakes stop me spotting new opportunities, or words to that effect.'

'Why were you thinking of him just now?'

'Envy, Pam, envy. One of the seven deadly sins. Envy of your house, your marriage, and your comfortable home. All things that I don't have, but my father would say that I could have if I got on and did something about it. That's what I was thinking.'

Pam looked at him thoughtfully. 'Do you think your job in TLC will help you to "get on and do something", as you said?'

'Roger may have told you how one letter out of ten we sent recently produced a new business enquiry from Les Tindall, but even if that's a fluke, why shouldn't other similar efforts also hit the bull's-eye? TLC can't survive for long without major changes, and where there are changes there are always opportunities.'

'In the meantime, shall we eat?' Roger suggested. 'I don't want to break up your train of thought, but I'm hungry!' So with freshly baked bread rolls and a steaming casserole set before them, all conversation ceased, and they ate until Pam's curiosity got the better of her.

'I'm being nosey now, Jon, but I understand that you're single again. Are you getting along okay, whatever I mean by that?'

'Absolutely fine, thanks.' And made his hosts laugh by saying, 'Please don't tell me that this old cottage once belonged to the village matchmaker who was one of your ancestors, or I'm off! Well, at least not until I've eaten this lovely casserole.'

'Do you like cooking?'

'Yes, simple recipes with easily available ingredients. I really try not to buy take-away convenience foods, except a few kept in the fridge for when I'm too tired or too late home to cook. Funnily enough in the freezer now there's a casserole I made, but it'll be nowhere as good as this one.'

'Jon,' said a smiling Roger, 'we can take a hint. Come again sometime.'

Back in Roger's car, Jon complimented Roger, saying, 'I like Pam, Roger, she's so pleasant and welcoming. Does she have a job – I forgot to ask about her profession?'

'Not full time, she used to be a nurse and now does some agency work. She wishes the NHS could itself recruit more nurses, and is puzzled why it doesn't. Or can't.'

'Where did you two meet?'

'Hospital. In the orthopaedic ward.'

'Oh, I get it, you fancied your nurse when she tucked you in bed at night and one thing led to another. The old, old story!'

'Not at all. She'd been nursing a patient in the next bed for a few days, and was fed up with his lewd remarks and groping. I got enraged with him, lost my temper, and hit him with my water jug, fractured his left arm and soaked his bed. There was a hell of a row, but as I couldn't be discharged they moved me along the ward. When the fuss died down, she came to thank me, and kissed my cheek. I said, "You can do that again whenever you like," and she did, and here we are together. Have been for years now. Both our kids are at uni, and we're proud of them. It was great on Christmas day when we were all together. Oh, I made a tactless comparison with your situation, Jon. Stupid of me. Sorry.'

'It's not a problem, and thanks again for the day and this evening, Roger, but here we are now, I'll see you at work in the morning.'

'How will you get there?'

'By bus. Eastbourne's buses are frequent and reliable. There's a stop over the road there, and at the other end I'll only have a short walk from the bus stop to the factory. Goodnight.'

'And to you.' But as Roger drove away Jon's envy of his home life hit him again

CHAPTER FIVE

The following morning, armed with his notes from the Oxenstone visit, Roger collected Jon from his office to report to the Guv, who looked up from his desk and enquired, 'Well?'

Nominated as spokesman, Roger reported, 'Actually, Guv, we think it was a good visit.'

'What do you mean "good"?' asked the Guv, in a genial mood. 'Do you agree, Jon?'

'Yes, Les Tindall was welcoming to me and especially to Roger whom he knew already. There were positive "vibes" all through the visit, and he gave us all the time we needed to make sure that any proposal was based on his needs, and not, as he said during lunch, based on what we wanted to sell him.'

'However,' said the Guv, 'I really didn't need to ask how the visit went because I already knew.'

'What?' the men demanded, in unison.

With a broad smile the Guv continued, 'You two had better sit down.' They did as instructed, glancing at each other in apprehension.

' After you left Oxenstone, Les Tindall phoned me to say that he was pleased with your visit and your obvious genuine interest in doing the right thing for his firm, and apparently you hinted at some new ideas, Jon. What was that all about, you haven't said anything to me?'

'Nothing specific, Guv, I just wanted to have his opinions of any new ideas or prototypes if the need arose as someone we could trust, and he agreed.'

'Fine,' the Guv acknowledged, 'but I can tell you now – and I can hardly believe this, because it's never happened to me before – Tindall also said that subject obviously to agreement upon details, I was to take his statement as a verbal "Letter of Intent" to purchase a conveyor from TLC, and in principle we could pencil a contract into our order book, and true to his word he's confirmed that by email. It's all very informal, and not contractually binding, but what do you guys think of that?'

They were speechless. After recovering, Roger offered, 'You could say we're delighted.'

'I haven't finished yet,' grinned the Guv, 'our friend Les also offered, I repeat *offered*, to lodge a cash deposit soon as an expression of good faith. I said that that wasn't necessary until the contract signing stage, although you both know very well that any cash is useful now. I thanked him profusely, but he explained that he wanted to do so to prevent the unnecessary grief that happened last time. What did he mean by that?'

Roger explained O'Flynn's intransigence in the matter of Tindall's last payment delayed by a bank, and that any order he might place would be conditional upon O'Flynn having no involvement with it.

The Guv looked shaken. 'Was he serious?'

51

'We believe so, Guv. We discussed it on the way back, and we agree that he meant it.'

'Afraid so, yes,' confirmed Jon, 'and we don't understand why Mr O'Flynn was unreasonable. TLC wouldn't have retained Oxenstone as a customer without the past goodwill that you and Roger have built up, but apparently Mr O'Flynn nearly blew it.'

After withdrawing into himself for a while, the Guv looked up at the men and said, 'Sorry about that, but it's clear that I have a problem to deal with.' Then with a huge grin he said, 'I have some other news for you, Jon. I almost forgot!

'Alice put a phone call through to me yesterday because she couldn't understand the caller, and neither could I at first. Assuming that it was someone from a foreign call centre trying to sell me something, I nearly put the phone down, but then I realised it was a man who wanted to speak to you personally. I have his number here, and you must call him back because I *think* he said he was one of the customers you'd written to in the mailshot. He spelled out his name, but I just couldn't get it right. It may have been Hugomvarla, but don't bet on it!'

Jon had nearly shot out of his chair, and laughing said, 'Have we finished here, Guv? I have a call to make! I'll leave you two to plan Tindall's machine.'

The phone number was international, and the line was surprisingly clear, but asking for the Hugomvarla's name resulted in background sounds as of human arguments. After a few minutes a voice said, 'Aylo?' Taking that as meant to be 'hello,' Jon tried again using 'Hugo' for short, and the previous voice replied 'Speaking,' in as clear English as the background noises would allow.

Encouraged, Jon said, 'My name is Jonathan Webb, are you the gentleman who telephoned my company yesterday?'

'Ah, Mr Jon, I am the manager of the mine which has your machinery. The machine was good, but not now. I saw your letter asking if it still works well.' The conversation was going somewhere and Jon asked, 'What is wrong with it?'

'It blew up.'

'Blew up? Christ!' exclaimed Jon, stifling a laugh. 'What do you mean "blew up"? We don't include explosives!'

'I know, but the rebels did.' Rebels? Jon's perverse sense of humour wasn't helping him, but recovering his composure, he started again.

'Excuse me for asking, but is Hugo your first name so should I address you as Mr Hugo?'

'No, just Hugo.'

Jon struggled on, commenting, 'Your spoken English is very good, Hugo.'

'Thank you, I learnt it at school, and practised it at the Camborne School of Mines.'

This was encouraging; maybe I've got a good contact here if he's a qualified mining engineer. 'Hugo, what did you mean "blew up"?'

'We have had many problems in our country, Mr Jon. Unemployment, low wages, corruption –

but I didn't say that, did I? There has been as you say in your country, civil unrest. Demonstrations against the old President turned into fighting and violence, and the government lost control because the police and army hadn't been paid for three months. You must have read all this in the press? Saboteurs got hold of explosives and started blowing up anything they didn't like or didn't understand, and did massive damage to one end of our conveyor because in their stupidity they thought as a machine it put people out of work. It is now useless, so we cannot work. Can you come and mend it?'

'Hugo, who owns the mine and its machinery?'

'The Ministry for the Interior.'

'Do you know who is in charge?'

'Yes, the Secretary for the Interior, Mr Gavuzzi.'

'Hugo, can you send me these rough details by email?'

'Not from here in the mine office, perhaps I can from my home. I had to keep your letter in the office, but I took a copy home. The soldiers who are guarding the mine now are suspicious of who I'm talking to. I have to go.'

With that, the line went dead. This left Jon optimistic if the Secretary's name was correct, but this was all far-fetched, like a plot in a film. When he tried to phone back the phone at the other end went unanswered, and finally he gave up trying. He returned to his prediction that mines needed products from TLC – or other makers – to help economic growth. Perhaps TLC was in pole position if the bomb-damaged conveyor could be repaired, or if not, perhaps was even one step ahead for tendering for a replacement. It was time for action. He went back to the Guv, enthused by the prospects ahead.

To his horror, there also in the Guv's office was O'Flynn, who with unnecessary rudeness demanded, 'Can't you see, Webb, we're having a meeting?'

Politely, Jon countered with, 'Good morning, Mr O'Flynn. I did not know, but Mr Catchmore was half expecting me. Excuse me,' and although O'Flynn said something Jon ignored him and left to see Alice MacInnes, seething with frustration.

'Excuse me, Alice, but I've unwittingly interrupted a meeting between the Guv and Mr O'Flynn, who was offensive. Please ask the Guv if I can speak to him later, or at his home this evening. Sorry to be melodramatic, but Mr O'Flynn annoyed me.'

The imperturbable Mrs Mac suggested, 'Why not go down to see Roger and have a cup of tea with him? A cuppa often helps, don't you think?' It was impossible for Jon not to smile at this smooth assessment, for clearly he had something to report to the Guv, and cleverly Mrs Mac didn't want him to leave the building. 'Alice, you are a very shrewd and sensible woman, and we all love you!' complimented Jon.

He sought out Roger who, with a quizzical look, said, 'Hello, hello, what's this visit to me all about? Are you on the scrounge again?'

No, just to update you about that phone call to the Guv yesterday, but before I go on did you know that O'Flynn's in the building?'

'No, oh Christ! He must have arrived after the Guv and I had done the first part of planning the quotation for Les. Why is O'Flynn there?'

'Don't know, but he's a bloody nuisance because I needed to talk to the Guv and you as soon as poss, and I assumed that you were still there. We need O'Flynn out of here. The chap who phoned yesterday is, or maybe was, the manager of the mine in Africa which has our conveyor, but he said it had blown up.'

'Blown up?'

'Apparently in the chaos before their new President was elected there were reactionaries, or rebels, rampaging around, and it seems that in their illiterate stupidity they thought that the conveyor took away work from men, not enabled work. A completely Luddite attitude, so allegedly they put explosives in one end. I've been asked to go and "mend it". It's now almost urgent for someone to go there to assess the damage because if we handle this situation well, we could get Brownie points from their ministry which would help new business. It may be that the whole of one end has been wrecked, or simply just the power supply. My contact is Camborne trained but he seems to be hemmed in by soldiers who denied him further use of the phone. Don't ask me why they're there, he didn't say, but maybe the new regime wants to prevent residual vandalism.'

'The point is,' an anxious Jon continued, 'could our installing sub-contractors be available to go there once I've found the problem?'

'Phew,' was Roger's first response. 'If I ask if their engineers are available they'll obviously ask what do we want done, and where, but even suppose someone phoned from the mine and said exactly what's to be done, who's going to pay? The customer? If so when, given the chaos? TLC? I don't think so, do you?'

Jon was pacing about in Roger's tiny office. 'I understand, but I'm totally frustrated. It makes sense for you or me to go there tomorrow – so to speak – but we obviously can't without the okay from the Guv, and we can't talk to him because O'Flynn's here, and I think it's important.'

'Why not ask Alice's advice, Jon? See if she can get O'Flynn away from the Guv for long enough on some sort of pretext.' Then, not waiting for an answer, he used the internal phone to her and said, 'It's Roger here. Could you come down to my office in the works please, it's fairly urgent … no, sorry I'll explain when you come.'

She arrived within minutes, and seeing the two men's expressions asked 'What's the problem, why so urgent?'

Jon explained. 'That man whose call you passed to the Guv is the manager of the mine in Africa which has a TLC conveyor they bought about three years ago. Well, it appears that during the political disturbances allied to the new President's election some rebels blew up the conveyor and it's now useless.'

'Blew it up?'

'Yes. He asked me to go there and "mend it" as he said, and I'm sure that if TLC reacts to this man's request we'll be favoured if we seek new business there. My point is that we can't do so without the Guv's say-so, and he's tangled up with O'Flynn and I will not discuss this when he's there. Roger and I hoped that you'd be able to help.'

Mrs MacInnes said nothing, but slowly a mischievous smile appeared. 'Do you know,' she said, 'I am grateful to you, Roger, for asking after me, you're quite right, I don't feel very well, and if you'll excuse me I am going to ask Mr O'Flynn if he'll be so kind as to take me home.' With that, she said no more and left, leaving the men speechless with admiration for this quick-witted woman.

CHAPTER SIX

Ten minutes after she left them, the Guv appeared in Roger's office, and with a frown demanded, 'What have you two done to Alice? She's been taken ill and Frank's taken her home.'

The other two looked at each other, then Jon admitted, 'She's quite well. It was a ruse of hers to get Mr O'Flynn away, so we could see you soon today.'

'She's a clever girl!' laughed the Guv. 'Come up to the office.'

They all took coffee which was routinely offered in the Guv's belief that it helped visitors to settle down. Even employees. One of Mrs Mac's jobs was to ensure that the machine was kept fully loaded.

'Right,' said the Guv, 'what's up?'

Jon explained, 'Guv, the phone call you took yesterday was international, so I checked from our mailshot file that it was from the mine where you sold a machine three years ago. The mine is now in The Democratic Republic of Lnugasha which I can't pronounce, so I'll call the country Zed. Okay?

'The mine manager's name is "Hugo" for short, and he'd received one of the letters we sent. He's a mining engineer, Cambourne trained, and his English is clear. He reported that their conveyor belt had performed well, but that recently it had blown up.'

'*Blown up*? What did he mean "*blown up!*"?'

'I've no idea, but he mentioned rebels, sabotage and bombs. But I thought it funny when he said "blown up"! Roger laughed when I told him.'

'So what do you two want me to do?'

Roger answered, 'We hadn't yet decided, but I guarantee that when I signed off the conveyor before it left here that there were no explosives or volatile substances built in it.'

'Well said, Roger, but what about "bombs" and "sabotage" as Jon's man said? And why do we need to get involved with this?'

'Guv,' Jon began, 'to get new business, as simple as that. Zed's economy is recovering from the murdered late President's autocracy, with its endemic corruption and economic isolation that other countries did nothing about, probably because there's no oil there. Now, however, the growth in global demand for minerals and metal ores together with confidence in the new President is bringing in billions of dollars of investments to Zed already. I've been following all of this in the press for months, and is one reason for my interest in TLC and for asking to join it.'

'Really?' interrupted the Guv, obviously pleased, but curious, 'Why?'

'When I saw your ad for a designer in the sits vac column of the local paper, I remembered when we first met months ago that you had told

60

me about TLC's products and that your main market was the extractive industries, so with the current frenetic investments in them I foresaw a good future for TLC, and here I am. Although TLC is underfunded, if you'll excuse me saying so, there's no cumbersome hierarchy here, so quick decisions are possible, as proved by the directors' ready agreement with Mr Phillips.'

For an anxious moment, Jon was worried if he was going too fast for the Guv, who, being a little set in his ways, might think that Jon was being 'pushy', so instead of suggesting that he should go to Zed himself, he changed tack. 'Guv,' he began cautiously, 'you asked us what we wanted you to do, and although I haven't discussed that with Roger, I suggest that you "jump on a plane" so to speak, and go to Zed to follow up this situation.'

Catchmore was puzzled. 'Jon, if this situation was here in the UK any one of us could go, but it's not, so who would pay for this trip to Africa? However, put that to one side for the moment, and tell me what we'd get out of it.'

'I can't be precise, Guv, but I'd predict that it would be profitable, and good PR. We don't know the condition of the TLC conveyor – it will either be repairable minor damage, or it'll be written off and need to be replaced. In both cases we could get some profit. I've no doubt that we'd be respected if we reacted quickly, and effectively got the mine working again.'

'An explosion doesn't suggest minor damage.'

'No, but we don't know who suggested "explosion". It could have been an excitable native who exaggerated hunting rifle fire, or a burst tyre, the list is endless. I can't get hold of Hugo again to ask his opinion, but I'm hoping he emails me. Do we have any trustworthy qualified contacts over there to give us an opinion?'

'Mmm, no,' admitted the Guv. 'What's your opinion, Roger?'

'I agree with Jon, Guv, and I do think that you or one of the other Directors should go, and as soon as possible.'

'Well, I'm beginning to be convinced, gentlemen, but as I see it the trip would cost money for no known return on it, and I can imagine Frank O'Flynn's reaction if I suggested it to him, for he would be emphatic, to say the least, that we couldn't afford it, and I would agree with him.'

So would Roger, but Jon with his new-found determination wasn't giving up yet.

'Guv,' said Jon, 'TLC can't afford it, but I can.'

'What the hell do you mean?'

'I am offering to pay for the air fares, hotels, incidental expenses, and so on out of my own pocket, with no immediate recompense from TLC. I have a pot of money in the bank which is doing nothing, and I can't think of a better way of using some of it. If you accept the idea, you wouldn't have to get Mr O'Flynn's agreement. I've no home commitments, and could go very soon, which is what I want to do.'

'Are you serious, Jon? Honestly?'

Roger interrupted, 'Guv, excuse me for butting in, because I *know* he is serious. On the way back from Oxenstone he stayed for supper at my home, and inevitably we talked about work. I don't want to embarrass you, Jon, because you're a modest guy, but, Guv, he's enthusiastic and confident about TLC's future to say the least.'

'Jon,' began the Guv, 'I say thank you, with amazement and some humility. Please clarify what you mean by "no immediate recompense"?'

'Oh that! If the trip's a loss maker, the loss will be mine with no refund from TLC, but if it succeeds and TLC makes a profit directly attributable to my work, then we'll talk about some recompense then. If I make a loss it won't be a waste, because the experience would be priceless.'

The Guv stood, and announced, 'I am delighted and, I admit, excited about all this. I know that this sounds stuffy, but on behalf of the company I formally accept your proposal, Jon. Now we shake on it, okay?' Both men stood, and shook hands in mutual pleasure. Then Roger said, grinning, 'I am a formal witness to that agreement, gentlemen, so you are both committed now!'

The Guv called his wife away from her admin in the next office. 'Millie, please come here right away, and find some glasses if there's some sherry left over, and if there aren't any glasses we'll use mugs!'

'What's happened, Henry?' she asked, finding glasses and a bottle in a cupboard 'and why are you leering at me like that?'

'I'll be brief,' he said as he poured the sherry. 'Remember that phone call I told you about? Well it was from the mine in Africa whose manager got one of Jon's mailshot letters. He told Jon that the conveyor belt they'd bought had been fine, but recently it was out of use having blown up.'

'Blown up? What do you mean?'

'We don't know exactly, Millie, but Jon is insistent that TLC should send someone to see the mine, and get the conveyor mended or possibly sell them a replacement if necessary. I agreed completely, but had to say that we couldn't afford to pay for anyone to go. Because he's adamant of the need for a TLC rep to go there, Jon has offered to pay all costs, with no obligation from TLC to refund him. What do you say to that?'

'Good Lord! This is outrageous. We can't have an employee funding our business in this way, Henry.' But she raised her glass to Jon in a toast, then in an uncharacteristic and unladylike fashion, she said, 'Bloody hell!' raising laughs from the others. Still looking at Jon, she asked, 'Jon this is incredible, and you haven't had time to think it all through, so what's it going to cost you?'

'Mrs Catchmore, it's less spontaneous than you may think. From the time Roger and I left Oxenstone to the time when my African phone call was cut off, I've been thinking about TLC's enviable track record of quality and ethics which would take a "start-up" years to get, but your record will go to waste if you don't keep trading creatively. It's just luck that I have some money to help TLC along and I haven't had time to work out the cost, so I'm just guessing at a few thousand pounds, maybe up to five.'

'You are prepared to risk, take a chance on, or whatever you call it, five thousand pounds?'

'Yes, Mrs Catchmore, but may we please stop discussing that, and concentrate on arrangements for the journey?'

'Quite right, Jon,' spoke the Guv with rejuvenated authority and confidence, which his wife was obviously delighted to see after his many weeks of depression about the business. 'We'll get down to work now and please think of anything you can, and write it down and we'll meet again tomorrow. Millie, please phone Alice this evening and tell her what's being planned, and ask her also to make notes. Another thing everyone, plus Alice, for the time being this project is confidential and not to be discussed beyond the five of us. Not with *anyone*, including the other Directors, until I say so. If Jon's absence is noticed, just say he's taking a holiday booked before he joined us. 'Jon, Millie and I will give you a lift home, but if we talk about this on the way, in fairness to you, Roger, we'll tell you tomorrow what's been said. I think that's enough for one day, so let's go home, okay? Sleep well!'

Once again, Jon's hand was shaken vigorously by Roger and the Catchmores, but Jon doubted that he'd sleep at all. Too much to think about.

***

Once in the car, the Guv asked, 'Jon, give me your postcode for the satnav please, we have your address of course, but not with us here.' Jon gave it, and they set off. 'Have you anything to ask or say just now, Jon?'

'Definitely. I really want to clarify that by paying for it I mean all of it, including any TLC costs attributable to it. For example, if you, or Alice and Roger contribute salaried time, then that should be charged to the project, same as phone calls, copying, and so on, because I will need help.'

Mrs Catchmore queried this. 'Jon, why are you so adamant about all that?'

'As a matter of principle because I said that I'd pay for it all, and so that nobody can say that I've been a drain on TLC. To avoid getting bogged down with too much detail you could always estimate such minor costs as copying and local phone calls, but please ensure that you enter nothing in the accounts until the end of the trip when I'll pay the total. I want the costs to be confidential until then.'

'I'll need to work from home sometimes, if that's okay if I tell you in advance? I'll keep a time sheet. When I go to Zed I must have full travel and health insurance, and public liability cover. As a provision for having to commit TLC to any form of contract could we think of some sort of authority for me to do that, which I don't have at present?'

The Guv asked for clarification. 'What do you mean exactly?'

'We've never talked about my level of authority within TLC, Guv. For example, I can ask you or Roger to order something, but I can't sign a purchase order, still less cheques, so if in Zed I find a company which could repair the machine at a reasonable cost, I can't give it the go-ahead. Do you see?'

'Mmm, I take your point. Millie and I will talk about it this evening. Meanwhile the satnav shows that we've reached your road, so we say good night and meet tomorrow.'

Jon watched and smiled as the Catchmores drove off with more positive things to think about than they've had for many months.

CHAPTER SEVEN

Jon had slept well, so he began to set off for work early, but remembered that he had no key to TLC's building. 'Oh bugger,' he swore, thinking that by the time he'd phoned Roger to ask what time he opened up, he'd have missed his bus anyway. 'Bugger!'

'Is that you, Jon?' Sybil called down from upstairs. 'I heard a voice.'

'Yes, I cursed because I haven't a key to the office, just when I wanted to start early.'

'Oh, that's okay. I thought for a moment you were trying to sneak a woman out before we woke up. We haven't seen you for a couple of days, nor a woman you've smuggled in, not that it's any of our business, dear me no, certainly not, you're a free agent here of course, none of our business, but while I'm on the subject, what's going on, Jon?'

'Good morning, sorry if I disturbed you, Sybil.' Then with their usual repartee, Jon retorted, 'Yes, you're right, Sybil, and it is none of your business, and now you've caused a delay and I've missed my bus, so I'll have to take a taxi, and I will deduct the cost from my next rent payment to you.'

'Please yourself, Mr Webb, but if you default on your rent we won't renew the tenancy, then where would you be? Eh?'

'Africa, possibly.'

'What?'

'Seriously, Sybil, it's a long story with a happy ending. Well, it is up to this point at least, but I may be away soon in Africa for a week or so. Can I bring you up-to-date this evening?'

'It sounds that your new job's going well, congratulations! If you'd like me to give you yet *another* lift to work I'll be down in two minutes, and on your way home you can buy the sherry because it's your turn to do so, having drunk so much of ours.'

As she pulled up at the TLC works, Sybil asked sardonically, 'What's this event today then, a champagne breakfast? Or are they actually *working* for a change?'

'Sybil,' said Jon, laughing, 'as you've been kind enough to give me a lift, I won't criticise your sarcasm, and that was funny anyway. Yes, I'll stop off later and get some sherry. I promise! Thanks for bringing me, and I'll see you later.'

***

The Catchmores, Roger, and Alice MacInnes, were already in the Guv's office, as also, to Jon's surprise, were Bryant and Phillips. 'Ah, Jon, good morning,' greeted the Guv.

'Good morning, everyone,' Jon said, looking at his watch, 'I'm not late, am I?'

The Guv smiled. 'Not at all. I phoned these gentlemen last evening to outline yesterday's events. By chance they were both able to come early today, and they've just arrived. It is important for them to be here when we discuss our plans, but first of all Jon, I want you to confirm the offer you've made about Zed because it's so unconventional and I wanted it to be restricted to the six of us.' Jon quickly realised that in saying that the Guv had made it blatantly obvious to him that O'Flynn was totally excluded from anything to do with his plan. As their Financial Director all plans should conventionally be submitted to him for consultation at the very least, so this indicated a serious split in the Board, causing Jon to wonder where the real power lay. He began his explanation, speaking with greater self-confidence now.

'It's quite a simple offer really. A telephoned reply to one of our mailshot letters came from the mine in Africa to which TLC had sold a conveyor belt. I have offered to pay all my expenses incurred in going to inspect it as it's out of use due to its allegedly having blown up.'

'Blown up?' Bryant and Phillips interrupted as one voice.

'Yes, absurd though it sounds!' Jon acknowledged. 'Someone from TLC should go there at the very least to report back, or better still to organise a repair to the machine, thus enabling the mine to work again. I'm told that the man in overall charge of mines is the Secretary for the Interior, a Mr Gavuzzi of whom I know nothing, but he sounds important, and a man to be on our side, which is the main reason for going. If, for example the machine is irreparably damaged, then presumably it will need to be replaced, so if there's a TLC rep on the spot we'd be best placed to sell a new one. In any case if we don't go and look, we'd always wonder if we'd missed an opportunity, and the customer might be annoyed by our apparent uninterest. I made my offer because I strongly believe that it's important to go.'

Phillips and Bryant regarded Jon in silence, then, 'You are serious about all of this, Jon?' asked Phillips. 'To pay for the cost?' These directors frustrated Jon. He was the only person there with ideas which should have come from them. Alan Bryant was the most decisive of the bunch, and as Jon was thinking that, he spoke.

'Jon, I like your initiative, well done, but there's one major point that you haven't covered for us. Suppose that you could organise the machine's repair, how would you pay for it?'

'I intended to raise that point this morning, Mr Bryant, but perhaps you have a solution?'

'My colleagues must agree, of course, but I suggest that you are authorised to organise repairs up to an agreed level of cost, to be paid by the company. That level to be, say, five thousand pounds. When the need arises up to that point, give the go-ahead, and then contact us asking for your decision to be confirmed back to the contractor. That'll show them that you're a decision maker with authority. If the cost proves to be above your level, contact us again.'

Turning to the Guv he then said, 'Henry, Jon's title is Chief Designer, but I suggest that we raise that if he needs more clout to get to see this Mr

Gavuzzi, who may be full of himself and won't deal with minions. What do we say to call Jon "Director of Projects", for the purpose of this trip. It doesn't imply a Board appointment or any seniority over other employees, but it will help him to open doors. What do you say?'

Looking taken aback by the speed of events, but with really no option to agree, the Guv said, 'that was quick, Alan, and I agree.' His wife and David Phillips nodded assent.

'Well, Jon, are you happy with that?'

'Yes, thank you, the arrangements are ideal now, and I acknowledge the limitations of the suggested title. Please make sure that Roger's people are assured that it doesn't imply any seniority over him or them. Can you do that, please?'

Mrs Catchmore was pleased. 'That's thoughtful of you, Jon, and it's appreciated. What are your immediate plans?'

'To think of all that needs to be done, Mrs Catchmore. Checking with my GP if I need jabs, checking flights, getting local currency, trying Hugo again, looking at the drawings and spec of the conveyor, hiring a satellite phone, and making contact with the embassy. Alice Mac's help will be invaluable soon.'

'Why do you want to contact the embassy?' she asked, astounding Jon with her naivety.

'For several reasons, and others that I'll no doubt find with time. Embassies have contacts, local knowledge of translators, interpreters, and help for UK nationals if they're in difficulties.

It's advisable to tell them in advance of business visits, which I've done before, even when going just to Paris on business. I may need a satellite phone if the line to the mine is cut and I couldn't otherwise contact the embassy, or indeed TLC for any reason. He turned his attention to Roger. We have to presume that the damaged conveyor is in fact one that TLC made, and is not a case of mistaken identity if its serial number and any other ID are damaged beyond recognition, and it's made by someone else. Can you let me have all the details of what was sent please, Roger?'

'Sure, they'll either be in the old filing cabinet in your office, or in the archives in No 2 Unit.'

'There's nothing in my office, and what's No 2 Unit?'

'It backs onto this building, and it's used for various stores and a small workshop when we can make repairs instead of sending them away to sub-contractors. Let's go and look while we're on the subject.'

They left the others to talk about whatever they had to talk about, but again Jon felt that he was making all the running in this situation, which was outrageous coming from a new employee. Well, they agreed with his intention with no argument, and when or if O'Flynn found out about it and disagreed it wasn't Jon's problem, despite expecting trouble from the man. No 2 backed onto the main factory, with just one single pedestrian door which was open. They entered and looked around. There were several benches, racks of hand tools, and shelves stacked with labelled boxes. No sign of rolled-up drawings in tubes. Jon wondered about the relevance of all this storage for small components, considering the huge size of the conveyors themselves. He asked, 'What's in the boxes Roger?'

'Small spare parts', he explained, 'but I've no idea what's in these packing cases,' kicking one.

Suddenly from behind a stack of cases a man appeared, aggressively holding an iron bar like a club and yelling, 'What the hell are you doing 'ere?' Then, recognising Roger, he changed completely and said, 'Oh, sorry, I didn't see it were you, Mr Martin. Can I 'elp you?'

To Jon, Roger explained, 'This is Keith, Jon, he works part time for TLC, but mostly for Mr O'Flynn who rents part of this unit for his own property business storage.

'Keith,' he asked, 'we're looking for some archived drawings, are they in that cupboard?'

'No, they ain't. There's nuffink of TLC's in there'. With that, he made a point of sidling up to the cupboard as if to stand guard over it.

Roger tried again. 'Any other storage that I can't see from here?'

'No.'

'Sure?'

'Look 'ere, Mr Martin, I've already told you there's nuffink in 'ere that's anyfink to do with TLC, cos you shifted all the stuff that was 'ere to the main factory when you were busy and needed it near you.'

'Right,' said a suspicious and baffled Roger, 'we've done here, Jon, I think? Thanks Keith.' And they left. Out of earshot from the man, Jon spoke for the first time since their arrival.

'Roger, there's something odd about that place, and that man. He was shifty, and hiding something. Did you see how he barred the way to that cupboard? And did you notice the stencilling on the packing cases? I think that it was in a Slovak typeface, but whatever it was I couldn't read it. I get the impression that O'Flynn is up to something, and it's nothing to do with commercial property or conveyors.'

'I agree completely, Jon. That bloody man is a menace to TLC, and I do not know, try as I might, why or how he's still on the Board. To tell you the truth, I'm embarrassed to have brought you down here, cos I think you're on the way to great things for TLC, and I don't want you to get pissed off and walk away.'

'Don't worry, Roger, I won't, because where there's chaos there are always opportunities if we look for them, okay?'

'Yeah, well, okay. But will you manage in Zed without the original drawings or specifications? How will you know if the machine there is one of ours?'

'I think I'll be okay, because don't forget that when we were at Tindall's plant I had a good look at his TLC conveyor which you thought was probably similar to Zed's.'

Struggling to concentrate on what he'd been working on before that distraction, Jon got on the phone to consult anybody he could think of for advice – the export section of TLC's trade association, any relevant UK government departments, and other bodies suggested to him as time went along. He contacted the British Embassy in Zed where he was put in touch with the Head of the Commercial Section with the glorious name of George Turbeville-Blyth whose reaction was surprise.

'You're asking for advice *before* you try to do business?' he asked.

'Of course,' replied Jon.

'Well,' George T-B began to explain, 'in our experience, Mr Webb, too many firms come out here without doing their homework, they get into difficulty, and expect us to get them out of it. If you come here I shall look forward to meeting you because it's refreshing to hear your approach. However, I'm sorry to be blunt, but at present I can't help you myself, but I'll transfer your call to Olivia de St Croix who will. Please wait a moment.' Jon was treated to some tolerable hold-the-line music until a pleasant voice came on the line.

'Mr Webb? Hello, I'm Olivia de St. Croix. How may I help you?'

'Good afternoon, Ms de St Croix, and thank you. I'm preparing to travel to Zed on business, and to be candid, I need all the help available. The embassy is one of my starting points.'

'Where is "Zed" please?'

'Where you are now, Ms de St Croix. I used that pseudonym to camouflage its real name, because our industry is rife with rumours and I don't want our competitors to know what I'm doing, and I can't pronounce the name of the country anyway.'

She laughed. 'I quite understand, but may I know the name of your company, and your particular responsibilities?'

'Of course.' He summarised TLC's history, its products, its reputation, his status, and his prediction of the firm's future, particularly in Africa, using the previous sale as a starting point.

'Thank you, Mr Webb, I'll be pleased to help you in any way that I can. I'm not employed by the diplomatic service, but am on secondment from Futurebank which is an investment bank based in London, and to which I'll return in a few weeks. My job here is to assist Mr T-B in any financial matters pertaining to relationships with the government.

'To help forestall any problems, I'll email you our guide to doing business in this country, but please bear in mind that the embassy is not actually in business so can't know everything. Politics are not included since the change of President. However, if we can help further we will, and if you come out here on business it will be our responsibility to be available. Will that suffice for the time being?'

'Yes, thank you. May I email you my business details, and use the embassy to contact you if I need? I know this sounds naïve, but I don't yet know all the questions that I need to ask.'

She chuckled at his candour and reassured him. 'Of course, Mr Webb, perhaps we'll speak again. Goodbye for now.'

'Thank you, goodbye.'

The business guide was only a five-page email, but valuable for its local information. Jon hadn't taken into account the political situation in Zed, and wondered why Olivia had emphasised 'politics are not included'. Nevertheless he emailed grateful thanks.

Also he hadn't thought of the personalities whom he may meet, and certainly not the distraction of female company. Well now, he thought, if Olivia looks as good as she sounds, I'd like to meet this lady, and as I'm paying for everything I could linger a while. After all, while I'm no philanderer, I haven't had any female company for over a year, so I'm not being unreasonable. Am I?

By late afternoon he'd had enough for one day, and left for home. He let himself out by the side door, and shut it behind him, hearing it lock. Only then did he realise the walking distance to the nearest bus stop for Eastbourne, and regretted declining Roger's standing offer of a lift, although to his surprise the roads of the industrial estate were fairly well lit, and he set off.

A couple of blocks from TLC he noticed that behind the buildings fronting the road, demolition was in progress although stopped for the day. He skirted round stacks of materials and plant to see what was in development, and walked to the beginnings of new factory building foundations. He was encouraged by the prospect of redevelopment of areas for new employment, but while the daylight faded there was sufficient to reveal that the foundations were of housing, not places of employment. 'Oh, bloody hell,' he exclaimed out loud, but to himself he thought people need houses, but if this slaughter of factories goes on there'll be nowhere for them to work. This isn't right!

'Oi!' a voice challenged him. ''Oo are you? What're you doing ere?' A rugged figure, wearing a vis jacket, loomed out of a shed. 'You're trespassing an' I can 'ave you arrested.'

'Sorry,' Jon offered, 'I was just walking to the bus stop and wondered what was going on here. I work in one of the factories back there. There seem to be houses coming here, are there any more factories to be demolished, do you know?'

'Dunno for sure, mate, you'll 'ave to ask someone else, but if I was you I'd make the most of my job cos I reckon the whole bleeding lot's coming down, ha, ha! Now, clear off afore the boss comes an' sees you, or I'll be in trouble.'

Polite as always, Jon reassured the man. 'Sure, sorry to disturb you, goodnight.'

The man's 'whole bleeding lot' worried Jon. The industrial estate needed an upgrade, but start-up businesses had spent money on improvements to their buildings. Had they bought the buildings or rented them? Or even bought the land on which they stood, which was unlikely, but how long would their tenancies be for if they rented, and above all what security did they have? Surely the overall plan wouldn't result in residential properties being randomly sited around remaining freehold-owned factories, unless those were at risk of compulsory purchase by the Borough Council? What about TLC's land and buildings? If they were at risk, what would be the point of expanding its business, unless of course there was a 'Plan B' in place to relocate, which Jon wouldn't know. If the security of TLC's site *was* in doubt, was Henry Catchmore hoping that the problem would simply 'go away'? Or, on the other hand, did he have such naive confidence in the future that TLC could afford to relocate anyway if needs be? Was that confidence built on the successes of recent events?

Jon concentrated so much on those thoughts that he nearly walked past the bus stop where another man waited, who asked, 'Hello, is your car in for service as well?'

'Oh, good evening! No, it was a car shared with my wife who now has it. I don't have one yet, and can't really decide what I want. Maybe a Land Rover, but it's not urgent. And you?'

'A bog-standard company Ford. There's nothing wrong with it, but the firm won't get me a courtesy car when it's off the road for service. Miserable buggers! If you're interested in off-roaders you could do worse than speak to my cousin. He refurbs and sells Land Rovers, and is pretty good at it. D'you want his number? Here, I'll write it on the back of my card.'

He gave Jon the card as a bus arrived, and said, 'This isn't my bus, I want the 135. Is it any good to you?'

'Yes, thanks a lot,' said Jon as the bus doors hissed open. 'If anything comes of this I'll tell you. Cheers.'

On returning home he swore. 'Oh, damn, I've forgotten the sherry for Sybil.' He shrugged off his coat, checked his answering machine, then phoned the Abbotts.

Eric answered. 'Hi, Eric, it's Jon downstairs. I'm probably in deep doo-doo with Sybil as I forgot to buy the sherry. In compensation, would you like to share a Chinese takeaway this evening? I can't be bothered to cook after all that's been happening at work, and I've a menu here to choose from.'

'That sounds okay to me, hold on a sec.'

Sybil came on the line. 'Good idea, Jon, pop up now and we'll decide what to eat, but you're not to pay for it all.'

They quickly chose their menu and phoned the order in. Sybil put plates in the oven to warm, and they settled down in comfort with a glass of wine in their hands to wait for its delivery.

'Thank you for this,' Jon said with warm appreciation. 'The last two days have been eventful so your company is a solace.'

'It's that bad, eh?' asked Eric. 'And what's this about Africa?'

'No, Eric, sorry, not bad, just fast moving and convoluted. I've put various ideas to my firm, which have all been seized on with alacrity, giving me the impression that the directors were lost in a sort of wilderness with no direction. In telling you this I'm not being disloyal, and to be candid I'd be grateful for your opinions. I hope you don't mind?'

'Not at all. What's bothering you in particular?'

'Remember that I left a large firm which either ignored suggestions from employees, or gave them no credit, so the suggestions dried up. TLC is quite the opposite. Every idea I've put forward has been accepted, which is surely abnormal, even in a small company. For example, there's a machine in Africa which has allegedly suffered serious damage and needs inspection, which I thought justified a visit from the firm, which won't, or can't, pay for the trip. I offered to pay from my own funds, and that's been accepted. I'm now beginning to feel that the firm can't operate without me, or is completely bereft of what's needed to progress a business, and that's simply unacceptable conceit on my part. I'd value your comments.'

Reassuringly, Eric said, with a knowledgeable smile, 'Jon, I think you're worrying unnecessarily. Let me explain by an example. Suppose you and a friend designed something, made a prototype, someone bought it, then asked you for another one. Word got around and orders grew so then you needed help to make them. Your wives helped for a while until it was obvious that you needed to employ someone full time, but then you and your partner get distracted by employment law and all the other ramifications of employing someone. You both waste time on a subject you know little or nothing about, manufacture slows, and customers complain about late deliveries. Then you meet an HR specialist, who looks at your firm and its prospects, helps with recruitment, conditions of employment, and so on. Before you know it, your problem's gone away, and you and your partner are back doing what you're good at, and the business thrives. The buzz word these days is "outsourcing", which benefits any and every type of organisation.'

'Sorry to interrupt, Eric, but you seem very knowledgeable about HR – or personnel management "in old money". How's that?'

Before Eric could reply, a bang on the main front door of the house heralded the arrival of their takeaway, so Sybil suggested, 'Let's enjoy this and think about what you've said while we're eating.

Jon insisted, 'Stay here, I'll go and get it and pay.'

CHAPTER EIGHT

The Abbotts liked the take-away. It arrived within the promised half hour time frame, it was still hot, and the delivery courier didn't hover about for a tip. Sybil served it, and the feast began.

'This is good, Jon, where'd you hear about these people?'

'Recommendation, it's the best way. Which reminds me, how do you know about HR?'

Eric had a good chuckle. 'Jon, I once worked in the personnel department of a large company, and concluded two things, no, three actually. Firstly, I disliked the firm's aloof attitude to its staff. Secondly, I thought that I could run a personnel department better, but I had to wait until I was professionally qualified to do what I really wanted, and that was to set up my own consultancy. Eventually I did just that. It was grim and hard work for months, but then one happy client introduced another and I was away.'

Those events weren't unusual. 'The third conclusion?' asked Jon.

'In the department was a cracking young lady about my age, whom I'd ogled for months but did nothing about it. Didn't dare, actually. As the day of my resignation drew near, I realised that I'd have to ask her out on a date, or I'd lose contact.'

'What happened?'

'Well, I did ask her, one thing lead to another, and here she is!'

'Sybil?'

The evening's amiability was undeniable, with Jon's gloomy worry about his job put to one side for the moment.

Eric picked up the threads of what he'd been saying. 'Jon, I said that I thought you were worrying unnecessarily, so now go back to the example of the start-up firm, which I think's analogous to your situation – a small firm getting out of its depth. You've told me that TLC has relied too much on repeat orders and recommendations for its business, but now in 2015 it's facing greater competition, and is unable to adjust, or doesn't have the people to do so. It's out of its depth in a way. Then an entrepreneurial character – you – appears on the scene by chance. You approached the CEO in the hotel where the seminar was held by asking "Can I join you?" Perhaps at that moment Catchmore thought of himself as a quiet and unassuming man, who wouldn't have done that, and realised that he needed someone pro-active like you in the business. You told us that he did most of the talking, he liked you as a listener, and you sensed that he began to trust you when he said "It's good to have someone to talk to." He said that because you interested him. Perhaps at your interview for TLC when he suddenly remembered you after many months, he realised that you were just the sort of character he wanted on Board to get new business. He liked the self-confidence that he lacked. Then let's guess this. Without your knowledge he then tells his co-directors what he knows about you, and persuades them to go along with fresh ideas that you come up with, and they have, and here you are! Isn't that reasonable?'

'I see the logic, Eric, but I'm not that good.'

'Jon, Jon, Jon!' Sybil said in frustration. 'You told us what your father's words to you were. In amongst them he was trying to tell you not to underestimate yourself. Why don't you just accept Eric's supposition and go along with the firm's support for your ideas?'

Eric looked stern. 'Jon, Sybil and I have seen many consultants transform the fortunes of small companies. What's the difference between that and what you are starting to do for TLC?'

'I see what you mean, Eric, but why did their ad specify that they wanted a designer?'

'Maybe Catchmore was trying to flush you out. Would you have applied for a job there if they'd specified sales manager?'

'No, but that seems to be my role now.'

'Agreed, but what's wrong with that?' challenged Eric. 'Forgive my bluntness, but your title as "Director of Projects" is meaningless within the company, but elsewhere you can explain its meaning however you like, depending on who's asking you at the time. Do you see?

'Look Jon, Sybil and I think that you've got yourself the sort of job that many would envy. Yes, it's insecure, but that's an incentive, not a millstone. Tell us, would your father have envied you?'

'I think that if I carried on fussing as I have, he'd be disappointed and frustrated with me.'

'Quite so,' said Sybil, and smiling at Jon she said, 'and so would we!'

'Well,' responded Jon, 'that's a threat if ever I heard one! Look, thanks for this evening, and for taking such an interest. As Henry Catchmore said to me, it's good to have someone to talk to. You're quite right that I should drop this cynicism and get on with my work, so if you'll excuse me I'll bid you good evening and go to check my emails and messages. And thanks again.'

***

The following morning dawned with an inspiring blue sky for a change, enough to cheer the dullest spirits as Jon enjoyed his walk to work from the nearest bus stop. It hadn't occurred to him to ask Roger for a lift because he needed the exercise, and didn't want to impose, but if it was raining he'd have thought differently, of course. Five minutes into the walk from the bus stop he came to the redevelopment site again, still with no indication of the company in charge. No name Boards, or claims for 'site safety awards', but men were now putting up hoarding to close the gap through which he'd snooped last evening. The secrecy was bugging him. Few people would protest against the development of a brownfield site, apart from Jon who was concerned about the loss of employment centres, so given spare time he decided to investigate, but not now.

Alice was already there when Jon arrived. She appeared in his office holding a shorthand notebook, a pencil, and wearing a smile. 'Good morning, Director of Projects, what is my master's wish this morning?'

'Oh, for heaven's sake,' Jon protested, laughing as he did so. 'Be serious, please!'

'Why?' she demanded, still smiling, 'I'm going to enjoy working with you, and if you don't also, I won't do it.' Then with a childish pout, she said, 'So there!'

The office had one chair, which Jon offered while he perched on a heavy packing case, left there for some reason. 'Alice, what's in this crate, d'you know? There's some weird printing on it that looks mid-European that I don't recognise. Someone must own the thing.'

'It's been there for weeks, I've no idea why. Would you like a cushion for your comfort and to complete the furniture?'

'You're in good form this morning, will it last?'

'Depends on what you want me to do. At home last evening I thought of a long list, not forgetting you'll get a bill for my time, and we're going to be scrupulous about that to prevent criticism.'

'I won't forget, but were you thinking of criticism from Mr O'Flynn?' She frowned. 'I didn't say that.'

'I know, but I've noticed that he's not involved with any decisions about my trip, and the directors are obviously keeping him in the dark, which is not correct as he's a director, in particular the FD. Anyway, enough of that, Alice. I've no written list so I'll tell you my plan for today. First, to phone the embassy in Zed because the email they sent didn't specify public holidays, which I want to avoid, and to ask if they've accommodation of any sort which I could rent. Also to ask about cell phone networks there. Do they know any industrial electrical contractors, and, don't laugh, Alice, bomb disposal experts?'

She nearly fell of her chair in hysterics. 'You must be joking, Jon!'

'No, that manager at the mine said that their machine had "blown up", as you know. If there'd been a second bomb that hadn't gone off, would you know what it might look like?'

Her face fell. 'Jon, I'm suddenly worried. Are you *really* sure you should go there?'

'Quite sure, Alice, and I certainly couldn't back off now. That last conveyor that TLC supplied was bought via an agent in Zed which was a normal export route, but nothing has been ordered since three years ago. Why? There's massive other investment in our type of machines going on over there but we've had none of it, and unless a TLC rep goes to investigate we never will. Don't you agree?'

'Yes, of course,' she admitted, 'but let's get on with everything. Here's part of my list. I'll ask about jabs you'll need, a visa, available flights, local currency – although you'll have to order it from your own bank, weather forecasts, is your driver's licence valid there, travel and health insurance, and public liability cover there as well. I'll start to deal with all that, Jon, and by the way, does this phone work? Mr Catchmore is supposed to have it checked yesterday.'

Jon pressed the green button to hear the tone. 'Yes, it's okay, I've already used it, and I'm going to give it a thrashing.'

She left him to make his significant first call, one which once again reminded him of his father whose influence never left. He noted the time when the call to the embassy was answered. For the record.

'British Embassy, good morning.' A female voice.

'Hello, my name is Jonathan Webb, from TLC company. May I speak to Ms de St Croix, please?'

'Please wait one minute while I transfer you, Mr Webb.'

Another female voice which Jon thought he recognised then answered. 'Olivia de St Croix speaking, may I help you, Mr Webb?'

'Oh yes, thank you, Ms de St Croix. Recently you sent me some helpful details about that country, and guides to doing business there. I'm now intending to visit, and thought it wise to consult the embassy before fixing dates.'

'I remember your call, Mr Webb, what can we do for you now?'

'To be candid, I still have no firm personal contacts there and I'm hoping that my first port of call could be to the embassy, in which case I would plan my travel around a date convenient to you. I wouldn't want to impose, but some local knowledge would be invaluable if I could consult with someone.'

'What exactly do you need?'

'Some names of local services for accommodation, local public holiday dates to avoid, taxis for cross-country travel, office facilities with internet connection, and contacts within the Secretariat for the Interior. I couldn't find any names here in the UK. I'm sorry to trouble you.'

'Are you travelling on government business, or for commercial purposes?'

'Commercial purposes only.'

'We can offer you certain facilities here in the annexe, for which there will be a charge to cover our costs. There is a bed-and-breakfast tariff, with possibly a light evening meal which is not guaranteed because it depends on staff availability. Telephone and internet connection is available, but with a charge for business international calls, and office facilities. May we know what you plan to do after you arrive, Mr Webb?'

'There is a mine about 30 kilometres from the embassy where there's a machine supplied by us which has been damaged we think by saboteurs, but I need to investigate it, and if possible to organise its repair. I will be seriously grateful for your help in finding transport to get there, and to suggest a repair company, and even – dare I ask – a contact in the office of the Secretary for the Interior who's overall in charge of the mines – or so I'm advised. I know that I'm asking a lot, Ms de St Croix, and am embarrassed to have to do so, but as I said earlier, we have lost our contact there and in effect I'm starting from scratch.'

'Mr Webb, we have limitations here as you'll appreciate, but can you hold the line for a few minutes while I make enquiries, or would you prefer to call back?'

'No, I'll hold on, thank you.' Jon was a great believer in not letting go of a contact that might suddenly be called away for some reason and not be there when you call back. To hell with the cost of the phone call! He was treated to some tolerable hold-the-line music while waiting, when she came back surprisingly quickly.

'Mr Webb, will you be here on the twentieth?'

Jon thought quickly that that might be a loaded question and a diplomatic hint that he should be there. If so, it could be to his advantage. Well, well.

'I could arrange to be, Ms de St Croix, but frankly because I need your help I am ready to fit in with any dates convenient to you, so yes I can be there. Why do you ask?'

'From time to time we hold informal evening receptions here for officials in government departments, local industrialists, and any UK exporters who happen to be here at the time, and there is one such event on the twentieth and Mr

Turbeville-Blyth asks if you would like to be invited. It is not a black tie event, and we don't yet know who'll be attending but it might be a good way for you to meet by chance some people whom you need. Your business visit here and presence at the reception will be evidence of UK business confidence in the economy of the country, so you'll be making a useful contribution to the evening. If you accept now, I'll email you the invitation if you don't mind that informality.'

'Yes, thank you, Ms de St Croix, I'll be pleased to come. As you say, it could be very useful, but as I have no experience of local circumstances I think it's sensible to arrive two or three days prior to the event in order to acclimatise, as it were, otherwise I'll be short of conversation!'

She found that funny, and with laughter in her voice, she agreed. 'That's a good idea, Mr Webb, just let us know your ETA and we'll be here to receive you, but I'm sorry that we can't collect you from the airport. There are plenty of taxis. So I will email the invitation, and we look forward to meeting you. Goodbye for now.'

Jon couldn't believe his luck. All through his plotting and planning for this enterprise his major worry had been how to make relevant contacts, now that Hugo at the mine hadn't emailed or phoned again. He thought himself lucky that none of the directors had asked him how, exactly, he intended to establish himself from a cold start. They weren't in a position to challenge him because he was bearing the cost, but in reality he couldn't have expected TLC to pay when Jon's only link was Hugo, a tenuous link at that.

He now had unanswered questions. The reception was informal, but just how informal? Thankfully it wasn't 'black tie' because he'd intended to travel light assuming that he'd be out in the countryside at the mine workings, so he'd take just one lounge suit. The more he thought about his planning, the more he realised how poor his preparations were, because it was all very well making the travel arrangements, but what had he thought he was going to do from the moment he stepped off the plane? It was lucky that no one in TLC had asked him, because without this development at the embassy he wouldn't have known what to talk about with other guests at the reception.

All these thoughts enhanced his respect for the people at the embassy, for they must have guessed at his naivety. But sure enough there was the invitation on his screen. After it was downloaded and printed with a second copy for the Guv he decided to check all his preparations yet again, to find what he'd missed, and to enlist Alice's help again. He found her with the Guv.

As usual, the Guv's door was open, but a light tap on it announced him. The Guv and Alice looked up with welcoming smiles.

'Oh hello, Jon, come in, take a seat. Coffee?'

'Yes please, white, no sugar.'

'How could I forget! Now what do you have for me?'

'There's an interesting development, Guv,' Jon began. 'You'll remember that I spoke to people in the British embassy in Zed prior to going there just to establish contact, believing that I'd need their help and advice if I went there. They've indeed offered advice, they can provide accommodation in an annexe to the embassy, and will give me personal advice before I approach any government departments.

'Best of all, I've been invited to a reception at the embassy on the evening of the twentieth to which various local politicians and businessmen are invited, and some from the UK.'

'Good Lord! How did you wangle that?'

'I didn't, they just invited me. It seems that during the previous presidency UK exporters were reluctant to go there because of the endemic civil unrest, and the unstable economy. However, a representative now from TLC appearing on the scene to do business there will be taken as an expression of confidence in their economy by the UK, so I will be a useful contribution to the reception. That seems to me to be an exaggeration, but I'm not arguing. Who knows whom I may meet?'

'So when are you leaving?'

'To arrive there on the eighteenth at the latest, so's to get to know the place a little, otherwise I'd be bereft of any meaningful discussion with other guests about local industry and culture. Is it okay with you if I leave then? I've no idea how long I'll be away, Guv, but I shan't be leaving any outstanding work here. Oh, I need to go to the bank tomorrow morning for currency. Okay?'

'No, that's fine, Jon, go when you need. Is Alice helping?

'Yes, you are, Alice,' Jon said, smiling at her. 'She's meticulously recording costs associated with the project, just as I asked, but I hope she's not too distracted from your own work, because I need to check everything again. For example, Alice, please will you arrange business cards for me? I need some for Chief Designer, and some for Director of Projects. Both should carry my private phone number also, please, and I obviously need them before I go. Oh, and Guv, here's your copy of my invitation which I'll acknowledge shortly.'

Having read the email, the Guv said, 'You must be really pleased with this, and you'll be pleased to know that Les Tindall has been as good as his word and by bank transfer has paid that deposit which he promised. Isn't that marvellous? I am so very pleased. Roger and I have continued work on an outline proposal for him which won't be too difficult because he doesn't want much variation from his previous machine, just interchangeable parts.'

'Are your Board colleagues pleased?'

Catchmore looked Jon straight in the eyes and said, 'I guess I know what you're driving at, Jon, and I can tell you that as a group they are pleased, with individual opinions varying of course.'

That was good enough for Jon, the implication being that O'Flynn was still dissenting, and if so when, if ever, was the man going to show an interest in TLC recovering from its doldrums? What more could any director want than a customer voluntarily paying a cash deposit against a verbal order, added to an employee with such a determination as to pay for a business journey on behalf of his company? Jon decided that if he returned from Zed with any quantifiable measure of success and O'Flynn was still negative that would prove that the man must have a vested interest in TLC's collapse. He wanted to voice these opinions to the Guv, but he would most likely side with a co-director with whom he'd worked for years, rather than with a new employee whom he'd instruct to get on with his work instead of speculating on matters not his business, and this wasn't the time to talk about negative issues anyway. There was always the thought, however, that the Guv shared Jon's suspicions and was watching O'Flynn closely but wouldn't or couldn't admit it. Jon wondered suspiciously whether O'Flynn had an interest in the redevelopment of the industrial estate which would give him more money than his investment in TLC, if he had such a thing? If so, was that the reason for his apparent uninterest in TLC? After Africa, he would try to find out, but how?

The days leading up to his departure on the eighteenth passed far too quickly for Jon's own comfort that he'd done all that he needed to do. He'd gathered all his TLC paperwork together, including his two sets of new business cards, but unfortunately not the working drawings and specification of the conveyor in Zed. Alice had been a great help, and gave him a tearful 'goodbye' when he left, but the Catchmores and Roger had been restrained and businesslike in their goodwill. Sybil Abbott hoped with her typical sense of humour as Jon was leaving home by taxi for Gatwick airport the following morning that he would return safe and sound because he hadn't yet paid for January's rent, and was he insured against all risks?

CHAPTER NINE

His first ever business class flight convinced Jon never to travel tourist class again. Easily said if someone else is paying, but the need to arrive as relaxed as possible would justify the extra cost even though he was paying. Anyway, I can afford it, he convinced himself, so why not?

He spent the flight time reviewing his preparations yet again. He had his satellite phone, his local currency, his business cards, enough clothes for two weeks, camera and video recorder, and rough maps of the mine site. He hadn't thought of anything else, except he'd forgotten to look in No2 unit for the specification of the conveyor belt.

Alice Mac was going to answer any further replies to their original mailshot. The Guv was attending to the quotation for Les Tindall, and the Abbotts would take in Jon's mail and look after his flat. Eric had relished dealing with Jon's request to investigate the ownership of the industrial site where TLC was sited, any planning permissions granted and pending, and if possible the ownership of TLC's buildings, or the lease if not the ownership. He had said to Jon, 'Bloody hell, Jon, you're not asking much are you?' But he happily agreed. It was something for him and Sybil to do.

Jon declined alcohol on the flight despite the freebies on offer, settling for reasonable food.

Finding nothing wrong with his preparations he wondered what he'd forgotten. No use now in planning what was going to happen next, he mused, nothing will turn out as expected, and being honest with himself he wondered if he'd truly embarked on this trip more as an adventure, than for the good of TLC?

***

Staggering about in the heat and humidity of the destination airport, he found a taxi of sorts whose driver rolled his eyes and swerved away when Jon asked for the British Embassy. The next driver was agreeable, but wouldn't stop talking over pop music on his crackling radio, claiming to have visited English towns never heard of by his passenger who suspected that he wasn't being taken by the shortest route. Finally they reached the embassy, which had the look of an old colonial style mansion, protected by closed iron gates manned by a muscular security guard.

'Please wait here for a few minutes,' Jon requested the driver as he got out and approached the man.

'My name is Jonathan Webb, and Mr Turbeville-Blythe is expecting me. May I come in?'

The guard looked stonily at Jon, and consulted a clipboard hanging on the railings. 'I have instructions here for you to continue to the house at the address on this card, and to return here when you are invited.'

Bloody hell, thought Jon, this isn't much of a welcome, but he thanked the guard and showed the card to the taxi driver. 'Will you take me to this address?' he struggled to ask over the racket from the radio, got a grunt in return, and climbed back in again, trusting to luck.

The house was a short drive from the embassy, with Jon hoping for a reasonable taxi bill. Paying in local currency, he had no idea what he'd paid or if he'd given a tip, but as the driver was still holding his hand out Jon assumed that he hadn't. Perhaps future business might help. 'Please give me your phone number so that I can use you again.' With alacrity the driver flashed his card, grinned hugely, gunned his engine and left in a cloud of fumes. The house was modern with a front door surrounded by prolific clematis. Jon's polite knock on it resulted in the appearance of a stout African lady wearing a bright smile and an attractive loose fitting full-length dress.

'You are Mr Jon, yes?' she asked, and without waiting for an answer stood aside for him to pass into the house. He went to pick up his case, but she protested saying, 'No, no, I take those.' He followed her in some embarrassment, not being in the habit of having a woman carrying his baggage, but he was then able to appreciate the interior of the house which was pleasantly cool and welcoming, with pictures by presumably local artists alongside the staircase and dotted haphazardly round the walls. His allotted first-floor room was bright with a view towards distant hills.

'Is okay?' enquired his guide. 'Will you like a cold drink? Orange, perhaps?'

'Yes please, madam,' he replied, startling the woman by his old-fashioned manners, but they had the desired effect as the smile enlarged, revealing splendid teeth. This welcome was an improvement over the embassy guard's 'You are to return here when invited,' which was rude and abrupt to a visitor.

The cool drink appeared in minutes and a grateful Jon asked, 'May I know your name?' not knowing the correct form of address. 'It is Evelyn, Mr Jon, and I am to tell you that Mrs de St Croix will be here to take you to the embassy in thirty minutes.'

'Thank you, Evelyn.' He unpacked his gear, showered, and felt more human now after his journey. Would this be a formal meeting at the embassy, or just an evening meal, or what? He supposed that visitors on export business were used to this sort of arrival routine, and going downstairs half an hour later found an elegant lady waiting in the hallway.

'Mr Webb?' she enquired, studying Jon. 'Welcome. Is everything to your liking?'

'Yes, thank you,' and looking at this lady's distracting appearance he thought everything's very much alright and to my liking, but get a grip on yourself, Jon, she's married.

'You are Ms de St Croix? Perhaps from the embassy?' Of course she's from the damn embassy you idiot. Try again.

'Evelyn here has been pleasant and attentive. The room is fine, the shower works well, and I feel quite refreshed after my flight.' He mentioned the shower to indicate style in his habits, but this attractive lady had unsettled him so his speech was clumsy, and collecting his wits with difficulty he said, 'I have to thank you for your help towards my arrangements to come here, it was invaluable and reassuring.'

'That's a pleasure, Mr Webb. Mr Turbeville-Blythe sent me to collect you for a light meal in the embassy garden this evening. He wishes to meet you now as he will not have time to be with you tomorrow. If you wish I can then be your local guide instead. 'Thank you, I have much to learn about this country, and I'm particularly looking forward to meeting Mr Turbeville-Blyth who also has been helpful.'

'Good,' and she thanked Evelyn for opening the door and shepherded Jon to a waiting car. At the embassy, the same guard leapt to open the gates saying, 'Good evening, sir,' to Jon's amazement. What a hypocritical turncoat, he thought, giving the guard a mere nod.

Turbeville-Blyth was waiting inside and greeted, 'Jon! It's good to meet you at last, how are things?'

'Fine, thanks, and again I thank you and your people for your great help with my preparations. There have been some developments that I haven't yet told you about. 'Good, and Jon may I explain that the Diplomatic Service has moved with the times and isn't as stuffy and formal as it once was, so we now use our first names in informal circumstances. At least we do here! I'm George, and Ms de St Croix's name is Olivia. Please use them. Let's go out on the terrace and have drinks. After you, Olivia,' and they took their seats in the shade of a palm tree.'

Jon didn't feel entirely relaxed in the company of these people and the unfamiliar setting, which despite George's reassurance had an air of formality. George was just over six feet tall, slightly greying stylish hair, slim and smart, grey assessing eyes, aged about fifty perhaps. Olivia was to Jon's mind a classic 'knock out'. At about his height and age and also slim, she wore a straight dark skirt, white blouse, dark hair swept back, and modest make-up. Jon wondered if these two were an 'item'. If so, lucky George.

A younger man carrying a tray laden with glasses and a jug of something joined them. George enquired, 'Is Pimms okay with you, Jon? And this is William Spence, who assists me in helping business visitors, so you may rely on him for detailed local issues. I should explain that he is on the permanent staff, whereas Olivia is on secondment from an investment bank in London as perhaps she's told you.'

'Good evening, Mr Webb,' William offered. 'Mr Turbeville-Blythe has given me some indication of your plans, which sound to be most interesting.'

'Thank you, William, and perhaps I may bring you all up-to-date with my present position?'

'Please do,' from George.

Jon launched into an overview of his task. 'I'll be recapping some things you may already know from email exchanges. I work as chief designer for TLC Ltd, which makes conveyors for mines, quarries, and other industries. I wrote recently to several TLC customers enquiring if our machinery was performing well so that we could quote them to potential customers, and those who've responded already report that they're all satisfied.' Jon amused his listeners by adding, 'One or two, however, made me laugh by phoning in reply to my letter saying, tongue-in-cheek, "Why did I ask, was I expecting trouble?" One customer thanked me for taking an interest in his fortunes, and is placing another order shortly.'

'Excuse me for being blunt,' William interrupted to a disapproving glare from George, 'but is that why you're here now?'

'That's my original reason, William, yes, but now not the only one. Our CEO, Henry Catchmore, pointed out that communications with certain parts of the economy here were not easy until recently. Or to be frank, he was nervous of the political situation, and was unsure what to do. However, the world demand for extracted minerals has grown, and I felt that despite former political difficulties here the country would need trading partners, and if TLC didn't try to export here, some other company would. The title "trading partners" in my book means suppliers, customers, and investors, some of which are already here from Asia. There was no time to lose, so the directors agreed that as Director of Projects I should come here to see if we could sell more machines.'

'Answering you further, William, I come to my second reason. I recently took a call from a man who announced that he is, or perhaps was, the manager of the actual mine here that had bought the original conveyor. He phoned me having seen my letter enquiring about it, but said that it was out of use therefore the mine itself couldn't operate. It seems that some rebels under the previous President's regime had blown it up.'

'Blown it up?' exclaimed George.

'That's what he said. Before I had a chance to ask more he urgently excused himself saying that some soldiers didn't like him using the phone, and the line went dead. I couldn't ring him back, and I don't know why the soldiers were there. It appears that the rebels were like the Luddites in 19th century England whose jobs were lost to machines, and so I guess that the rebels thought that the mine's output should be moved by men, not by the conveyor. They stupidly didn't realise that by destroying the conveyor the mine itself would shut down, putting miners out of work.'

'When was this sabotage, Jon?' asked George.

'I couldn't find out, and as an instance of rebel activity it wasn't reported in the UK press, or if it was I didn't find it, and I also don't know if the conveyor was indeed one which we had supplied.'

'But surely that manager would know that it was one of yours, or he wouldn't have phoned you?' asked George, thinking logically.

'That's a correct assumption if it was the only conveyor at the mine, but if it was one section of a flight of two or more machines it may not be made by TLC. I can only find out who built it by going there, and if it is ours I can hopefully organise its repair, but if it's not ours maybe I can at least do something to help.'

'What could you do?' asked Olivia.

'I don't know, because I don't know the extent of any damage. The worst case scenario is that the machine is irreparable, but if – and it's a big if – merely the power to it is cut there may be local engineers capable of mending it under my guidance. To be candid, I hope that if one way or another I can get it up and running again, someone in high places may consider TLC favourably if new tenders are invited. Price isn't everything, but the attitude of suppliers can be.'

His audience was thoughtful, until Olivia asked, 'But, Jon, if after you've been there and concluded that nothing can be done short of replacing the whole machine, or a major part of it, and there's no budget for emergencies at the mine, won't the money spent on your visit have been wasted?'

'That's been debated at length within TLC, Olivia. The directors agreed that there's a market for us here, so part of my job is to make contact with potential customers and to put it crudely, to sell them something. That will take time, during which TLC has to establish a name for itself which could result from our efforts at the mine, and if so some decision-maker at some time might remember us favourably. People have long memories for favours done in business, and you can never achieve that relationship by advertising, however much you spend.'

George had been listening with polite interest. 'Jon, I assure you now that we will endeavour to get you a good introduction to the Secretary for the Interior, and to the Minister for Mines.' Then seeing his watch he exclaimed, 'Good heavens! Look at the time, and we haven't eaten. Could we make do with sandwiches for once? It's all your fault, Jon, for being so interesting. William, could you please go and ask in the kitchen if some can be rustled up? Any preference, Jon?'

'No thanks, but I'm sorry if I've taken too much of your time.'

'Not at all,' reassured George, 'but what is your plan now?'

From the bag that he'd brought with him when expecting a meeting, Jon produced a geological survey map. 'I need to get to the mine, which I believe to be about thirty kilometres from here. It's not marked on this map, but it's somewhere here'. He circled an area where he thought there to be mines or quarries. 'To get there I'll probably need a four-by-four vehicle and driver, as a taxi in effect, if there is such a thing. Do you know of one?'

Helpful as ever, back from the kitchen with the promise of food, William announced,   'The embassy gardener has a brother who has a pick-up truck like that, if that would be any good, Jon?'

'Why not, I don't mind getting bumped about! I'd be happy to leave early tomorrow.' The sandwiches arrived, brought by another member of staff, and William left to enquire about the truck.

George said, 'I'm sorry about this, Jon, but I must be here tomorrow, and I can't spare William. Will you be okay on your own, with the help of the driver?' Having no choice, Jon accepted that, but before he could answer, Olivia announced, 'I'm happy to go with you, Jon, if you'd like. I do have a little knowledge of local dialects and conventions which might be useful. Would you mind, George?'

'No, fine by me,' he said.

Jon was delighted at this prospect. 'Thanks, Olivia, but are you sure? I've no idea how long we'll be away from here, or what to expect, but it won't be a normal day's work for a lady – that you can bet on!'

Olivia was quite sanguine about the prospects. 'That's not a problem I assure you, Jon. I don't spend my life sitting in offices, when I'd prefer to be out and about in the countryside, and I'm used to the mud and work on my father's dairy farm.'

William returned with the news that the pick-up would be at the lodging house at eight a.m. with a full tank of fuel, even maps. Helpfully Olivia offered to ask Evelyn to prepare packed lunches and bottled water supplies, and remarked, 'I'll see you for breakfast at seven, Jon, okay?'

'Fine, but how will you get to the house?'

'I'll be there already. I'm staying there.'

'Oh, I see. As it's only ten minutes' walk away shall we go together?'

Well, well, thought Jon, this lady possibly has a room near mine. I must be on my best behaviour, don't say or do anything unbecoming to a delegate for UK business which George had already suggested I will be at his reception.

Having gone to their separate rooms at the house, Jon concentrated on his kit for tomorrow. His business cards and passport as ID, copies of TLC papers relevant to the conveyor without unfortunately the drawings and parts list that he and Roger couldn't find, the satellite phone fully charged, money, and a compass he'd remembered at the last minute.

After a good night's sleep, he met a rather different-looking Olivia downstairs, dressed as if for going on safari. A green shirt with long sleeves, combat trousers with many pockets, tough-looking boots, no spectacles, a small canvas shoulder bag, and wearing an expression which implied 'Don't you dare say anything sarcastic.'

He didn't, but he was increasingly drawn to Olivia by the way in which she conducted herself. 'Good morning, Jon, sleep well?'

'Yes thank you, and I hope you did too. After thinking about that pleasant evening and packing for today, I was gone the instant my head hit the pillow.'

Evelyn had prepared a breakfast of fruits, yogurt, and coffee which they ate on a similar terrace to that at the embassy, and also produced generous lunch packs of food and water. The pick-up arrived on time, and as they prepared to leave the house Jon stopped by the front door. 'Olivia, please wait a moment, what do we know about this driver? Can we trust him?'

'He's worked for the embassy for a few years before I came here, mostly driving, I understand. He's driven the Ambassador several times, and the President once, I'm told.'

'Which President?'

'Ah, I see what you're getting at. I don't know, but we'd better get going before he drives off in a huff for being kept waiting.'

CHAPTER TEN

They loaded their gear in the back of the truck, giving great care to the satellite phone. Three seats were across its cab, and with his usual courtesy Jon held a door open for Olivia. 'Thanks,' she murmured, 'but you go on the middle seat please, Jon, I don't want to squash up against this driver, or have him fumbling between my knees for the gear stick.' The driver heard that and was clearly disappointed.

A thought struck Jon. Whispering in her ear he said, 'We mustn't leave him alone in the truck with the keys in case he decides to drive off abandoning us. I don't trust him yet.'

After two hours of steady driving over mostly unmade roads when Jon had to admit that the driver was careful, the land became barren and remote. Dusty dead vegetation was on both sides of a track which ran along a dried-up river bed, obviously not having carried water for decades. As they emerged from the end of a narrow gorge, both sides of the road were bordered by high wire fences restricting the width of the road and closing off any possibility of U-turns. Frequent signs on the wire warned DANGER, KEEP OUT.

'I understand the warning signs, but those fences wouldn't keep intruders out,' suggested Jon, thinking of the saboteurs.

'Mr Jon, they are also to keep wild animals out,' corrected the driver. 'The wire will go all around the mine area.'

'Oh, of course.'

Before long a full-height closed wire gate with a STOP sign on it blocked the road.

'Switch off and wait, please,' Jon instructed. Through the wire could be seen a wide open area at the foot of rocky hills, with a line of dusty trees on one side of the area and scattered buildings on the other. Jon thought that he could see the conveyor where it emerged from the mine.

Sounds of raised voices came from a brick hut outside the gate, and suddenly a group of shouting soldiers erupted from it, brandishing rifles they pointed at the truck. For some reason this absurd scene struck Jon as something from a James Bond film, and unfortunately he laughed. That just made matters worse, and he was hauled out of the truck, shouting to Olivia to get back in and lock the door as he was frogmarched towards the hut. A swarthy soldier in presumably an officer's uniform emerged, shouting to Jon in some foreign tongue, and waving his arms in emphasis.

'Sorry,' Jon protested, 'I don't understand.'

'English?' demanded the man. 'I know your language; why are you here?'

'I have come to visit the mine and to mend a machine.'

'I do not believe you. You have come in a stolen vehicle. I think you are lying.'

'I have paid the driver to bring me here, and I know nothing about his vehicle. The longer we stand here arguing, the longer it will take to get the mine working again. I am not a soldier or a politician, I am an engineer come here to help your mines. Will you please tell those men to put their rifles down, they are dangerous. Also, please open that gate and we will be on our way. There will be trouble for you if you do not do so.' That last remark was very bold, and Jon had no idea what he had meant by it, but by now he was a perspiring bag of nerves.

'No, I will not open it, I do not know who you are, and I do not trust you. The guns are not dangerous, they are not loaded.'

'Not loaded? What use are they then?'

'I do not have to explain anything to you.'

'And I do not have to explain anything to you either,' retorted Jon, 'but we are willing to show you our identification, provided you show me yours.' He folded his arms across his chest and stood his ground, glaring at the man. 'I require you to open the gate to let us pass to go forward to the mine over there,' pointing to what he'd guessed it to be. He was actually extremely nervous, and hoped he hadn't overdone his belligerence, especially as his adversary was taller, broader, and more muscular than he.

The officer was disadvantaged. 'We have used all our ammunition shooting for food.'

These men were in some sort of trouble, and Jon was curious. He turned and waved to Olivia, beckoning her to join him. After a noisy argument between her and the driver she left the truck.

'What was that row about?' Jon asked.

'He didn't like it that we didn't trust him to stay and while I understood his fear of the guns I warned him that the embassy wouldn't hire him again if he left us.'

'Do you have authority to say such things?' asked Jon.

'No, of course not, but here are the truck's keys.' Ata girl! thought Jon, then addressing her in front of the officer he explained,'Olivia, this gentleman speaks English, and has explained that the guns are not loaded because they have used their ammunition in shooting for food.'

The men were told to put down the guns. Jon's next question was obvious. 'Why have you had to shoot for food?' he asked in a manner he hoped would soften the tension. 'We have been here for three weeks, but with supplies for only one. We were sent here to protect the mine over there from rebels who are so isolated that they have not heard of the new President and the changes he has made, therefore they continued shooting and bombing. We chased them away once. We were supposed to be relieved after one week, but have heard nothing, and nobody has come. We have no radio.'

'What have you been shooting to eat?'

'Birds, mostly'.

'You've been shooting *birds* with *rifles*?'

Jon was impressed. He had shot much vermin with a shotgun, but had never heard of birds being shot by rifles. In Wild West films, yes, but not elsewhere because it's virtually impossible, unless the birds are perched.

'What happens when you report your situation to your superiors?'

'We cannot. The telephone is out of action and our vehicle does not work and we cannot fix it. I sent two men to go for help a week ago but we have heard nothing. Perhaps the rebels found them. I cannot risk these men here to walk many kilometres in this heat with little water, so I decided to wait for help to arrive. Instead we have you people who are no use to us.'

Restraining his anger at this stupid insult, Jon asked, 'Where is your vehicle?'

'Come,' instructed this upstart, beckoning Jon to follow. A vehicle track led behind the hut where stood a battered and sad-looking Land Rover in an area of dense scrub. Jon turned to Olivia and said, 'If I can get this old girl going we'll need to keep it running immediately to charge the battery if it's on its last legs. Can you drive one of these?'

Olivia frowned at Jon as if she'd been insulted. 'Yes, of course.'

He raised the vehicle's bonnet making gritty squeaks, and propped it open. He saw immediately what the problem was, showing that neither this officer or his men knew the first thing about engines, but he decided to make a drama about starting it up to prove to these characters that the mine also needed his expertise. He made the usual fluid level checks;

116

coolant water, brake fluid, and engine oil level. He found a clean stick and poked it down into the fuel tank. Good, enough there. The officer didn't know what Jon was doing, and stood watching every move, scowling all the time.

'Olivia, I've no idea what the battery charge is, and I may only get one chance with the starter, so please jump in and if it starts drive it away for a bit, but keep your foot on the gas and don't stall it, and then drive it back here.'

Borrowing some rudimentary tools from the pickup, Jon repaired a broken wire to the coil, thanking his lucky stars that this wasn't a diesel which he knew little about. At its third reluctant cough the engine started. He closed the bonnet, Olivia revved it for a few moments, then engaged gear and drove away into the scrub.

Panic and shouting among the soldiers was immediate. Jon's arms were seized and forced behind his back, the rifles were waved about, and the officer produced a pistol. The pickup driver dived for cover under his vehicle.

The officer screamed, 'Tell that woman to return here immediately!'

'Don't be bloody daft, she's out of sight behind those trees,' Jon shouted back. She was indeed, but taking her time. Jon could still hear the Land Rover's engine running and in a few minutes Olivia drove back, laughing hysterically.

'Hell's bells, Olivia, what were you *doing*, there was panic here?'

'While I had the chance away from these men, I was having a pee.'

'Christ, Olivia, talk about different priorities!' protested Jon, helpless with laughter.

They left the engine running, and standing looking at the officer Jon asked, 'Well?'

The officer still didn't trust them. 'Will it go again?'

'Yes, but not for long,' Olivia answered. The officer was clearly sexist. 'You are a woman, how would you know?' He demanded.

'Because there is not much petrol in it,' she replied, obviously keeping her temper with difficulty as a good and true representative of the Diplomatic Service should faced by this fool.

Jon's emotions had been churning after he'd just realised in this very moment that maybe in this unbelievable adventure he'd unexpectedly found the sort of exciting and capable woman he would like as his partner. He gazed at Olivia in silence for a moment or two, not daring to say anything, for this would be completely the wrong place and time.

'Jon,' she asked, looking directly at him, 'are you okay?' After what to Jon seemed minutes, but were just seconds, the corners of her mouth twitched and she smiled with her eyes, and he thought, does she know what I'm thinking? How could she do that?'

He literally shook himself, and with a Herculean struggle brought himself back to reality. 'No, not really, but yes,' he said to reassure her. 'I'm thinking what to do next for these men. Olivia, how much fuel is in the tank?'

'Using my dad's Land Rover as a guide, I'd guess at enough for forty miles on normal roads, say thirty over these.'

'Thanks. Switch it off please, then re-start it to show that it will, but then leave it running to charge the battery.'

After that simple exercise with the engine, Jon faced the officer with whom he'd planned a serious confrontation, but now his attitude had softened, and all that he wanted to do was to help the men. After his brief reverie just now he was in the mood to help anybody and everybody to do anything, encouraged and distracted by the possibility of a relationship with Olivia. I'm supposed to be here as a tough negotiator for TLC he protested to himself, but I don't feel tough at this moment. So he intended more support for the officer who was clearly subdued by results, and who offered an apology.

'Mr and Mrs English,' he began, 'I say that because I do not know your names and I wish to apologise for my bad behaviour towards you, and also for my men who only acted as I instructed. Thank you for mending our vehicle which will hopefully take us to safety.'

He launched into local language addressing his men at length, who when the officer had finished, startled Jon and Olivia with salutes. He then announced, 'My name is Makwasni – please call me Mak.'

Significantly the gate was opened for them to pass, but Jon had other ideas.

He said to the officer, 'Thank you, Mak, call me Jon, and this lady is Olivia. I am from England to repair a machine at the mine, and I hope that it can work again. Mrs Olivia is from the British Embassy and with her local knowledge is to assist my work. Okay, Olivia?'

'Near enough,' she granted.

'How far away from here is your nearest base?' Jon asked Mak.

'Seventy kilometres, I think.'

After consulting Olivia, Jon had to say that, 'We do not think that you have enough petrol to get there. Do you have a telephone number for your superior officer?'

'Yes, of course.' Mak frowned.

'Would you like to telephone him for reinforcements or supplies?' Mak looked at Jon as if he were mad, but the answer being obvious Jon produced his satellite phone, and after several attempts at connecting to his superior, Mak was in full flow while Jon worried about battery life and the cost, and also wondering how to save the number against possible need. Mak was in high spirits. He handed the phone back to Jon, who ended the call. 'My colonel is sending men, water, and food. He tells me to thank you.' Then spoke again at length to his soldiers reporting the conversation which resulted in them standing, clapping, and saluting their officer.

Jon gave his visiting card to Mak, saying, 'Come and see me if you are ever in England, and until then we wish you good luck and safety.' Handshakes were exchanged between everyone, including the taxi driver to his consternation, and with some reluctance on Jon's part as this small adventure was over, they left for the mine.

As they set off Jon asked the driver, 'Was this vehicle actually stolen?'

'Yeah, but not by me. I bought it from a dealer who'd got it from a thief who is now in prison. The dealer gave me papers from his insurers showing that the truck was now his to sell, so I bought it. I do not break the law, Mr Jon, I do not like you to think that I would.'

Jon said, 'No, I did not ask if you'd stolen it. I asked if it had been stolen – there is a difference, and also I want to compliment you upon the way you have been working today.' And then, anxious about a misunderstanding developing between him and this African driver, added, 'Thank you, and by the way we don't know your name. What is it?'

'It is Dave, Mr Jon.'

'Dave? Just Dave?'

'It is enough, Mr Jon.'

'Thanks, Dave,' Jon acknowledged. It occurred to him how easily even a small innocuous mistake about the truck's origin could become a major issue between cultures. They approached the mine cautiously, aware that rebels could be squatting in the buildings ready to hijack returning employees or anyone else carrying supplies. 'Switch off, please, Dave, and we'll wait to see if anyone comes.' After five minutes

Jon decided, 'Okay it seems all clear, but we'd better watch out for animals which may have been foraging for food waste thinking there's still some around.'

Dave went round to the back of his truck, producing a shot gun and cartridges from a steel box. Jon and Olivia stared. Tactlessly, Jon asked him 'Are you any good with that?' Dave retorted, 'Of course. How do you think the embassy gets fresh game for its dinner parties?' And smiled when Jon admitted, 'I'm not going to ask you any more questions!'

As they'd already seen through the wire the area inside the gate had been widened into a large area for trucks, three of which were still parked there. It was a good sign for Jon that power cables ran from a larger building and disappeared over the horizon supported by wooden poles. Maybe the lines haven't been cut, he hoped, perhaps there's still power here. Dave stopped near to the conveyor which was accessible. Jon wanted to work alone when looking at the machine with no interrupting questions. 'Olivia, would you and Dave have a general look round while I search here, please? I'm sure you'll be safe with him. Keep your gun with you, please, Dave.'

Jon had expected explosives used to put the conveyor out of action permanently, making it irreparable, but at first sight he presumed that there had been no explosives because of evidence of a major electrical short circuit, which would have *sounded* like an explosion due to the high voltage of the incoming supply. The damage had clearly been deliberate.

'This was madness!' he exclaimed. Whoever had done this knew he was taking a dangerous risk to say the least. It must have been an experienced electrical engineer, and definitely not an ignorant rebel, who could have killed himself. The damage was to the electrical supply to the conveyor's switchgear, which was wrecked, as was the safety cabinet enclosing it. Whoever did this knew that it could be repaired, so why put the conveyor out of use temporarily? Surely if Hugo was the manager of the mine – claiming to have qualified at Camborne – he would easily conclude the same cause of the alleged "explosion", and could have had it repaired? Why hadn't he done so? Why was he nervous of the soldiers seeing him phoning for help all the way from the UK? Perhaps he wasn't near the switchgear at the time of the so-called explosion and the 'soldiers' prevented him going to investigate. Another realisation hit Jon; were the 'soldiers' who had frightened Hugo in fact rebels in stolen uniforms? Where was Hugo now, and when was the mine deserted?

Jon considered his position. His remit was to generate new business for TLC, not to detect and solve crimes in another country. However, back at TLC it was agreed that if Jon could ingratiate himself with Zed's hierarchy by getting the conveyor, and the mine, going again it would help TLC's new business negotiations. He therefore decided to end the speculation of the-who-and-the-why of the sabotage and concentrate on getting it repaired. He had been sitting on the ground going over all these aspects staring at the conveyor all the while. There were too many mysteries here, none of which made sense. Olivia returned with Dave, and interrupted with, 'Jon, shall we have something to eat? We're hungry.'

'Good idea,' agreed Jon. 'Dave, if you didn't bring anything to eat, please share some of ours. Did you two find anything?'

'Nothing of interest,' Olivia answered. 'It looks as if the whole place was abandoned in an orderly manner. Three offices have filing cabinets which are locked, there's a canteen of sorts with freezers and fridges that have been cleared of perishables. There's a workshop with machine switches left in the 'off' position, but we didn't go into the mine workings. It is like Neville Shute's book *On the Beach*. Have you read it, Jon?'

'I have indeed. It was too prophetic for my comfort, but when you've finished eating please look at the damage here and without any prompting from me, please say what you see, and what you think happened here.'

Dave said, 'There has been a very bad fault in some live wires,' and Olivia expanded on that with, 'It seems to me from the scorch marks in and around the damaged area that there has been a major short circuit.'

'Exactly so,' agreed Jon. 'And I don't think that there is anything more that we can do here, except please take pictures on your phones, I will need them later.' Results from both were good.

'Another thing troubles me,' said Jon. 'When the people here left, which way did they go? Is there another gate? If they had used the same gate that we did, surely Mak would have said something to us, which means that they had left before he and his men were posted here.

'I've decided that it's not my problem either to answer the question or who did the damage here, or why, that is for the overall management of the mines to do. Can either of you think of anything else we should do here?'Olivia and Dave shook their heads, with Dave seeming to be very pleased to have been consulted.

'Right,' said Jon with authority, 'let's go home. Dave please note down the distance we travelled both ways, and slow down by the gate.' As they did so, Mak and his men emerged.

'Mak,' Jon asked, 'were there people here when you came?'

'No, Mr Jon.'

'But you said that you'd chased some rebels away, where had they been?'

'We do not know, they tried to get in through the gate which was locked, but we came out of the hut and they ran away. They were dressed in army uniform, but not our army.'

'Do you know why they wanted to get in?'

'No, I am sorry, I cannot help you, but I am very pleased to have met you all.'

'Thank you, Mak, perhaps we'll meet again. Goodbye.'

And to more salutes the pickup left, and waves were exchanged. After travelling for a while, Olivia enquired, 'You're quiet, Jon, what are you thinking?'

'Nothing makes sense here, but Dave, if you have any opinions please tell us, because I don't consider you to be merely a driver.'

They were now back in open country, and seeing a clump of trees ahead, Jon asked Dave to please pull over in the shade and park while they talked about what he'd been thinking. Glad to be away from the truck and its lack of air conditioning, they piled out.

'I think that I have completely misunderstood the reason for the damage, and what I seriously want to know now is, are there other mines in Zed which have also been damaged?'

CHAPTER ELEVEN

Continuing his ideas, Jon began. 'Dave, you haven't been told all the details behind my visit, and if you've questions please wait until I've finished, but as you're obviously intelligent you're likely to think of something new.' Olivia smiled at Jon's pleasant manner towards this driver.

'I came here to either get the conveyor repaired, or replaced, hoping to get a contract for one or the other, but when I saw the machine I knew that it could be repaired, so why was it damaged in the first place, especially as it was done in such a way as to minimise the cost of that repair? The saboteur must have been an experienced electrical engineer.

'We come to the who, the when, and the why. Mak told us that he assumed the men he chased off were rebels wearing uniform from a different army. Suppose they weren't soldiers at all, but men wearing combat gear similar to Olivia's here which can be bought anywhere? Sorry, Olivia, nothing personal! But unlike Mak, Hugo probably wouldn't have known the difference, so perhaps it was actually one of them who damaged the conveyor.

'There was nothing in Hugo's phone call to suggest that he was subject to violence. He hadn't expressed surprise at the "soldiers" being there, just that they "are guarding the mine", so didn't seem surprised when they cut the phone call to me. He said that the conveyor had been "blown up", but hadn't heard an explosion himself and we now know that explosives weren't used, although perhaps in fairness to Hugo it was reasonable for him to suspect they had. So when was the damage done? Not at night with animals prowling in the dark and an insecure security fence. So perhaps very early one day a bunch of camouflaged men broke through the fence, one of them damaged the conveyor, then they waited for Hugo to arrive for work to whom they explained that the sound of an explosion had brought them there. They probably lied to Hugo saying that some tourists on safari reported it. They then prevented Hugo going anywhere near the conveyor on the pretext of the risk of a secondary bomb, and waited for him to stop operations and close the mine completely.

'There's probably a routine procedure for that, including a report from Hugo to his superiors. When the mine was cleared of everyone we can presume that Hugo locked the security gate and left. Eventually Mak and his men arrived after instructions from the overall mine authorities to guard it. What a boring job, with nothing to do until we arrived.

'Nothing has been heard of Hugo since. Presuming him to be alive, he's either being held against his will or he's joined the rebels, or he's hiding from them. I hope that it's the latter, but what were those men intending to achieve, and have they actually achieved it? I have an idea what it is, or was, but I'll leave that for now because I think it's extreme, and that all the above events took place under the late President's regime, but what do you two think of what I've said so far, please?'

Olivia had been listening intently. 'I follow your reasoning, Jon, and I don't argue with it, but I'm baffled by the suggestion that someone deliberately damaged something with the intention that it could be repaired later after having served some useful purpose.'

'Dave,' said Jon, 'what do you say?'

'Mr Jon, I agree with what Ms Olivia said, so I don't now suggest what I was going to say before you'd finished.'

'What was that?'

'The mine was put out of action, so nothing could be removed from it. But suppose someone wanted not to take materials out, but to put something in?'

'Go on.'

'Well, this mine has an entry at ground level as we have seen and small electric vehicles can drive in and out. There must be many spaces – galleries, I think they're called – which could be used for storage.'

'Storage of what?'

'Wine, or anything which needs constant storage conditions, stolen paintings, for example. Or documents, armaments, security papers, laundered money, gold. Many things.'

'Good Lord! Dave, what an imagination! Are you serious?'

'I am, Mr Jon, because the men we think are rebels had got to the mine in Hugo's absence before he arrived for work and before Mak and his men came to lock the gate. If you think about it, the conveyor delivers ore to the trucks which drive away to unload at the crusher then they always come back empty, but suppose they stop on the way somewhere to load up with things to store in the mine? If they did that in small amounts of some sort, the mine manager Mr Hugo may not be able to see.'

Jon was impressed. 'I follow your reasoning, Dave, and I think that an internal search of the mine is quite urgent. We're not going to get involved, except that when I report your idea to the mine authority I'll make sure that you get the credit for it, not me.'

Jon went on. 'When trying to make sense of all this I had an idea of the purpose of the damage and its consequences, but I need to ask you a question, Dave, and please speak freely when you answer. People in business have reacted positively to the election of the new President, but what do people in Africa generally think? As I've said please speak freely, this is not a trap.'

Despite Jon's reassurance, Dave was obviously sceptical, and reasonably so because under the previous regime nobody, but nobody, dared to say what they thought of the government, let alone the President. To do so, and be caught, meant prison at the very least.

Dave looked from Jon to Olivia, and back. Finally and Jon thought, bravely, he spoke.

'I wouldn't have answered you before today, but I saw how you work and now I trust you. I think that when you said "people in Africa" you meant *ordinary* people, but were too polite to say so. Many black people still dislike the whites for historical reasons, some of them justified under colonial rule, but now most white people and governments overseas want us to prosper, and encourage democracy in our country.

'I haven't said this before to anyone, but the last President didn't understand democracy, or if he did he ignored it and he ruined the country by corruption and his bad treatment of the people. We're all pleased with our new President, and are hopeful for the future, Mr Jon.'

'Thank you, Dave, for trusting us. Your opinion's relevant to what I say now. I think the renegades damaged the mine as part of a campaign to damage the economy. I don't know if there are other damaged mines, or other affected industries, because the closure of just this one mine wouldn't have a major impact, but if there *was* a campaign of sabotage, before long the whole economy would be in a worse condition than it was already and grind to a stop.

'Perhaps I'm exaggerating, but suppose I'm right. Ultimately the population would rise up and the unpopular President would be overwhelmed. Would that be a fantasy? There are of course flaws in my argument. For example, a campaign would entail prodigious central organisation, which would be impossible to build up because of the President's numerous infiltrated spies.

'Alternatively, the idea of sabotage could spread by word of mouth, which could be rapid among disaffected people, especially between the "small worlds" of the same industry.

'So, Olivia and Dave, do you think that my theories are plausible? If they are, and because there is a new President and his people are settled and confident, we could tell the mine owners that the conveyor can be repaired and the damage is unlikely to be repeated.'

'Well?' Dave asked, 'Who do you think did all the damage, Mr Jon?'

'I have no idea, but although they were doing criminal damage I can't think of anyone who could identify them, still less who'd want to prosecute them. I'm new in this country and couldn't know.'

Olivia had been really pensive. 'Jon, I see one flaw in your argument. Suppose the campaign wasn't centrally co-ordinated, or couldn't be, as you surmised, then there wouldn't have been one spokesman to blackmail the President saying "resign or else". Also even if there *had* been anyone, he'd have been shot. Your theory therefore hangs on the assumption that eventually the populace would have at last taken matters into their own hands. Do you think that's a possibility, Dave?'

'Yes, I do, Ms Olivia. I know that I'm only a driver, but I do read newspapers and listen to what passengers are saying. Eavesdropping, I think you call it. There have been uprisings called Arab Spring which began in 2010 in Tunisia, and spread to other countries not always with popular results, but it could happen here, yes.'

'Jon,' said Olivia, 'Dave clearly has his "finger on the pulse" here, and an uprising against the President would be likely, as you've suggested, but we don't know if there was damage elsewhere of sufficient severity to be catalytic. Using your phone I could ask George T-B to make enquiries while we are travelling back.'

'Good idea, Olivia, here it is.' She was surprised by the rapid connection to the embassy, and the good luck of T-B being back there that day.

'Good afternoon, George, it's Olivia here … yes, fine thank you. We would like your help, please … No, not from the mine, from Jon's satphone. We think that we know why the mine here was damaged, and it would really help us if you could find if there was similar damage to other mines, and to other industries … Yes, I could make enquiries myself if you're snowed under … Yes, I know you always are, but you have contacts that I don't. If there *are* similar instances, it would be of great significance to Jon in any meetings with Mr Gavuzzi … Oh no, not in precise total, but are they numerous … Yes, they may be unreported. Oh, thank you, George … Yes, we'll be back today. Thank you very much. Bye.'

Giving Jon back the phone, she remarked, 'I think that George took the hint that Jon needs the answers soon. One does not say "urgently" to him because he thinks that only calls to the emergency services are urgent. If anything else is said to be "urgent" he thinks it's because someone has forgotten to do something. He's mostly right.'

By now, the sun had moved around and they were out of the shade. Despite the heat in the truck they set off to return. The drive was faster now that Dave was familiar with the tracks and roads. All three of them were engrossed with their thoughts, which always seems to make anyone's journey shorter and they were surprised to arrive back at the lodging house before sundown. Unloading their gear, they sensed some regret that their eventful day should end, leaving Dave appreciative that his status as a driver had been ignored enabling him to become an equal participant in the adventure. Jon offered his hand. 'Dave, thank you for your work and your contribution to our task, we have enjoyed your company, and I'm in no doubt that we will meet again. I don't know what I shall be doing from now on, but I look forward to the possibility of needing you. Thanks so much.'

Olivia reinforced all that. 'I'm sure that we will see more of you, Dave, particularly here in the embassy, and I also thank you for your ideas and hard work. I'll see you again soon.' She surprised him by her handshake, which was generally unheard of at the embassy between such different levels in the hierarchy.

Dave nodded to the two of them, and drove off smiling broadly in pleasure.

'I don't know about you, Olivia, but I fancy a shower, a long drink on the terrace, and something to eat if Evelyn could oblige.'

'I think she could, Jon. Would you like me to see if George can join us for drinks, but I know he won't stay long as he has a dinner date this evening?'

'Yes, brilliant,' was Jon's eager response. An evening with Olivia. What a prospect! 'Shall we meet on the terrace in an hour? Okay? Good.'

***

Refreshed and feeling human again after the eventful day, Jon waited on the terrace for the others, making notes. Darkness had closed in before George arrived, bearing a bottle of Hock. 'Good evening, Jon, this is all I could find as everything else is locked up for the night. Is Evelyn getting you some supper? If you're settling here for it, I'll light this oil lamp.'

'Hello,' greeted Jon, shaking hands, 'I prefer German wines, so you've done the right thing, thank you, and Evelyn is getting something.' They settled round a circular table apparently made of a native timber that Jon didn't recognise.

'Olivia not here?'

'Washing off the residue of a dusty day probably. It took me a long time.'

135

'Tell me about your day please, Jon.'

'Of course, and I'll write up a long report tomorrow. Could I use one of your computers and a printer, please?'

'Sure, come along to the embassy in the morning, and see William. He'll fix you up, but give me an outline now, if you would.'

'The mine was about 30 kilometres miles away, I think. I asked the driver to record the distance. Incidentally, his name is Dave, and I recommend him unreservedly. By the end of the day he and Olivia and I had melded into a working team. I'd use him again anytime.

'We were accosted at the mine by a group of soldiers who'd been abandoned by their higher command. They were there to protect the mine from rebels, but they seemed to have been forgotten, having no supplies, radio, phone, food, or transport. At first they were hostile, to say the least, but by using my satellite phone they organised their rescue, and we left them happy. It was at times a hilarious, or an alarming experience.'

Olivia appeared in the doorway to the house, silhouetted and glamorously backlit by the room lights behind her. The men courteously stood in welcome.

'Good heavens, Olivia! What's that you're wearing?' asked George.

'It's just a full length loose-fitting dress, George, I obviously wouldn't wear it to the office as it would be quite unsuitable. I had the idea for it from Evelyn, and loved the idea of the enormous reproductions of colourful local flowers, which aren't easy to see in this late evening light.'

Jon made a social blunder. 'Is it one of Evelyn's?'

'*Jon*!' protested Olivia, 'it certainly is *not!* Although I did buy it in the market from the same woman who had made hers.'

'Sorry. I bet if you took a load of those to a music festival back home they'd sell out in minutes, but if you wore one to Glastonbury it'd look odd over muddy wellies!'

'Back to business, please, Jon can we resume where you left off?' asked George. 'I have to leave soon.'

'Of course. Olivia I'd just told George about Mak and his men, and how we left them. From there, George, we went to the mine, found the conveyor, and I immediately knew that explosives hadn't been used. The so-called explosion was the sound of a massive short circuit which could have sounded the same.'

'Quite possibly,' confirmed George, 'once when I was working on my old car I carelessly dropped a spanner across the terminals of a fully charged battery; there was terrific bang, and part of the spanner melted.'

'Exactly. Olivia and Dave had been searching the buildings and reported that the mine had been abandoned in an orderly manner; everything was clean and tidy, no perishables left in the canteen, toilets left clean, and so on. In other words it was easily reusable. Added to that, the damage to the conveyor could easily be repaired. So the questions were, who would do damage knowing that it was repairable, and why do it?'

'There's more behind my reasoning than I'll explain now, but I suggest that the damage was part of a widespread campaign against the economy to damage it beyond the capabilities of the President to organise its recovery, therefore presumably he'd have to stand down. All that's been pre-empted by his death, and the new President's election.'

'A flaw in my argument is the "widespread campaign" theory, because under the old regime nobody trusted anybody for fear of the President's spies, so I can't see how a network of saboteurs could be built in secrecy. However, George, if you can tell me that other mines or factories have also been damaged, my theory bears water and you can understand why Olivia phoned to ask you to find out.'

'Don't forget, Jon, that she asked me only three or four hours ago, so I haven't finished my enquiries, but so far there have been two mines, a quarry, and a water pumping station reported to me.'

'A water pumping station? For human consumption, or irrigation?'

'Mains water to two villages. The effect would be immediate, obviously, but apparently some small mobile pumps are getting some through. That's all I can tell you now.'

'Thank you, George.' Then after deep thought asked, 'When was it known here that the President had died?'

We can't be sure. He'd gone to Mexico for medical treatment, but died there from an unknown, or more likely, undisclosed illness. His remains were flown back for a funeral in the manner of his tribal custom which was attended by all sorts of sycophantic diplomats torn between condolences and laughter at the irony of the death. But um, six weeks ago, I think.'

'This sabotage could have stopped then, while the culprits waited upon events, and it would probably have ended with the new President's inaugural speech promising changes, on their assumption that the dead President's gangsters would be rounded up.'

'Do you think, then, Jon,' asked an equally pensive Olivia, 'that the risk of sabotage continues?'

'When I said "gangsters" I meant his henchmen who under the umbrella of "security officers" would have been his enforcers, running protection rackets, frightening people away from polling booths, and reliant on him for money. Their source of money died with him, so now they've no money, but time on their hands. Men like that are dangerous – no money, nothing to do, frustrated, and no leadership to control them. If there is more sabotage, it will be by them simply releasing their pent-up violence. As I said, dangerous.'

Evelyn had been watching and tactfully waiting while Jon was talking, but the sight of food stopped him immediately. 'It's only a light bean salad, Mr Jon, Ms Olivia, I'm sorry if I've interrupted you.'

'No problem, Evelyn, if you produce food like that again, interrupt me any time!' thanked a smiling Jon.

Ever the practical diplomat, George had an obvious question. 'Jon, I go along with your theories and your clever logic, but what are you going to do next?'

'The key to that is Mr Gavuzzi. He's overall responsible for the mines, apparently, so his authority is needed before any repairs are done, and there is no more that I can do here without that authority. So, George, I seriously need more of your help. It's possible that I could approach his office for a meeting with him, but that could take days. Would you be prepared to introduce me personally to him, on the basis of what I've told you now, and my credibility?'

George's reaction was spontaneous. 'It will be a pleasure, Jon. If he doesn't come to the reception, or if that's not the right time and place, I'll do so afterwards, but please give me a couple of your business cards. I have an idea that he may be at the dinner tonight, but we'll see. Talking of which I really must go now.'

'Thanks that's immensely helpful, George,' said Jon, smiling at the thought of how he and Olivia might spend the rest of the evening in an otherwise empty house.

CHAPTER TWELVE

Olivia and Jon remained sitting across the table from each other in the gloom of the dimly lit terrace, listening to the sounds of the African night, occasionally watching suicidal moths flying near the oil lamp now burning with a smoking flame.

'That lamp's going to go out soon,' said Jon, stating the obvious, 'but this is a very pleasant way for an eventful day to end.'

'End?' Olivia asked softly, and suggestively. 'Is it to end now?' She was gazing at Jon with the same mischievous expression which had so unnerved him outside the mine.

'It's beginning to get a bit chilly out here, would you prefer to go indoors, Olivia?'

'There's a coffee maker in my suite. Would you like a coffee, Jon?'

'Thanks, I'll just tidy up here and see you in a few minutes.'

Ever the gentleman, Jon had given her private time before he joined her, but then realised that he didn't know which rooms along the corridor were hers, or even if the other rooms were occupied at this time of night. Consequently he almost tiptoed along, and peering tentatively round the first open door he came to found to his relief that it was hers.

Her room was identical to his, not large, but adequate for both expected and unexpected guests to the embassy, and was more like a hotel suite. 'It's the same as mine,' he observed, failing to find something sensible to say.

'Really? Has yours got a woman in it too?'

'No, but there is space for one.'

Olivia moved across the room to him and stood directly in front and close to him. She looked up and asked quietly, 'And who might that one be, Jon?'

He looked down, with his fingertips lifted her chin up a little, and kissed her gently.

'Mmm,' was all she said, then, 'this room of yours, would I do?'

'Not really, Olivia, it's too far to walk.'

'Do you remember George's last question?'

In these circumstances, why would he want to remember?

Taking his hand, she lead him gently into the next room of the suite which proved to be her bedroom and quietly asked 'George asked you what you were going to do next. Well?'

Neither of them said anything, because nothing needed to be said for quite a while. There was no rush, no hurry, just the pleasure of mutual discovery. After a while when she lay with her head in the crook of his shoulder, and an arm across his chest, Olivia said, 'Thank you, Jon, that was lovely.'

'I can only think of one thing to say after that, Olivia, and you must tell me – please – if I'm going too fast, but I'm going to say it.'

She lifted her head and looked at his face. 'You sound very serious, tell me.'

'Do you remember after you'd had your pee in those bushes and you'd driven back with the Land Rover and I was gazing at you and you asked me if something was wrong?' His answer all coming out in a nervous rush.

'Yes, I was concerned.'

'I was thinking that quite unplanned and quite unexpectedly I'd met a woman who I would like to have as my partner for a very long time.'

Silence. Each with their own thoughts. Did he mean it? Has he said that to anyone else before? Have I annoyed her? Did I go too fast? Was I being soppy? Why did he say that? What do I know about him? Is he married? Is she married? Is he being honest? Would this damage her career? By "a very long time", did he mean marriage? Christ, does she think that I want to marry her? Well, do I? What's his income, does he earn enough for two? Why the hell do I need to know that?

'Jon, I have another question.'

'Oh.'

'Would you like a coffee?'

'That question comes as a great relief, Olivia, you've no idea, yes please!'

Gathering up her bath robe which magically could be found by the bedside, she disappeared and shortly returned with two mugs.

Jon complained, 'You didn't ask me if I take sugar.'

'Well, do you?'

'I don't remember if I do or I don't, and at this moment I don't care.'

'Why can't you remember?'

'I've no idea. Something seems to have distracted me.'

'I have another question, are you married?'

'You go straight to the point, don't you, Olivia? No, recently divorced. We both behaved in a civilised manner, but it's a pity.'

'Why is it a pity?'

'Well, people fall in love – if you'll excuse the cliché – marry, all seems well, then something happens or a new interest arrives, or a new person, and the original sharing of interests is no more.'

'Which new person?'

'One of her colleagues at work, but in fairness to her I was becoming more interested in my job, although less tolerant of her self-centred histrionics. You will not hear me speaking ill of her again.'

'Jon, have you done before what we've just done?'

'What, with you? No, I'm sure that I would've remembered.'

She put her coffee down, and hit him with a pillow.

'My turn now, Olivia. Is Ms de St Croix really Ms, or Mrs, or Miss? I know that she's not a maiden in the old-fashioned sense. I had wondered about that, but we know the answer this evening.'

Another strike with the pillow.

'"Mrs" is a smokescreen, Jon, an attempt to indicate that I'm not "available".'

'Not available? I'm sure that's not right, if my memory serves me.'

'Okay, selectively available.'

'So what are the approved indicators from your selection? Have you made choices before?'

'Yes, very few, but not as interesting as this one,' and she turned to Jon, putting her arms round his neck, kissing him and smiling with happy laughing eyes. 'You'll do,' she said, and they slept. A well-deserved sleep at the end of an incredible day.

***

They were awakened by the raucous ringing of the bedside phone. Out of habit, Jon went to pick it up. '*No, Jon, stop!*' Olivia squeaked, 'guests aren't allowed in these rooms!'

She grabbed the phone from him. It was Evelyn. 'Oh hello, Evelyn … Oh, good heavens, I seem to have overslept! Thank you for reminding me. What? Not answering his phone? Yes, possibly in the shower. I'll go and bang on his door soon. What? When did he phone …Oh, thanks. Bye.'

'Phew! Jon, you'd better get up and out of bed and down for breakfast in half an hour, George is joining us for a breakfast meeting!'

'Olivia,' Jon began, 'George isn't daft. Didn't you notice how he watched us during the evening? He must have guessed that our working day may develop into something more, but Olivia, I promise you I hadn't even give a thought to the evening ending as it did, but I don't think George would be surprised that you had company last night.'

They exchanged smiles and Jon left in a rush.

He dressed with lightning speed, and was down for breakfast in twenty minutes taking his notes from yesterday with him. Evelyn appeared brightly dressed again. 'Good morning, Mr Jon. Mr Turbeville-Blyth will be here shortly, and has asked me to lay a table on the terrace. 'The same terrace table they had used the night before had been laid with cutlery, good quality napkins and a large vase of exuberant local flowers. Jon spread his papers ready for the meeting, hearing Olivia and George talking in the hall way. He liked circular tables; best for meetings as all participants could see each other.

'Good morning to you both,' he offered, trying not catch Olivia's eye. 'Sorry, I'll make space for you.' He shuffled his papers together. George looked at them and unfortunately remarked, 'You look as if you've been at it all night, Jon.'

Olivia had a sudden and violent sneezing fit, grabbing a napkin and hiding her face behind it, spluttering. Recovering, she apologised, 'Sorry – hay fever, it's these flowers.'

George looked at her with a smile, obviously not believing a word of it. He opened the meeting. 'Mr Gavuzzi was at the dinner last evening, Jon, along with fifteen others including the Minister for Industry, so I didn't have more than five minutes with him before dinner was announced. If you have dealings with the Minister have patience and be careful. I don't think he liked your title including "director" because I guess that he's very left wing. He's also taciturn and stolid, joining uninvited into my conversation with Gavuzzi when I gave a résumé of your report.

Gavuzzi listened to me in silence, asking no questions, no change of expression, and no reaction at all. He was hard work and impossible to fathom, so when I'd finished I was astounded when he said, "Please tell Mr Webb to make an appointment with me tomorrow."

'I suggested that he could meet you at the reception, which was a mistake because he countered that with, "No, a meeting in my department where there is privacy." He and the Minister then left me to mingle with the others for cocktails before dinner, but he wasn't seated next to me. Neither was the Minister, thankfully!

'So there you have it, Jon, an entrée into the upper echelons of government, as you needed.'

'I'm unsure how best to thank you, George, because I could not have asked for more.'

'As I said, thanks to me aren't needed. Whether the repair goes ahead or not, you've effectively supported this embassy's work in cementing good relations with a foreign power, which although was probably unwitting when you set out, your work is thanks enough. What do you plan to do now, Jon?'

'Well, phone to make an appointment with Mr Gavuzzi, but before doing that I should prepare a proper written report as a provision against him asking for a copy. On the other hand, if he says "come now" I'll go with the promise of a report for him later today.'

'Jon, supposing you phone him, and he does say come right now, could Olivia start drafting the report while you're away, as she was with you throughout the day? What do you say, Olivia?'

'Yes, fine. Jon could leave his notes, but take my mobile phone, Jon, to show photographs of the damaged machine.'

'Oh, good Lord, I forgot!' admitted George, 'your driver printed off photos taken on his mobile and dropped them into the embassy last night! Sorry, Jon, but I'll get them sent round right away.'

'Brilliant! Thank you, so please don't forget how helpful he was all day yesterday as I told you.'

'No, I won't forget, and please let me know how you get on with Mr Gavuzzi. I will be at the embassy all morning if you need me.'

***

Jon phoned the Secretariat, gave his name, and was put through to Gavuzzi office. A woman answered, 'Mr Gavuzzi's office.'

'Good morning, my name is Jonathan Webb and I wish to make an appointment for a meeting with Mr Gavuzzi. I believe he is expecting me to call.'

'One moment, please...' Then, 'Mr Webb, can you be here at 2 p.m.?'

'Yes, thank you, I'll be there. Goodbye.'

Olivia had been riffling through Jon's papers. 'Jon, I haven't found anything with the actual address of the mine we went to. Do you have it?'

'There should be a copy of the letter I wrote to the mine weeks ago. I took the address from the delivery and billing documents which were in the office file. Blast! I left it there! But Olivia, we only need to know the name of the mine and Gavuzzi could identify it from that. I forgot to write it down, but Dave might know. This is embarrassing. Anyway, we have two hours at least to write a report of events and my speculations. It'd be great to have your help.'

They began writing an outline of the facts of the previous day, and were remarkably adept at separating business from pleasure. No winks, no innuendos, no touching of hands, and no out-of-place proximity, therefore William's sudden arrival caused no discomfort.

'Mr Webb, I understand that you are going to a meeting with the Secretary for the Interior, do you need a car and driver?'

'Oh yes, please, William, thank you. While you're here, I'd like your advice on what to wear. I've brought the minimum of luggage including just one suit for the evening reception, and most of the rest is informal wear. What's the least I can get away with for my meeting, because I don't want Mr Gavuzzi to think that I don't change for evening receptions, so I can't wear the same suit all afternoon and the evening. Have you suggestions, please? Don't forget my name's Jon.'

'Mr Webb, sorry, Jon, we seem to be about the same size in clothes, would you like to borrow my navy blazer?'

'Are you sure? That would be so helpful.'

'Okay, I'll be back with it in about half an hour. I'll bring a couple of ties as well.'

'That's brilliant, thanks, but there's something else I haven't discussed with George, and that's the charges for my stay here; yesterday's driver, phone calls, meals and so on. I have the means to pay, so who do I talk to about it?'

'Mr Turbeville-Blyth has a sense of humour. He instructed me how to answer that question if you asked. He told me to give you a blank sheet of paper, saying here's the bill, and to walk away, just like this,' and he went.

Jon watched pensively as William disappeared into the building. 'Olivia, if I am ever in the company of anyone who criticises our Diplomatic Service I predict that I'll get angry and defensive of it. Also, one of its virtues is the possibility of making new friends, would you agree?'

'Perhaps you're right, but as I'm here only for a short while I have few opportunities.' Then looking at Jon directly with a straight face, she continued, 'But I don't look for them now.'

Thinking of no adequate response, he settled for returning her gaze in mutual silence, eventually breaking that silence but not breaking the spell of the moment, and said, 'I meant what I thought at the mine, Olivia..'

'I know you did, Jon. Say it again in a year or so, would you please?' Self-restraint escaped them at last as they reached for each other in a silent embrace, until Jon said, 'My CEO's last words as I left were, "I'm sure that you'll come back with a good result." I'll tell him he's a clairvoyant.'

When Evelyn gave a light, tactful cough, they realised that she had been watching them, for she approached wearing a smile as large as a basking shark's. 'Would you like coffee or tea or something, Mrs Olivia, Mr Jon? Or do you have everything that you need?'

'You are a kind lady, Evelyn. I think tea, please, yes, Olivia?' Evelyn had worked at the embassy for several years, through difficult years and good times, but apart from Mr Turberville-Blyth, he guessed from her expression that no white man had ever before spoken to her in such a polite and respectful manner.

Bringing them back to reality, Olivia asked, 'Do you think your report's okay as it is, Jon?'

'Yes, I do actually. We don't know what Gavuzzi expects but all the facts are there, and I think that if we spent hours jazzing it up it would lack credibility because he knows that we've only been back for a few hours, so it's only a draft. I'll ask William to stick the photos on to backing paper.'

As before, Jon marvelled at the embassy staff's ability to appear like genies at exactly appropriate moments, for here was William with his blazer, some ties, and a cravat. The blazer fitted near enough, and Jon reported, 'I've just found these car keys in one of your pockets, William.'

Dropping his diplomatic façade, William exclaimed, 'Oh, bloody hell, I've been looking for those bloody things for two days so I've had to walk to the office!'

Jon couldn't help himself, 'Language! William, language! But thanks again. George has some photos for me, so after I've selected some, could you please have them stuck on an A4 sheet to match our notes?'

'Of course,' he agreed, withdrawing in embarrassment at his faux pas.

With an apologetic cough, Evelyn appeared holding an envelope. 'Excuse me, Mrs de St Croix, but a messenger just brought this for you. I'm told it's a fax message which may be urgent, so I've interrupted you.'

Olivia opened the envelope and read the fax in rising alarm. She looked nervously at Jon.

'Jon, yesterday there was an extraordinary event in London when we were away at the mine. My PA, Janice, took a call on my office phone from Mr O'Flynn who was abusive and obscene, demanding "Why the f... isn't she there? And you can tell her to mind her f... business and we don't want your f... bank's money", and slammed the phone down.

'Janice had no idea who this foul-mouthed man was, but she did a search on O'Flynn and found that he wasn't well known in financial circles, and not at all in the City, but appears to have some involvement with property.'

Jon gaped at her. 'When did you know? Not before last evening, I hope?' He looked unreasonably angry.

Olivia was irritated by Jon's silly question. 'No, Jon, only this morning, just now, you saw me open the envelope!'

'Sorry, Olivia, that was a reaction, not a sensible question. May I try again? Please tell me why you didn't know earlier. What made O'Flynn try to phone you in your office?'

Olivia was equally blessed with an ability to forestall a disastrous situation. She actually smiled. 'This could take a while, Jon, do you have time?'

'For you? Forever.' He smiled at the world's silliest sentimental word.

'I need to explain about my employer, Futurebank Inc. Like all banks, it makes money by borrowing money and lending it on, but it's not a high street bank so doesn't have a retail section. You probably hadn't heard of it before we met?'

'Oddly enough, I think I had, but it didn't register. I read the financial press avidly, looking for snippets relevant to my work, which is how I concluded that it's worth coming here.'

She continued. 'It's a large part of my job to research companies to check their needs. That's why I knew something about your company before you came here. George hadn't heard of TLC before your first phone call to him, and asked me to find out what I could so that the embassy could behave properly towards TLC. For all we knew, it could have been a large conglomerate or a small start-up.The bank has numerous information sources, both published and unpublished, and even more numerous contacts, especially in other banks. I don't have the authority to agree loans, my job is to report and recommend to the directors whether we should lend or not.'

'Isn't it frustrating for you, Olivia, if they override your recommendation?'

It happens when they have additional facts from their own sources, not privy to me. All of us in the bank have memories like sponges, soaking up data and names on a "just in case" basis, just like the CID remembering villains who turn up again after hiding for years. Sorry, I digress. I was curious about the name TLC, which although not exactly an acronym had to be the initial letters of something, but surely not " tender loving care" which didn't suit a maker of machines to move rocks about. So I phoned the company.'

'You *phoned the company*? Who did you speak to?'

'A very pleasant lady named Mrs MacInnes. Who is she?'

'She's the Guv's secretary. What did you say?'

'I told the truth. I said for whom I worked, saying I was researching companies who may want finance at some time, and gave her my London phone number. She seemed to be very quiet at the prospect of extra finance, and explained that their CEO, Mr Henry Catchmore, was absent on a short break, but that I could speak to a Mr Frank O'Flynn, the Finance Director, and gave me his number. We ended the conversation pleasantly. Who is the "Guv", Jon?'

'The CEO, my immediate boss.'

'Thank you. I've nearly finished. From that conversation, and from your pleasant manner of speaking over the phone, for some reason I quite liked TLC and made more enquiries. I was curious that its listed directors didn't mention a Webb on the Board, although you must be relevant to be coming here. I decided that "Director of Projects" was merely titular, but all that was before you came, Jon.'

'When did Janice tell you about the O'Flynn incident, Olivia?'

'I haven't spoken to her. She probably sent this fax for me c/o the embassy because she knew you were here, and that it might help me to be cautious of what you say about your company.'

He skimmed the fax quickly, and said, 'I think that Janice acted intelligently. Please tell her I said so, and I am truly sorry at being short with you earlier. Please tell me that that incident's behind us, especially before I go to meet Gavuzzi.'

'Jon, it is certainly behind us, and it was partly my fault for not thinking quickly enough when I read the fax. But can you tell me, please? Is TLC in financial difficulties?'

'In a word, yes, depending on what we mean by "difficulties", which is vague. There is some relief from a customer who has sent a large cash deposit with a new order, on the proviso that O'Flynn is not involved with the processing of his order.'

'Why?'

can be aggressive and offensive, as Janice has learnt. He's aloof to the staff, who can't understand how he came to be on the Board. For some time now I have suspected that if TLC went under, it would suit him, but I can't think how he would cause it, or how he'd benefit. If I'm right, then O'Flynn would be livid at the possibility of Futurebank providing funds to TLC to keep it going, hence his unwarranted attack on Janice.

'I also think that he voted against my work here in case it succeeds, which is absurd, but I have to tell you, Olivia, that I joined this company because of my confidence in its future. TLC is in the doldrums now because the directors were happily trundling along getting repeat orders from existing customers, and new ones from recommendations, and it's my belief that they just didn't foresee the present competitive market coming. They had no one to look for new business, or the experience to do so. I seriously hope that O'Flynn's attack on Janice won't mean TLC being stigmatised within Futurebank, because it has a track record of ethics and propriety.'

'Why are you particularly troubled about TLC's reputation within the bank?'

'Well, it would be undeserved, for one thing, but it's common sense to build business relationships through contacts at any level.'

'By "any level", did you mean me?' She looked displeased.

'No, sorry, that was clumsy, I meant me. I am not on the Board, neither do I have any involvement with the company's finances, although this enterprise in Zed is an exception because I have authority to commit the company up to a discretionary limit; otherwise I couldn't get anywhere with this project. As things stand back in the UK, all I could do is to suggest you as a suitable first contact in the bank.'

CHAPTER THIRTEEN

Gathering his papers and his thoughts together, Jon took the car which had arrived promptly, and thanked the driver who would wait until his meeting finished. The Secretariat offices were housed in an apparently former mansion since converted into official use. It was well-maintained, judging from the landscaped gardens at the front, and its paintwork in good condition. Jon presumed that all this was to impress visitors. It did.

The interior was equally impressive. Acres of white paint reflected light from high windows, probably the originals, and the whole effect was cool and calming against Jon's expectation of a brittle and forbidding atmosphere. He was shown into a small conference room where seven or eight men mingled, giving Jon no idea who was who.

Tentatively he enquired, 'Mr Secretary?'

'Ah, Mr Jon!' offered a well-built African man of about Jon's height, approaching with a smile. 'Let me introduce my colleagues.' He took Jon to them each in turn, giving their name which he forgot instantly, but luckily remembering George's advice that the Minister for Industry could be cold and distant. He was, shaking hands reluctantly.

'Gentlemen, be seated. Mr Jon, please take this seat,' indicating the one next to him. The table was made in sections to allow different shapes, in this room an octagon near enough to Jon's favourite circle. The Minister sat directly opposite him, but other than those two men there was no indication of anyone's title or level of authority. Don't ask, Jon thought; wait to see what happens.

'Now, Mr Jon, your Mr Turbeville-Blyth gave me a verbal report last evening of why you came here, and what you have found. I have already told my colleagues here, but now tell us all that in your own words.'

Jon had decided that in meetings he would always go straight to the point, not saying anything needing interpretation. They all knew that he was there on business, so why not be honest and say so?

'Mr Secretary, Minister, gentlemen. Thank you for receiving me. I have come here on business, to see if my company, TLC Ltd, can supply machinery for your mines and quarries, but I emphasise that in our company profit isn't everything. The company has a long history of good relationships with customers, so when I learnt that nobody had visited you since you bought a conveyor three years ago, I decided that we should be represented here. However, please don't let me mislead you, because I also predicted good business opportunities as your economy flourishes. Those *were* the principle reasons for my visit – courtesy, and potential profit.

'Is my blunt manner of speaking acceptable to you?'

The Secretary looked at the others in turn for their reactions, receiving smiles or nods in return. 'It would appear Mr Jon, that you may continue.'

'Thank you. As part of my planning to come here I wrote to several of our customers at random asking for their opinion of the machines they had bought. I have copies of their replies here,' holding up the bunch of them to show the meeting. 'I don't have all the replies yet, but so far they are all good reports, and one customer is ordering his second machine. All that, I trust, is evidence of the quality of our products.' He looked around at the listeners, seeing no signs of scepticism.

'I received no reply from your mine to my letter until we had a phone call from a gentleman who said he was the manager of the mine which had bought the conveyor I'd asked about. He reported that it had worked well, until it "blew up", and that puzzled us all in TLC because we don't use explosives!

'I can't give you a verbatim report of my conversation with him whose name is Hugo for short, but the gist of it was that because the conveyor was out of action the mine itself had to shut, putting men out of work. He asked me to come here and mend it, but his phone suddenly cut off and I couldn't get back to him. However, as I wondered if there had been sabotage elsewhere in the country in those times I presumed that explosives had in fact been used, which *could* mean that the machine was totally wrecked beyond repair.'

The Secretarycoughed gently, and said, 'Excuse me for interrupting, Mr Jon, but I can assure you that Mr Hugomvarla is well. He did not witness the damage at the mine, nor heard the explosion because he was away at the crusher, but he sent a comprehensive report to the Minister here that the mine was out of action, and that he'd closed it. He acted properly in every way and has been promoted to be in charge of two mines elsewhere in the country. He did well to telephone you. Please continue.'

'Thank you, sir. Because of my firm's good reputation for customer care, we felt obliged to travel here to see what we could do to help the mine to be productive again, and that is unrelated to seeking new business.

'At first sight of the machine yesterday I knew immediately that it could be repaired, because the damage was only to its electrical supply. Someone who knew what he was doing had caused a major short circuit which could have sounded like an explosion to a layman, but why would anyone do temporary damage knowing that it could be repaired? It then occurred to me that it was perhaps part of a co-ordinated campaign of sabotage in your country intended as a form of protest against the government, but that's speculation.

161

'You will appreciate, gentlemen, that I have left many details out of this summary of events, so I will answer any questions. We are, however, at the point where provided that there are suitable facilities and contractors here, that conveyor could be restarted, and I will be happy to organise the repair should you wish. In the meantime, thank you for receiving me this afternoon.'

Jon then realised he had been quite unmindful that his was the only white face in the room, and therefore hoped that he'd been accepted by the meeting on the basis of what he said and how he'd said it, showing respect to them. His own philosophy was that appearances were inconsequential, it's how people behave that matters. He felt comfortable with his behaviour and what he had done in this completely new experience.

It seemed that the Secretary might agree with some of that. 'Are there any questions for Mr Jon?' Heads shook. 'Mr Jon,' he resumed, 'as you might expect, we would like to confer in your absence for a short while.' Addressing the Minister, he requested him, 'Minister, would you please take Mr Jon to the relaxation area and arrange refreshments?'

So Jon and the taciturn Minister for Industry walked a short way to a room where two other people were presumably enjoying their afternoon break, until the Minister waved them out of the room. His touch on a switch produced a young lady with an order pad, and the Minister enquired, 'What would you like to drink, Mr Jon? Unfortunately, a pint of bitter is out of the question!'

Laughing at the joke, but more with release from tension than amusement, Jon replied, 'Just mineral water, please, Minister. Do I take it that you have been to England?'

'Once, to study at the Camborne School of Mines for a short while. Why do you ask?'

'Because you struck me as having an interesting background of a technical nature. Were you at CSM on a postgraduate course? My class at technical college visited once during our apprenticeships, not to study mining or geology, but to be shown career choices.'

'Are you an engineer, Mr Jon?'

'Yes, mechanical. My task at TLC is to update our designs, which is why visits to customers are important to learn what they need. I will be grateful for any ideas that you might have.' As before, the Minister's expression gave nothing away, and Jon asked himself how it would be possible to get past this man's inscrutability. He was as stolid as a sphinx.

'Mr Jon, you told us that the so-called explosion was an electrical short circuit. As you are not an electrical engineer, how could you repair it?'

'I couldn't. I offered to organise or manage its repair, using local people wherever possible.'

'But you are a director of your company, yes?'

'No sir. I am "Director of Projects", which is a suitable title and level of authority when speaking to customers, or for signing contracts. I am not on the company's Board of Directors, but I can make decisions at their level. For example, if necessary I can spend money to repair your machine, with no prior guarantee from you that we'll be repaid!'

The Minister grinned mischievously, and challenged Jon, saying, 'Good, please go ahead!'

'Okay, sir, when shall I start?' Jon smiled back.This repartee had apparently broken the ice, for this was the first sign of any humour in the Minister's demeanour. Jon took the opportunity to press a possible advantage by showing interest in the man's background.

'Minister, may I know about your experience in mining, for example has it been in copper?'

'Yes, originally, to help support my family. My father was a miner, but he was hurt in a mine accident working for a company which gave little compensation for his injury. He was given a poorly paid job at the mine so I had to leave school to earn money for food. I hated the company for their miserable treatment of their workers, and especially their directors who nobody trusted.'

'Were you a face worker?'

'Yes, and the conditions were bad, very bad.'

'I can imagine, Minister. When you were in England, did you visit the old mine at Morwellham Quay?'

'Yes, the conditions there were terrible, and you British should be ashamed of the treatment of the miners in those days.'

'It wasn't only miners who suffered, sir, there were children in factories, working up chimneys and so on. My own apprenticeship was nothing like that, but we did start at seven in the morning and lost pay if we were a minute late. How did you progress from face worker to going to Cambourne?'

'Same as anyone, Mr Jon, hard work, reading books by candlelight, and applying many times to go on courses. It seems that our backgrounds are similar. My name is Hogarth, please use that when we are alone, and I will call you just Jon, not Mr, okay?'

'That's fine by me, and if I may say, I'm enjoying your company.' The Minister laughed when Jon then said, 'Perhaps you'll come to England and we could enjoy a pint of good Sussex beer!'

A delegate to the meeting knocked and entered. 'Minister, could you return to the meeting for a short time please?' The Minister surprised Jon by leaning across the low coffee table to shake hands as he left, leaving Jon with his mental arithmetic working out the probable cost of repairing the conveyor in case they asked. He had no idea of local labour prices or availability, or of spares. It would all be a guess, he realised, and O'Flynn wouldn't like this. And laughed out loud.

Five minutes later, the Minister had reappeared unannounced in the doorway behind Jon.

'Something's made you laugh, Jon?'

'Oh, hello, Hogarth, yes. It was a funny incident yesterday. I'll tell you about it sometime.'

'I look forward to that, but now please come with me to return to the meeting.'

On his return to the room, Jon sensed that the atmosphere had warmed towards him. The Secretary was definitely the most senior man, because he had kept one of the sides of the table to himself, and Jon as the guest business visitor.

'Thank you, Mr Jon. Before I continue, could you be here for another meeting tomorrow morning if necessary?'

'Yes, Mr Secretary, that is no problem.'

'Good. We have decided that we will ask you to organise the repair to the conveyor, and we understand from the Minister that you have the authority to do that without reference to your colleagues back in the UK. Is that so?'

'Yes, sir.'

'When could you start?'

'In principle, right now, but please let me explain. I have no office or telephone here, or contacts among possible contractors. It would be most helpful if you could lend me someone to help me if necessary, a room with a telephone, and transport of some sort with a driver because I will need to return to the mine. I must go back to the embassy to extend my accommodation, and to tell them and my company that I will be remaining here for a while.'

'What is your estimate of the cost of repairs?'

'Not less than five, but not more than eight thousand dollars US. This is very vague, I know, but I suggest is reasonable in the circumstances.'

'Are you prepared to sign an agreement to that effect on behalf of your company?'

'Yes. I have the authority to do so.'

'Good, then shall we meet again here at, say, 10.30 tomorrow to conclude formalities? I will send a draft agreement between us to you at the embassy later this afternoon. Until then, we will meet again this evening, I believe?'

'Yes, thank you Mr Secretary, Minister, and gentlemen. Goodbye for the time being.'

CHAPTER FOURTEEN

The patiently waiting driver took Jon back to the embassy, where he found both Olivia and George in the building's large dining room helping to prepare for the reception later.

Stopping work, George said, 'Well?'

'Very well, actually, George. They have asked me to organise the conveyor's repair. A draft agreement is coming here later today, and I'm to go there again tomorrow morning to sign it and conclude formalities. The Secretary and Minister will definitely be here this evening.'

'Congratulations!' George exclaimed, 'I am so pleased for you. What do you say to that, Olivia?'

'Jon's done well, and I'm pleased to've taken a small part in it. It beats working in a bank!'

George asked, 'Tell me, how did you get on with that frosty Minister?'

'We had a few laughs.'

George's diplomatic façade collapsed. 'How the hell did you do *that?*'

'Piece of cake, George. No seriously, we broke away from the main meeting while the Secretary was cloistered with other delegates, and he was okay when he knew that we had a few things in common. I'd worked my way up from an apprenticeship, and he from being a face worker in a mine. It was he who cracked the first joke which was quite funny, and broke the ice.'

'Who were those other delegates to the meeting?'

'I've no idea. I instantly forgot their names the moment I was introduced, and none of them spoke while I was there. I'd decided to be up-front with them all, and made it clear that while I was there to help, I was also looking for profitable business, and they said they liked that approach.'

'What are you going to do next?'

Jon couldn't stop himself looking at a smiling Olivia as they both remembered that same question last night and what happened after it. 'Are you okay, Olivia?'

'Yes, just happy for you, thanks.'

'George, the first thing to arrange is a longer stay here, and if I may, the use of an office and phone so I can report to base. Are those possible, please? I will of course pay if you ask.'

'Yes, but wait until after your meeting with Gavuzzi tomorrow when you know what he wants in more detail. What if he asks you to organise repairs to any other similarly damaged machines? You could be here for weeks if they are dotted around the country.'

'I'd thought of that, and in a way I hope it doesn't happen. Because there's a lot to do back home.' What he really meant, and couldn't say, was that he didn't want to work in the UK if Olivia remained here, and he didn't want to remain here if she returned to the UK. What a dilemma.

'I know nothing about repair resources and capabilities in this country. Either I could pick up the phone here and find a contractor who'd continue the work after I'd supervised the first repair, or there are suitably trained people who could be organised into one new unit which I could help to set up.

'To be candid, George, I'd prefer the first option, then I could focus on new orders back in England but, as you advise, I'll wait until the end of the meeting. In the meantime could I share William's office and phone, please?'

'Of course, I warned him that this could happen. It's three doors on the right down that corridor.'

The line to TLC was free of interference and crackling. A man's voice answered.

'Guv?' asked Jon.

'No, the name's O'Flynn.' Oh Christ, thought Jon, what the hell is going on if a director is answering the phone? This is awful news, who on earth let him use it? He could speak to customers! Suppose Les Tindall happened to ring!

'Who's that?'

'Jonathan Webb, Mr O'Flynn.'

'What the devil do you want, Webb?'

'I rang to give Mr Catchmore an update on progress.'

'Mr Catchmore's not here. He's visiting the works manager who went into an area nothing to do with him, to look for something which you asked for. If you'd been minding your own business there wouldn't have been an accident. You've been nothing but trouble since you came. You are supposed to be a designer but I've seen no sign of that work, and now you've gone away on holiday.'

Jon all but protested at "holiday" but thinking quickly and carefully he thought, don't defend yourself, keep calm. Easier said than done. Don't argue with this man. 'I will return soon, Mr O'Flynn, and we can discuss this then.'

'No that's not necessary. There's no need for you to come back, because I'm dismissing you now. Your employment is terminated, and you will have that in writing.'

'What?' said Jon, and in a moment of high adrenaline retorted, 'No, Mr O'Flynn, you cannot do that, you don't have the authority to do so.'

'*What! What did you say?*' shouting in rage.

Jon had no idea if he was right or wrong, but didn't care. 'You are a non-executive director, you don't have line management authority, so you are out of order. I am not dismissed, I am working on behalf of the company, which I don't see you doing. Goodbye, Mr O'Flynn.'

Jon's anger with this man, and all of his frustrations since he joined TLC were boiling up inside him. Its lack of enterprise, lack of financial controls, lack of marketing, and above all he alone having the guts to think of this Zed enterprise. Anxiously hoping that his raised voice hadn't been heard in the embassy, he cut the call, absolutely shaking with rage and frustration, not caring a damn if he could be sacked for insubordination or insulting a superior. He'd no idea if O'Flynn had any sort of executive authority, and for an absurd moment he laughed, wondering what his father would have said about this latest performance by his son. He slowly calmed down, which took many minutes, but taking a chance that O'Flynn had left TLC, he phoned the office again. Alice answered.

'Hi, Alice, it's Jon Webb here, is this a good time to speak?'

'Oh Jon, Jon, when are you coming back? There's no good time to speak, it's awful here!'

'Whatever's the matter?'

'You haven't heard?'

'How could I? What's going on?'

'Mr Catchmore is visiting Roger Martin in hospital. He's in a bad way, and we're seriously worried. Roger told Millie that he was going to No2 unit to look for something, but then he was violently attacked.'

'Alice, I rang half an hour ago and O'Flynn answered. He was shouting at me, blaming me for Roger being attacked. How was it that O'Flynn answered the phone, who let him do that? We had an argument, and he sacked me. Is he still there?'

'No, he stamped off in a filthy temper, not saying goodbye, or anything. He'd turned up unexpectedly, and started looking in all the offices for something but wouldn't say what. When he came out of your office he came into mine to use the phone, but when it rang he picked it up and answered it. I thought that he was damn rude – if you'll excuse me – and I walked out of the office leaving him too it. Fancy just snatching my phone! I went to find some antiseptic wipes after he'd used it. What do you mean, "He sacked you"?'

'Just that, accusing me of not having done any work, and going off on holiday.'

Alice said nothing for a few moments until saying quietly, 'Jon, he doesn't know what you're doing, does he? Nobody's told him.'

'So it seems, but what's this about Roger being attacked?'

'He was attacked, as I just told you. Someone must have dragged him out of the No 2 building and just dumped him in a nearby ditch while he was unconscious. A woman walking her dog found him, or the dog did, and the only word Roger's spoken sounded like "keeve", and we don't know what that means. Neither do the police. When are you coming back, Jon?'

'I don't yet know. Could be two days, could be two weeks. I may have a better idea tomorrow.'

'Two weeks? Why?' She was far from her usual calm and collected self, but on the face of it, Jon thought, what could he do there that was more important than being here?

'There's good progress here, Alice, I have agreed a small contract to get the mine repaired, and I have a good relationship with the overall boss of the mines. I cannot leave here yet. What could I do by being back there?'

'Oh, dear. Please talk to Mrs Catchmore, she's heard who I'm talking to.' A slightly less unsettled voice said, 'Hello, Jon, Millicent Catchmore here. Did you just say something to Alice about a contract?'

'Hello, yes, it's looking promising, the Secretariat has asked me to get the conveyor repaired, and I will agree a contract tomorrow. I will obviously email you the details. But how is Roger?'

'Awake, but sedated. Henry has been with him several times, and the doctors say that he will recover. We'd all like to catch the swine who hit him.'

'He said one word "keeve". Did he mean "Keith" who works at No 2?'

Silence from Mrs Catchmore, then, 'Of course! Aren't we fools for missing that! Well done, Jon, now we can get somewhere. Look, I want to get on to the police right now. Can you phone again tomorrow?'

'Yes, but give Roger and the Guv my best wishes, please.'

Completely perplexed, Jon found his way back to where George, Olivia, and now also William were working. He found a chair.

'Good Lord, Jon, you're as white a sheet, what's wrong?' a worried Olivia asked, and the others stopped work.

'Our works manger went to our No 2 unit and someone attacked him, knocked him out, and dumped him in a ditch. I don't know if there was water in it. A dog belonging to a passer-by found him and he's in a bad way in hospital. The police have no clues, but I guessed who did it. I told the Guv's wife, and she's on to the police now.'

George asked gently, 'Who is the Guv?'

Olivia answered, 'He's Jon's boss, the CEO of TLC.'

Jon looked up at her. 'Roger Martin is the works manager. He and I went to No 2 looking for some archived drawings just before I left to come here. When the employee who works there saw me and Roger looking with suspicion at some strange packing cases, he challenged us by shouting until he recognised Roger. He was holding an iron bar as if it were a club. Olivia, he reports to O'Flynn.'

George was naturally puzzled until Olivia explained further, but in view of the great help that Jon was getting from the embassy she couldn't explain about O'Flynn's rudeness as one of the directors in case it affected TLC's goodwill from the embassy. That was far-fetched, but not impossible. 'Mr O'Flynn is a difficult man with connections to the firm, George, that's all.' Time was pressing, and the reception room wasn't ready yet, so George asked Olivia, 'Could you please take Jon to the small rest area and make him a cup of strong, sweet tea?' In other words please get him out of here, we're running late.

In the rest area Jon said, 'Thanks for the tea, Olivia, but please go back to what you were doing and help George. I'm terribly embarrassed about the interruptions I'm causing to the embassy's routines and worried that I could outstay my welcome. Please go, and I'll see you later at the reception.' He didn't want to be the first to arrive at the reception, nor did he particularly want to think any more about TLC today. Those simple letters sent to some customers early in January had triggered all the dramas of the last few weeks, with their unlikely and inconceivable consequences. With a wry smile he thought, my last year with Jane was more predictable than this lot!

There were so many 'what ifs' swirling about in Jon's head that this evening was a pleasure to look forward to as a complete break. Except, of course, for obligatory discussions with the Secretary and the Minister whom he'd unexpectedly found he actually quite liked. He wanted a clear head; or alternatively, a few glasses of bubbly wouldn't go amiss. Ah well, a long shower and a change of clothes will set me up, he thought. He dressed carefully in his one and only suit. When he arrived at the reception, several important-looking people were already there, greeting each other, none of whom he already knew, and in alarm Jon realised that he wouldn't recognise the Ambassador nor did he know his name. In a panic, he almost grabbed William's arm when passing with a small tray of drinks.

'William!' He whispered hoarsely, 'Help!'

'Jon!' William squeaked, 'I say, steady on, you nearly spilt this lot. Yes?'

'I haven't been introduced to the Ambassador, I don't know his name, I don't know what he looks like, and don't know if he's here yet!'

'Relax! He's not here, and he hasn't accepted although he may pop in if he hears that anyone he thinks to be important is present, but there's something you could do for me if you would, please. I wouldn't recognise either the Secretary or the Minister, so if you get the chance would you introduce me as George's assistant? I probably won't have any dealings with them in my daily duties, but one never knows.' Jon was pleased. 'I'll be glad to return your help, my friend.'

The room was steadily filling up with guests. Jon guessed that as a newcomer he wouldn't know any of them and was quite content to linger unobtrusively to one side. The trick here is, he thought, don't stay in one place, move around a bit to eavesdrop and maybe join a group. Someone will get curious and ask who I am when they're bored by their usual contacts. George was working hard as the host, and Olivia was drifting about with canapés and other nibbles.

The noise level rose gradually until one had to almost shout in listeners' ears to make oneself heard. Why, asked Jon, invite so many people if you can't hear each other? George politely introduced Jon to a few people who bored him instantly with their chit-chat. Struggling with his good manners to listen to them while glancing around to spot anyone interesting, he realised that a woman who'd been gossiping to him about some other nonentity, was watching the arrival of the Secretary and the Minister, and immediately lost interest in Jon. Fine by me, he thought.

There was no doubt that most guests seemed to be wary of the two men, whose movement about the room seemed to Jon to be like Moses parting the waters, or Henry VIII powering his way through a crowd of dancers to reach his latest paramour. After a while he realised that they were heading his way. Don't speak until you're spoken to, he advised himself.

'Good evening, Mr Jon,' greeted the Secretary, 'are you pleased with your day?'

'Yes, good evening, gentlemen,' Jon returned, becoming aware that nearby guests who'd previously ignored him were showing interest, so he enjoyed himself by speculating that they were probably wondering who is this Brit we've not seen before, and why is he on good terms with Gavuzzi? But then, he wondered why the hell were these two men grinning at him? If grinning was an Olympic event, they would have got the gold.

The Minister made the puzzle worse. 'How is the squash, Mr Jon?'

'Squash? I don't understand, sir.'

'Well, you were in the Oxford University squash team, yes?'

'No, I didn't say that.'

'Oh?' The Secretary's eyebrows had shot up. 'Your blazer said so.'

'Pardon?' Then realisation dawned. There was a badge on William's blazer pocket when he went to the meeting.

'I get it now, gentlemen, you're laughing at me, aren't you? There I was in the meeting professing honesty, but all the time in borrowed clothes!'

The three of them laughed equally, all differences of status ignored. The two men slapped Jon on his shoulders, and shook hands. Out of the corner of his eye, Jon saw William and waved him over. 'Gentlemen, I want to introduce William Spencer to you. He owns the blazer I borrowed. William, this gentleman is the Secretary for the Interior, and this gentleman is the Minister for Industry.'

'Good evening,' welcomed William, and with his quick wit added, 'We are pleased that you came. If there's anything that you need, please tell Mr Webb, and I'm sure that he can borrow it from somebody.'

More laughter followed, and by this time it was obvious to Jon that various other guests were envious of him and William getting along so well with these visitors, who by reputation were notoriously starchy. From across the room Jon noticed that George seemed delighted by the scene which had set off an unusually relaxed ambience, when in walked another tall, slim, distinguished-looking man, elegantly dressed, who stopped to speak to George.

William murmured to Jon, 'That's the Ambassador who's just arrived, talking to

George,' but openly to the Secretary he said, 'Excuse me, Mr Secretary, but our Ambassador's just arrived.'

'Ah, yes, I see. Thank you, Mr Spencer, but Mr Jon,' he said, handing Jon an envelope, 'here is the draft agreement that I promised. We meet tomorrow as arranged, but now I must talk to other guests here,' More handshakes followed, then Gavuzzi worked his way back through the throng to speak to the Ambassador, who greeted him with a broad smile.

The Minister lingered, wanting to say something, and took Jon to one side. 'You told me that you had been an apprentice, but the blazer suggested you'd been to Oxford. I don't know if apprentices then go to university, or if graduates take up apprenticeships. Do you?'

'I've no idea, Minister. I know I wasn't entirely honest in that respect, but in everything else I spoke the truth to you all. Someone once said that "if you never tell a lie, you don't have to remember anything" which is a good maxim to follow. When planning to come here, I packed clothes suitable for crawling about mines and damaged machinery, and just one suit, this one, for this reception, but nothing suitable for the unexpected meeting. It would have been disrespectful to you if I had turned up in shirtsleeves. So I borrowed the blazer.'

'That's appreciated, but back to business now, eh, Jon? I doubt if you've yet had time to contact anyone to mend the conveyor, but that man near the windows wearing a heavily striped jacket may help. But I have to circulate now. See you tomorrow.'

Jon stayed where he was, noticing that some guests were sidling up to him, clearly curious about this well-connected person. Two or three predatory women 'of a certain age' hoped for introductions but Olivia interrupted their arrival with canapés, a glass of wine, a wink for Jon, and a smile. 'Well done,' she whispered. The striped jacket tried to look casual as it weaved its way to reach Jon.

Its owner said, 'Good evening, Mr Webb, my name's Stone, Alan Stone. The Minister seemed to point me out as he talked to you. I understand your company makes mining machinery, yes? And I wondered if we have business interests in common.'

Jon knew that that expression was usually a euphemism for 'Can I sell you something?' Well, let's find out if he could. 'What is your business, Mr Stone? We don't make a range of mining machinery, just conveyor belts.'

Stone's resumé was amazingly relevant. 'We're into construction, out-sourced maintenance services, heavy industrial plant movements, power transmission lines and ancillary services, but not in residential markets. We started out as builders and grew from that as satisfied customers asked us to branch out to do different work. There must be thousands of firms who've grown that way. Please take my card.'

Jon's mind was racing ahead. Could Stone's firm repair the conveyor's electrics, install another one if ordered, and could it be a local agent for TLC in the future? All this was possible if Stone and his firm had credibility.

'Have you done much work for the Minister? By the way my name's Jon, please use it.'

'That depends on what you mean by "much", Jon. In money terms, not many millions, but we've been careful never to go beyond our capabilities. By that I mean we avoid being tempted to go for large contracts which *might* have been profitable.'

'Excuse me quizzing you, Alan, but perhaps our companies could do business here. I'll certainly give you the background to my visit, and my company, but first I want to show you a photograph.' Catching George's eye he managed to get him over.

'Hello, Alan,' said a smiling George, 'I trust that you two are getting on okay?'

Jon answered for them. 'We are, George, and is it possible for either you or William to bring me at least one copy of those photos that Dave took on his phone? It'll be most relevant to our discussion.' He had looked at George with an unblinking expression hoping that he would understand the importance of his request.

George nodded, left, and returned in minutes with all the photos.

'Thanks,' said an appreciative Jon.

He selected a close-up of the damaged conveyor switchgear, showing it to Alan Stone. 'What do you think happened here, Alan? I assure you that I'm not playing games, I need to know if our opinions coincide.'

Stone looked at it pensively for a minute, then offered Jon the best news he could have. 'There has been a massive short circuit, and I suggest that it was caused deliberately.'

'Sure. Is it irreparable?'

'Certainly not, of course it could be repaired. Maybe with new parts from the UK.'

'Could your firm do that?'

'I'm sure that we could, but I must point out that as I'm not an electrical engineer with enough experience I'd need to have one of our men look at it. Can I keep this photo to discuss with him? But, Jon, assuming that we could do the repair, what happens now?' At this point, Jon knew that he was beginning to get out of his depth. He knew he could agree a plan with Stone to get the conveyor working, and was authorised by TLC to pay for it, but that was just the beginning of possibilities in this country. He made a decision. 'I think it's likely that I'll ask your company to do the repair, Alan, obviously provided that the price is acceptable. Incidentally, here's my business card, which I'll explain.'

'Thanks, what does "Director of Projects" mean?'

'It implies a level of authority needed for current tasks. I'm not a Board Director, but within limits can commit the company as if I were, concerning contracts for example. Most importantly, it's effective in discussions with potential customers. It works, as perhaps you've seen this evening!'

'It certainly does! Gavuzzi won't deal with people whom he holds to be below his status, so your title was well chosen.'

'Anyway, Alan, after this first repair, I can think of other ways in which we could work together, but to be candid I'd have to consult my CEO and his colleagues. The Minister indicated that we should meet, so that implies that we both have credibility with him, therefore, speaking bluntly, we can take each other at face value. Does that offend you?'

'Certainly not, I agree with you. What did you mean by "other ways", Jon?'

'I have another meeting with Mr Gavuzzi tomorrow morning. If he gives me formal instructions to get that repair done, I'll tell him that I will probably appoint you as a sub-contractor. You will get paid by TLC. But, Alan, if Mr Gavuzzi asks me to investigate other damage elsewhere, and asks TLC to organise repairs, I would need time to plan before committing myself or TLC. Presumably we could work together as on the first repair, but if your bills were to exceed my discretionary limit I could not instruct you. Terms of payment would have to be agreed, and so on. There are legions of "what ifs" in this potential partnership, wouldn't you agree?'

'I do indeed, Jon, but touching on terms of payment this government pays on time; there's been only one case when it drifted up to sixty days, which is very good indeed. I suggest that we meet again after your meeting tomorrow and talking to your people back home. Agreed? Phone me when you're free.'

'Yes. I must say that this is an enjoyable evening, except that my glass is empty!' They managed to hijack William, got their drinks, chinked their glasses with traditional 'cheers', and merged into the crowd.

Jon decided to consult Olivia about Alan Stone's company. Could she ask her London colleagues to run a check early tomorrow? Then another difficulty struck. After Olivia had told him she worked for Futurebank, he had wondered if it could help TLC with funds. Until now it had been too early to suggest that to Olivia, but after all his results in recent days, perhaps now would be a good time to sow seeds. The obstacle that struck him was O'Flynn's bad reputation that could fall upon TLC. Futurebank would or might become nervous of any involvement, and shy away. Then with some pessimism it dawned on him that Futurebank would consider TLC too small to be a client. Okay if it needed millions.

Thankfully he noticed that guests were beginning to drift away from the reception and that Gavuzzi and the Minister had already left. Very soon he was the last there, and offered his help in clearing up.

'Are you sure, Jon?' George enquired. 'I don't remember anyone offering before.' Between the four of them, and two staff members whom Jon hadn't met, the room was back to normal in no time. 'Well now everyone, George offered, would anybody like a drink to round off the evening? There are some wines already opened, so please help yourselves. If there are any nibbles left, Olivia, please round them up on one plate. Anyway, thank you all for a successful reception, and for your hard work. Are you pleased with your evening, Jon?'

'I certainly am, and thanks for inviting me. At first I felt conscious of being the outsider that I was, but the Secretary and the Minister soon changed all that. I met Alan Stone through their suggestion, which will save me days of wasted time searching for the contractor I need. Yes, George, it was thoroughly pleasant and effective for me.'

'What are you planning to do now?'

'I have another meeting with Mr Gavuzzi tomorrow morning, but as I don't know what he wants to discuss there's not a lot I can do yet apart from phoning my company with a progress report.'

'Do you want William's office again?'

'Are you sure, George? Is that okay with you, William?'

'Not a problem, Jon. If I may say so, you helped the evening along with that raucous laughter coming from you and those Ministers. We can send you back to your lodgings by car and collect you in the morning at nine to take you to your meeting. Would that be good? There's a car available now if you'd like to take it, but I'm leaving now and wish you good luck with your meeting tomorrow.'

'Thank you, I'd like a car tomorrow morning but this evening I'll walk back, thank you.' Once they were alone, Jon tentatively said, 'Olivia, I really need a huge favour, may I ask?'

'Ask away.'

'I have that meeting with the Secretary in the morning, then with Alan Stone afterwards to see if we can agree to his firm repairing the conveyor. Here's his card. Is it possible for you to arrange for a check on his firm before I meet him at, say, noon? He claims to have a good credibility record in this country, but I really must be certain of that.'

Olivia was looking smug, grinning at him from ear to ear. 'I already have, and he's okay.'

'What? How? When?'

'Well, it's a verbal check. Good enough if you're not giving him a line of credit. In between doing the hospitality bit, I was watching you and those government Ministers talking and noticed the short stocky one indicate Mr Stone to you, who then approached you. Assuming that you might be talking business, I offered the same Minister some canapés as a ruse to get into conversation with him. He was a bit gruff, but melted when I explained that I'd been to the mine to help you, which seems days ago. Anyway, I explained your search for a repairer, and the Minister pointed Stone out to me, saying, "He's your man, he does much work for us," and then walked away.'

'Oh, that's clever, Olivia, what a brilliant piece of news to end the day, thanks so much.'

'Ending the day, are we, Jon? Didn't we say something like that the day before yesterday?'

By that time of the evening Olivia and Jon were showing signs of needing sleep, and tacitly agreed to forego any further "events" as they put it, each wanting recovery time after a long and eventful day, but agreeing to meet for breakfast. A quick hug sufficed.

CHAPTER FIFTEEN

As he went to leave, a thought struck Jon, and luckily William hadn't left the embassy for his home. 'I'm embarrassed to ask, William, and I've a cheek to do so, but could I borrow your blazer again? It was a great success, especially when you cracked that joke in the reception. I'm certain that those government Ministers will make fun of me again at the meeting tomorrow, which will be helpful. They're not as aloof as we first thought.'

William grinned. 'Do you know, Jon, I was half expecting this, and if it's okay with you I have another one with a clay shooting club badge on it. Would that be useful?'

'You bet! Which club is it? Clay shooting's my hobby.'

'Oh, it's a small club that you won't know of, and nothing special, but our club and another club held a grand competition last season, and we decided to show off and have some badges made. They created great rivalry and sarcasm from the other teams, especially when we lost! Shall I have it sent round to your digs in the morning? Our driver can bring it, wait a few minutes for you, and then take you on to your meeting.'

'Please, if it's no trouble. This is brilliant service, William, thank you.'

In the morning the driver arrived promptly with the second blazer, which fitted, then took Jon punctually to the same offices as for his previous meeting. The Secretary and the Minister were both in the meeting room, together with several others, to whom he was introduced. He had no idea if they were the same men he'd met previously, so said to the room as a whole, 'Good morning, gentlemen, I'm very sorry if I've forgotten any of your names,' hoping that would suffice.

He saw that the Secretary was grinning at him. 'Well now, Mr Jon, I see that this morning you are wearing a different and interesting item from your wardrobe. Or perhaps Mr Spencer's wardrobe?' His staff, of course had no idea what the Secretary was talking about, and he confused them even more by asking, 'What is it that you shoot, Mr Jon?'

Jon took an outrageous chance with their sense of humour, by answering, 'Government Ministers, mostly, sir!'

At that provocative remark, the staff looked absolutely terrified of what the Secretary would do next but he roared with laughter either at Jon's joke, or the sight of his quaking subordinates who'd never dare to make fun of their superiors. Lapsing into his native language he put them at their ease and smiles developed. Of course, Jon had no idea what he'd said.

The Secretary shuffled his papers and remarked with a smile, 'That was an unusual start to any meeting, don't you all agree, gentlemen?' Naturally everyone nodded and agreed.

The Secretary turned to Jon. 'Are you in agreement with the terms of our draft agreement, Mr Jon?'

Jon had studied the agreement carefully before retiring to bed, and accepted its terms proposing that he should have the machine repaired at TLC's expense, then after its satisfactory re-commissioning the Secretariat would pay up to eight thousand US dollars within thirty days. Also, TLC, as the sole contractor, would inspect and report upon any damage to ten other machines in the Secretariat's ownership within thirty days from the signing of the agreement, for which the Secretariat would pay two thousand US dollars per machine report. TLC would then submit quotations for any repair work.

'Mr Secretary, I find the terms acceptable and am willing to sign. However, there are two simple caveats, one of which is that my company is permitted to sub-contract inspections and repairs to a local contractor, one approved by you, of course. Also I have difficulty with the thirty days allowed for the reports as I don't know where the machines are sited.'

'Which contractor do you have in mind, Mr Jon?' asked the Minister, smirking slightly, as if he didn't already know, or guess.

'Stone Industries, Minister. I met Mr Alan Stone last evening at the reception, and learnt that the Secretariat has entrusted contracts to him to your satisfaction. On that basis, and the need to get the mine working again quickly I have decided to use his company subject to an agreement which I expect to conclude with him today.'

'Has he visited the mine, to inspect the damage?'

'No, Minister, but his analysis of it from photos satisfied me of his competence.'

The Secretary took the contract document from his folder, but before signing it, laid his pen down, and looked round the room, particularly at his subordinates to whom he spoke again in his native tongue for a few minutes. When he'd finished, there was a murmured discussion then they looked at Jon and applauded.

'Mr Jon,' began the Secretary, 'I reminded my staff that you have come to our country to make a profit, and asked them if they are satisfied to do business with you. However, we are all agreed that you have shown an apparently genuine interest not only in our economy, but also in our people. For those reasons we look forward to a long partnership with your company. Mr Jon, I will extend the inspection period to sixty days, will you agree?'

When Jon had nodded, smiled, and said, 'Yes, Mr Secretary,' Gavuzzi made the alteration, initialled it, signed the contract and its copy, passing his pen and the papers to Jon for him to sign also. That small ceremony over, Jon could not let the moment pass unrecognised, and asked, 'Mr Secretary, may I say something?'

'Yes, of course.'

Jon stood up, and making sure to look at them each in turn as he spoke, said, 'Gentlemen, I appreciate the Secretary's kind remarks. We in my company have a philosophy that business and pleasure should be mixed wherever possible and appropriately. Roughly speaking, we work eight hours a day, we sleep eight hours, and we have eight hours left in the twenty-four in which to enjoy ourselves. However, I ask why not let enjoyment and work overlap where possible? That's to say, make business itself enjoyable, or at least a pleasure? I assure you all, gentlemen, it is a pleasure to be among and work with you all. I am pleased with the outcome of our work here, and on behalf of my company I thank you formally for your decisions.' He resumed his seat.

'That is all good, Mr Jon, and as I indicated already, we shall meet again. For now this meeting is ended.'

To Jon's astonishment the Secretary's staff all filed past him to shake his hand, murmuring remarks in their own language. After the minions had left the room, the Minister for Industry grinned hugely at Jon, saying, 'You don't know what they said do you, Jon?'

'No idea, Hogarth, what was it?'

'Most said "well done", others said "thank you", and the rest asked if you have any jobs going!'

'Good heavens, Minister, I didn't imply that! Anyway, now could we celebrate somehow?'

193

With the Secretary beckoning and leading the way, the three men returned to the relaxation room, whereupon the Minister pulled keys from his pocket and opened a drinks' cabinet presumably denied to lesser staff. 'Still no pints of English beer, I'm afraid, Jon, so what will you have?' And they spent an informal half hour, each pleased with the results from unexpected events and spontaneous decisions. With due courtesy, after a while Jon reminded the others of his meeting with Alan Stone, and after promising to contact them later in the day, he left to join the driver for his next meeting.

It was the same car, but a different driver, who leapt out to open a rear door for Jon.

'Dave!' he exclaimed, 'this is a pleasure, what's going on?'

'Thanks to you, Mr Jon, I've been given more responsibility and a small pay increase. Please get in.'

'I'd prefer to sit up front with you.'

'No, you are important to us, and should sit in the back. It's more dignified.'

With reluctance and embarrassment at being driven about in this regal manner, Jon settled in where indicated, and was driven off to Stone Industries.

'What did you mean "thanks to you"?'

'You gave a good report about me to Mr Turbeville-Blyth, who was pleased with that and with the photographs I left for you. I was called in to the embassy this morning and was asked if I would like to assist you while you are here.'

Jon's reaction was pleasure for the man, but who was going to pay for his services? The embassy was responsible only for diplomatic expenses, not to fund businesses. He'd take it up with George T-B later, because he certainly hadn't budgeted for all this.

'That's good, Dave, thank you. I don't know my plans from day to day, but for example if I go back to the mine it may be with another company. The one I'm meeting now. I don't know how long my meeting will last, are you instructed to wait for me?'

'Yes, that's not a problem, and here we are.'

Stone's buildings looked modern and well set out. The car pulled up in front of a single-storey office block, past which could be seen a yard with several heavy machines parked. There was no sign of life until a young African lady emerged and approached the car as Dave opened the door for Jon.

'Mr Webb, sir?' she enquired, a smile lighting up a pleasant face.

'Yes, good afternoon. Mr Stone is expecting me but unfortunately I couldn't tell him when, because I've come from another meeting which ended twenty minutes ago. '

'My name is Yasmine, I'm Mr Stone's secretary and PA, and I know about your arrangements and that your time wasn't fixed. He's away from the office, but will be back shortly.'

Looking up she added, 'I think that's him now.' Jon followed her eyes, seeing and hearing a modest-sized helicopter which came down and disappeared behind the buildings.

'Yes, Mr Webb, he'll be here in a minute.' With no indication from her to move, Jon just waited until a Land Rover roared from behind him through the gate into the yard, and Alan Stone leapt down.

'Jon! Hello, my friend, sorry to keep you waiting.'

'Hi Alan, where've you come from? Yasmine suggested that you were in that chopper which went down behind the buildings in the opposite direction! Are you trying to confuse me deliberately before we've even started?'

Stone and Yasmine laughed, with Jon smiling at his own joke.

'Certainly not, but it's good for you to have a laugh after being stuck in a meeting with those boring officials, isn't it?'

'Actually, it wasn't boring at all, Alan, good progress was made, and the three of us finished up having a scotch in a sort of private room.'

'Scotch? As in whisky?'

'Yes, as in Scotland, not that Russian poison.'

'But they don't drink, Jon, this is unheard of!'

'Oh,' said Jon, in a degree of alarm, 'perhaps I'd better keep quiet about that, although I must say that we got on very well, and I enjoyed their company.'

'Bloody hell! Enjoyed their company? I suppose you're now going to tell me that they've signed a contract with you, eh?'

'Yes, they have.'

Alan Stone went quiet, looking subdued, as if he'd underestimated Jon. 'Look, let's go indoors,' he suggested, 'we don't want to talk out here. Yasmine, we'll use the small meeting room, and please go and ask Roy to join us and bring the photos with him. Come on, Jon.'

The meeting room was not 'small' in any sense, having space enough for a dozen or so chairs with various circular tables, a coffee maker, a digital projector, and an effective air conditioner. Numerous framed photographs depicting Stone Industries' contract achievements hung on the walls. Stone moved some chairs to positions where participants could see the projection screen, as well as each other. Jon wondered why.

Another man entered, and Stone said, 'Ah, Roy, this is Jonathan Webb from TLC. Jon, please meet Roy Howell our Chief Electrical Engineer.' The men shook hands, assessing each other.

'Right, everyone,' Alan Stone began. 'We're all here to discuss future possibilities between our companies which Jon and I began last evening, which seems a long time ago because much has happened since, according to Jon. Yasmine will take notes as we go along. Jon, perhaps you'd care to give us an outline of TLC and how you came to be here.'

'Certainly. TLC are the initials of the founder of the firm, and don't suggest "tender loving care" which isn't synonymous with rugged working machinery. The firm has a good reputation for making conveyor belts for quarries, mines and so on. My background is in designing internal conveyors for factories, so I have less experience of typical TLC machines, and in fact joined the firm in the last few months,' stopping short of admitting to weeks. 'I will answer any questions you have, so please stop me at any time.

'After joining as Chief Designer I researched existing users by writing to ask for any comments about the TLC machines they'd bought, in case they had novel ideas to build into new models. I had a reply from the manager of a mine here in Zed – which is a pseudonym for its unpronounceable real name – who said that their TLC machine had been okay, but that it had blown up.'

'Blown up? Were they his exact words?' laughed Roy.

'Exactly, Roy, and I also laughed when he said so, but then took the matter seriously when he implied sabotage, but the phone was cut and I couldn't get him back. We didn't want this situation to be unresolved in case a major machine malfunction jeopardised our reputation for quality and so on, therefore I came here to investigate and to make contact with the owners of the mine, which is the Secretariat for the Interior. The plan was to investigate, report, and if possible organise a repair. Also, to be candid with you, to help in such a way as to get Brownie points from the Secretary to put us in pole position if he went out to tender for new machines.'

'Did that work, Mr Webb?' asked Yasmine. 'If you don't mind me asking?'

'I think it did, judging by the wording in a contract which I have. Anyway, I visited the mine and concluded that the damaged conveyor could be repaired. Subsequently I had a meeting with the Secretary, whom I met again at the embassy reception with the Minister for Industry, who indirectly hinted that Stone Industries could manage the repair, and from that I met Alan. That's how I've come here.

'Subject to us agreeing to the way forward I will give Stone a contract for the repair Alan, unless you or Roy have any questions. Over to you now.'

Alan Stone was grinning like the proverbial Cheshire Cat. 'Jon, you're not the only one who's been busy. Tell him, Roy!'

Roy Howell spoke with confidence. 'I thought that we have the skills and the people to repair your machine when I saw the photos, but having now actually seen the damage I know that we can. Look, here's the first shot. It's not very sharp because we had to scan the print that you gave to Alan.' Up it came on the projector screen.

Jon was taken aback. 'Whatever do you mean "having seen the damage", you don't know where it is? Do you?'

Alan Stone chipped in. 'Jon, part of one of those photos you gave me showed one of the mine's trucks in the background. Show him the next photo, Roy, thanks. It's a bit blurred as you see, but that name on its cab enabled us to identify the mine, so we knew how to find it. I phoned the Minister's office this morning, who gave its location, and Roy and I went to have a look. That's where we'd come from in the chopper as you arrived.'

'Christ, Alan, how do you afford one of those?'

'We can't, it belongs to a friend who hires it to me with a pilot from time to time. I must say we had fun and games when we got to the mine and landed inside the perimeter security fence. A whole squad of soldiers appeared from nowhere brandishing rifles and shouting. There was an officer of some sort with them who thought we were invaders or rebels, and got very excited. I managed to shout to him over the soldiers' racket, saying that we were there for Jonathan Webb, and he instantly shut up and told his men to settle down. It's just as well that they did, because the pilot was all for "getting the hell out of here" as he put it, and had almost begun the engine start up procedure.'

Seeing the grin on Jon's face, Stone continued, 'It's all very well for you to laugh, Jon, but it wasn't funny at the time. We were worried about the chopper getting shot at.'

'There's no need to worry about that, Alan, their rifles probably weren't loaded. I've been there before, don't forget, and got to know that officer fairly well. The soldiers were isolated from supplies and a radio link, but I lent them my satellite phone, so by now resources are on their way. I'll tell you all about it when we've time. Meanwhile, this is all very pleasant, and I admire your initiative but can we get down to business, please?' He continued, 'Do you have a proposal for the repair?'

'Yes, although obviously we haven't had time to write it out for you, we made an estimate on the way back, which Roy has in draft. Show him please, Roy.'

Jon scanned the handwritten notes, going directly to the total cost, and laughing at what he read. 'You say 3,000, but you don't say which currency, Roy!'

'What? Oh, sorry, pounds sterling, Jon. I wrote in the helicopter with some difficulty.'

'You're proposing to restore the conveyor's functions, but if you left off replacing doors and so on and merely repainted them, could you bring the price down a tad? I'm not nit-picking at your price, but it's a good plan – I think you'll agree – that Mr Gavuzzi doesn't think we're loading the price with cosmetic costs, although if he wants an "as new" appearance we can give him the option.'

'I understand,' agreed Roy, 'reduce the price by £200, please.'

'Right, gentlemen, I accept this draft,' said Jon. 'When could you start, and how long would you need to complete the job?'

'Subject to spares availability from local sources, we could start within seven days. If we have to wait for spares from the UK, say ten days. Roy thinks we could have the conveyor up and running seven days after either case, *but,* and I mean "but", Jon, that presumes we'd have no interference from those characters with their guns. We'd need help or authority from the Minister to have the power line checked, and we haven't priced for that. There was no power at the mine.'

Without showing his feelings, Jon was thoroughly satisfied with the outcome of the meeting. There had been a measure of humour in both of his meetings that day, all to good effect, and to TLC's advantage. The Guv would surely be pleased, which mattered to Jon, who for a moment thought of O'Flynn and how he'd be useless with these people in Zed. He wanted to wrap up the day's work and have a break, but first to report back to the Guv, who by now must be wondering what was going on.

'Alan, I think that we've finished here for the day, and please put in writing what I've seen in Roy's draft, plus your terms of business. You can email it to me as a formal proposal, which I can sign and fax back to you. That could wait until the morning in case either of us thinks of anything else. Is that okay with you?'

'Yes, fine, Jon, but I have another proposal. Roy and I and our wives would like to take you out to dinner this evening, and to keep the balance, perhaps your colleague Mrs de St Croix would care to join us. What do you say? We could collect you from where you're staying at, say, seven?'

'That is a thoroughly pleasant suggestion, Alan, which I accept for both us. Thank you, and we'll see you later. Goodbye for now.'

After genuine smiles, and handshakes all round, Jon returned to the car, and left. Using his satellite phone, he called the embassy, asking for Olivia.

'Hello, Jon, are you okay?' she asked.

'Yes, absolutely fine, and I'll tell you about the day later. Meanwhile, I've accepted an invitation for us to be taken to dinner by Alan Stone and his chief engineer, together with their wives. Alan specifically invited you. I hope you accept. Or to put it another way, I really hope that you do. We'll be collected at seven.'

'That sounds like good business hospitality, Jon, and yes I want to come, thank you. What's the dress code? Long? Short? Or trousers?'

'Sorry, I've no idea, didn't give it a thought, but anything that you've worn for embassy events perhaps. Nothing startlingly revealing, please.'

'Spoilsport!'

CHAPTER SIXTEEN

Consulting his watch, and working out the time difference with the UK, Jon took a chance that the Guv was still in his office, so borrowing William's office and phone, he rang TLC. Alice MacInnes took the call.

'Hi, Alice, it's Jon Webb here, phoning to report to the Guv.'

She sounded subdued and off-hand to him. 'Oh, hello, Jon, how are you?'

'Fine thanks, I have some news for the Guv. Is he still there?'

'No, he's resting at home. You should be here.'

Alice's attitude wasn't at all as Jon thought it might be. He didn't expect to be treated exactly like a sort of conquering hero, but she seemed totally preoccupied.

'Alice,' Jon asked anxiously, 'what's wrong?'

'What's wrong? *What's wrong*? None of this would have happened if you hadn't gone off to Africa. You should come back and sort it all out, and apologise for the trouble you've caused.'

This was ridiculous. Alice was not the Alice he knew. Not the same person who'd helped with the earlier mailshot. Not the same enthusiastic helper for his enterprise. As gently as he could, he asked again.

'Alice, please tell me what's happened.'

'Jon, I'm sorry if I was short with you just now, really sorry, but it's awful here. It would help if you were here, because there's no one else.'

Come on! Jon wanted to shriek at her, get to the point, for heaven's sake. He was suddenly alarmed that the confidence in TLC that he'd portrayed in meetings was hollow, and would be taken as a sham, and his achievements would fall apart, together with his credibility. He reluctantly began to believe that he should fly home immediately, but this was the wrong time to leave what he'd started, and if there was a mess in TLC, it wasn't his job to resolve it. Where were the directors?

He tried again. 'Alice, please start from the beginning.'

'Mr Catchmore was livid about the attack on Roger, and now the man who allegedly did it is in custody. He's responsible to Mr O'Flynn who asked why the man wasn't at work. He was told about Roger's search, and then found out of course that you weren't here.

'He went absolutely berserk when told where you were and what you're doing, or hoping to do, and that developed into a dreadful row with Mr Catchmore. Mrs Catchmore managed to contact Mr Phillips who rushed here to support Mr Catchmore against Mr O'Flynn. I have never heard or seen such a dreadful argument. I agree with you, Jon, Mr O'Flynn wants you to fail, and he's not interested in TLC's future. Why is that? Suddenly, in the middle of the argument, O'Flynn stopped shouting, and just stood there snorting and sweating like an angry bull, and shouted, "Right, Catchmore, this is the last straw, you may as well pack your bags, shut up shop, and piss off." I was there, I heard him. What did he mean?'

'I don't know, Alice, but I really can't rush back just now because I …'

'Sorry to interrupt you, Jon, you must have a reason, and Mr Phillips and Mr Bryant are both helping. I shouldn't have asked you to come.'

'Where's the Guv?'

'After that argument Mr Catchmore was taken ill with stress, and he's been given firm instructions by two doctors to rest and forget the business for a while, which he cannot do, as you'll imagine. Millicent won't leave him at home alone. But did you say you've some news for him? Would it cheer him up?'

'I hope so, and please let Mrs Catchmore decide if he should get it. Tell her that we have a contract signed by Mr Gavuzzi – the Secretary for the Interior – for the repair of the damaged conveyor, and that I have an agreement to be signed tomorrow by a contractor who'll do the repairs. We are having dinner tonight in celebration. I estimate that TLC's profit will be acceptable for the repair, and as a separate issue I will also charge to go and inspect and report on machines at other mines.'

'Have you got all that, Alice?'

'My word! Jon, you have been busy! I'll phone Mrs Catchmore straightaway. Can she call you back?'

'Not really, I'm using the embassy's phone, or one of them, and I worry about being a nuisance, but I'd like to know if the Guv is cheered up by it all. Oh, and Alice, I won't email the details to the office in case O'Flynn sees it, but send it to you at home and you can send it on to the Catchmores if you think that's wise. I must hang up now and get changed for the evening. Excuse me rushing.'

'Thanks for phoning, Jon, and again I'm sorry I was rude, but you've cheered me up no end. Bye for now.'

Jon sat back in the borrowed chair, puffing out his cheeks in a huge sigh. William wandered in casually, and took the chair opposite Jon which was normally used by visitors. Jon made to rise.

'No, don't worry, Jon,' William reassured him, 'stay for a moment and recover. I wasn't eavesdropping, but I couldn't avoid hearing you. Is there trouble back at the ranch?'

'William, you and George and Olivia, not forgetting Dave and Evelyn, have been so helpful that I'm happy to tell you that my mission – it that's what it's called – has been, or still is being, really successful. Unfortunately there's a non-exec Finance Director who for some reason was dead against me coming here, and I don't know why, neither do his Board colleagues, and it's thought that he doesn't have the firm's interest at heart. He will go absolutely nuts when he learns of what's been achieved here, and apparently he has already caused our CEO to be laid up with stress.'

'Will your concern about that man distract you from your work here?'

'I was thinking about that as you came in just now, and no, it won't, William. I could worry about the company's future and suffer a "doom-and-gloom is it all worthwhile?" mentality, but no it won't be a distraction. Quite the reverse. Yes, I'm worried about our CEO, but he'll recover, I'm certain, and it occurred to me that even if that director couldn't be voted out perhaps we could re-structure the company – don't ask me how – or fold it and start again with the same employees and so on, like the proverbial phoenix, to which we could sub-contract the contracts I got today. So, no, William, to answer your question again, I'm quite motivated by it all. Strange, isn't it? But if you'll excuse me, I really must change for the evening. Alan Stone's taking us all for dinner somewhere.'

'Ah, yes,' said William, remembering, 'I came to tell you that Olivia phoned Stone's secretary to ask for the dress code because you weren't really helpful, intimating that she should not go looking like a tart, and she learnt that you're going to a country club where Stone Industries has a membership. I've been there, and it's good. You'll like it. Meanwhile, I'll give you a lift to your digs, and lend you the other blazer. Okay?'

'William, you are brilliant, you really are. Thank you.' Jon liked William and his occasional absent-mindedness.

Olivia was waiting in the hallway of the house as Jon leapt out of William's car and ran up the front steps. She pointed to her watch. 'Jon, you'll have to hurry, it's gone six-thirty, and I'm told that Stone is always punctual. You're looking flustered, what's the problem?'

'Come up to my room, and I'll tell you while I change.'

'Pardon?'

'No seriously, Olivia, I want you to know what's wrong, but not for Alan Stone to hear it.'

She found a chair in his ante room, while he dived in the shower for five minutes, and rushed about changing. 'You'll remember O'Flynn who was rude to your Janice? ... Oh, blast, this is my last clean shirt! ...Well, when he learnt that I'd come here hoping for new business a furious row broke out between him and the Guv, which became so violent that his secretary Alice MacInnes needed to get another director in to support the Guv. It finally ended with O'Flynn shouting that Henry Catchmore should "pack his bags, shut up shop, and piss off". I can only conclude from that that he meant liquidating the company.

'That won't happen, Olivia, but even supposing it did, the company could rise again like a phoenix, as I explained to William who'd overheard my end of my call to Alice. I'm really not worried about O'Flynn affecting my future, Olivia, he's just a temporary aggravation. Oh, look, it's five to seven, we'd better go down. Incidentally I've got a signed contract for the conveyor's repair, plus some other work, and will probably sign up with Alan tomorrow for his firm to do the work.'

She stopped him half way down the stairs, looked at him and said, 'Brilliant, Jon, congratulations!' and unashamedly held his hand to go and meet their host for the evening.

***

Alan Stone was waiting by a people carrier, and seeing the held hands he grinned, and mischievously remarked, 'Ah, it's a good thing that we're all going together in this old bus, isn't it, then we won't have to separate you two! Come and meet the others.'

Mrs Stone and the Howells had politely left the vehicle for introductions, and at first sight of the way the wives conducted themselves Jon realised that they were no strangers to this type of business event. They were both aged in their fifties, slim, smartly but simply dressed, and, he thought, elegant. He guessed that they also worked in Stone Industries. Genuine smiles and firm handshakes were exchanged all round.

To Jon's embarrassment when introducing him, Alan Stone said, 'Ladies, this is the man of the moment, he's made a name for himself with Gavuzzi and his Minister, and done business with them when he's only been here for a few days.'

Smiling broadly, Jon said, 'Mrs Stone, Mrs Howell, I protest at Alan's remarks. I couldn't have done it without Olivia's help, and then Alan's and Roy's. I know what Alan's game is,

210

he's trying to butter me up so he gets a better price from me tomorrow. Always assuming, of course, that I do actually need his services. We'll see!'

They sorted themselves into the vehicle and set off. 'It's not far,' reassured Roy who was driving, 'ten minutes or so.' The country club looked quite ordinary at first sight, except that as people were coming and going no distinction between them of race or colour was apparent. It was quite multicultural, and the interior was decorated and furnished in a style which reflected the traditions of the country. A circular table had been reserved, and the group was welcomed by an immaculate maître d'. 'Good evening, Mr and Mrs Stone, Mr and Mrs Howell, Ms de St Croix, Mr Webb, welcome to the restaurant. If you take your places, I will fetch someone to take your aperitif orders.'

Jon smiled at Stone, and observed, 'That welcome was a slick bit of marketing by the club, Alan, well done.'

'No problem at all, Jon, he knows me, Pam and the Howells, and I just gave your names when I booked. You'd have done the same.'

They took their seats in no set places. Aperitifs were ordered, arrived, quickly consumed, and glasses refilled. Conversation among them sprang up uninhibitedly, and the evening progressed well.

After the dessert, Jon tapped his glass to gain attention, announcing, 'I want to propose a toast to us all. We're all here after some successful

211

work, and something of an adventure for me as a newcomer, so it falls to me to make this toast.' He raised his glass, waited for the others to do the same, and said, 'To us all.' Glasses clinked where reachable across the table and 'to us all' was repeated, with accompanying smiles.

Alan Stone looked round the group and asked, 'Does anyone mind if we talk business?'

Pam Stone purported to grimace, and groaned. 'Oh dear, not that, please! Alan, you're too early, Jon hasn't had enough to drink to take you seriously! Olivia, what do you say? Should we or shouldn't we?'

Quickly latching on to Pam's joke, Olivia settled the matter. 'I think that we should, because I think Jon wants to talk about some ideas and unless we let him get it over with early we'll be here all night.' Grimacing at Olivia, but also smiling, Jon said, 'That's right, but do you mind, Pam?'

'No, of course not, I was being silly. Carry on please.'

'One of the reasons for my visit was that we had nobody here to look after our interest, a problem which seems to be solved, having met Alan. Was it really last evening? I can't believe how much has happened since then. Sorry, I digress. You note that I didn't say "interests" plural, but that's what I'm about now. TLC doesn't have any representation in this part of Africa, or indeed anywhere in Africa, so I tentatively raise the possibility of a longer term association with you. I don't have the authority to conclude such an agreement with you, so I'm just exploring.'

'Our companies have disparate interests, but common ground. We both have good track records of credibility, we're both small, that is, less than two hundred employees, we're both ambitious, we work hard, communicate well, and enjoy working. When I said "representation" I meant creative selling, looking for new business, and not merely waiting for enquiries to come in. May I know who does that for your company, Alan, apart from you?'

'I do, Jon,' said Pam Stone, looking at Jon with steely eyes, as if to imply don't you dare say 'that's a man's work', but he wouldn't have done that anyway. Oh, good,' he said, 'I was just going to ….'

'Why "oh good"?' she interrupted, suspiciously.

'Being married to Alan, you spend more time with him than an employee would, or could. I visualise you at home and one of you saying "I've just had an idea …" and off you go into a useful discussion. An employee would have to wait to talk to you, by which time the spontaneity of such a moment is lost. It's happened to me many times, especially because my then wife wasn't the slightest bit interested, and by the next morning I'd forgotten what the idea was. You've all done remarkably well in the last fifteen years.'

Roy Howell was a quiet man, given to thinking carefully before speaking, a trait that Jon liked.

He asked Jon, 'Which range of products do you have in mind, Jon?'

'So far TLC has specialised in the type of product that you've seen, Roy, or variants of it, that is to say, bigger or longer and so on. Each one is made to order, but by using standard components order turnaround times are relatively quick. There will be new and novel variants for other industries, which I can't talk about yet.'

'Commercial secrets I suppose eh, Jon?' asked Pam.

'Not at all,' he assured her, and raised a laugh by revealing, 'I don't yet know what they'll be, so I can't say! If we work together, that has to be approached carefully because the last thing to do would be for either you or we to exaggerate business prospects. We have a modest factory, mostly used for the assembly of sub-contracted manufactured parts, although we could, for example, double our present production.'

Jon noticed a raising of Alan's eyebrows as he looked enquiringly at his colleagues, receiving imperceptible nods in return. 'Jon, we don't rush into new projects quickly, but neither do we waste time. We've had enough time and information to agree among us that we wish to develop a partnership with your company, based upon what we've seen and heard from you. We understand that we'd have to go to the UK, or your people would have to come here, or both, unless you can conclude formalities. Is that likely?'

'No, Alan, I'm not a director of the company, so I couldn't commit.'

'But you have certain authority here, yes?'

'As I explained to you, my title as "Director of Projects" is to help open doors to such people as Mr Gavuzzi. My early working life as an apprentice engineer interested the Minister far more than a status symbol, and he and I had a laugh about that. I have with me a formal declaration from the company of my authority to engage any company that I might need. You may have a copy of it.'

Janet Howell hadn't said a word throughout these exchanges, but now she had a question. Jon dreaded any question about TLC's finances. If he lied, he would eventually be found out to be deceitful, but if he was truthful, or too honest, it could scupper the whole enterprise. 'Jon,' she asked, 'forgive me for asking, but my notorious woman's instinct tells me that you are reserved about something.'

Oh Lord, is she going to ask about money, or to discuss the financial aspect of any agreement with our Finance Director O'Flynn? He desperately needed to sidestep that question. 'Yes, Janet, I am. As I've said already, TLC is a modest company, smaller than Stone Industries. It would be unfortunate for our association if you wanted from the outset to move too fast for us. So, Janet, as our agreement goes forward I would suggest that we do so one step at a time. Get the cash in from the first, then work on the next step, so to speak, get accustomed to working with each other, and review policy frequently.'

'Thank you,' she said reassuringly, 'I think that that's perfectly reasonable.'

Jon took control again. 'I'd like to suggest this. We've had a pleasant evening, but I suggest that we think over all that's been said, and I will be at Stone's offices tomorrow to review Alan's proposal for the conveyor's repair, and go from there, because meanwhile, I can't think of anything to add, except to ask for the bill here.'

Alan Stone pounced. 'Not a chance of that, Jon, the meal's on us. Speaking for Stone Industries, this evening is an investment of time and money not "entertainment" that the taxman would allege, although it's been fun. We'll drop you off at your lodgings and see you when? Ten o'clock?'

At the house, they all left the vehicle to say courteous 'goodnights', shaking hands and kissing cheeks, loaded up again, and Roy drove off. Jon and Olivia watched them out of sight, when he asked her, 'What do you think of that, Olivia?'

'In a word "successful" but, Jon, I know you well enough by now to know that you were alarmed that Janet was going to ask about TLC's finances.'

'I was absolutely shaking, I don't mind admitting, and it was as well that we were all seated or I might have fallen over! Something's got to be done about the firm's working capital before we get in too deep with Stone. I'll have to go back to the UK very soon, because I can do nothing about that here. Bugger it. Meanwhile, let's go in as it's getting chilly here, and maybe Evelyn's still there to make us some coffee.'

'I see,' said Olivia, with a grin, 'gone off my coffee, have we?'

'Not at all, and I'm not as tired for this time of night as I thought I would be.'

CHAPTER SEVENTEEN

The next morning, Jon sorted his priorities, using the reception area as an office. There were no emails to his laptop from Alice Mac, which he hoped was a good sign. His satphone was fully charged and he wouldn't have to use the embassy phone to call the office, as he did now. Mrs Catchmore took the call. 'Hello, Mrs Catchmore, it's Jon Webb here, how's the Guv?'

'Oh, hello, Jon, it's good to hear your voice, is all well?'

'Very much so, thanks, but I've been worried about your husband. What's the news, please?'

'He's much better, thank you, Jon, and I'm confident about leaving him at home. Recent events overwhelmed him, as you can understand, but you're not to be blamed for his worry, not at all, Jon. In fact, the opposite's the case, because he's quite excited to hear your news and in that respect he's younger in spirit. He is most optimistic for the firm's future, but to be candid with you, it is Mr O'Flynn who's causing serious difficulties.'

'What's happened?'

'The police are questioning Keith, who very nearly killed Roger, and obtained a search warrant for No 2 unit presuming that he was hiding something from Roger. When we leased this office and factory building we also leased No 2, but subsequently sub-let it to Mr O'Flynn for his business storage purposes because we no longer needed it. However, there was some residual archival TLC storage still in there which Roger had gone to look for. Remember? The police did indeed find hidden goods. There were two crates which they opened to find stun guns …'

'Stun guns?' Jon interrupted

'… which are apparently legal in some countries, but the police want to know why O'Flynn wants them, and is he trading in them. The problem is that because TLC holds the main lease, and that O'Flynn is a director of TLC, the police presume that the stun guns could be there with our knowledge. They aren't, of course, but I don't think the police are being unreasonable. The thing is, O'Flynn can't be located, and his wife doesn't know where he is; at least, that's what she says.'

This was incredible news, and Jon sensed urgency.

'Mrs Catchmore, there's a wooden crate in the small room that I use and I've no idea what's in it, neither does Alice, but she said it had been there for some time as the space was used for storage until I came along. I was sitting on it one day when she was in there with me and I'd lent her my chair. If the police are in TLC's offices and see it they're bound to ask what's in it if it looks the same as the other two crates, but to be on the safe side show it to them voluntarily and let them take it away. They'll give you a receipt.

Whatever you do, don't open it! I think that you'd better get legal advice very quickly.'

'Good Lord, Jon, I need the support that the other two directors are giving me, but this is becoming a nightmare and I'd be glad to see you here. When are you coming back?'

'Probably not for another week, I'm afraid. I have to see work on the damaged conveyor belt at least started, and also see some other machines to write an initial report for the Secretariat, but I need to come back soon to discuss a possible agency for TLC here. Please don't worry, Mrs Catchmore, and I know that's easily said, but I'm sure that everything will turn out for the best eventually. Please give my best wishes to the Guv, but I have to go now.' They exchanged closing greetings, and ended the call. For Jon, all manner of situations came to mind, and occupied him as Olivia walked in.

'Oh, Olivia,' he offered, realising that he should have looked for her earlier. 'I was wide awake at five and crept out not wanting to disturb you.'

'Hello to you, too, Jon, where've you been? I was expecting you for breakfast.'

'I was here, on the phone, expecting to make just a quick call to the office which turned out to be dramatic. Please join me, and I'll explain.'

'I have to say that you're looking confident, Jon, tell me about it, but don't forget your meeting with Alan Stone at ten.'

'There's a drama going on back at TLC. You remember that our works manager, Roger

Martin, had been attacked and virtually left for dead in a ditch, yes? Well, he recovered briefly and sufficiently to name his assailant who is now in police custody. The police became curious about the attack, wondering if the assailant had something to hide in the building where the attack took place. They got a search warrant, and lo and behold found two crates which they opened and found to be containing stun guns. I have just told the Guv's wife that there's another crate in my small office which looks similar to the other two.'

'They're a bit like Tasers, aren't they? Are they illegal?'

'I don't know, but to shorten the story if I may, the attacker is a nephew of O'Flynn who's a director of TLC, as you know, and the building is one that TLC sub-let to O'Flynn for storage purposes some time ago. Not unreasonably, the police began asking if TLC had knowledge of the stun guns, which of course it doesn't, or rather didn't. Mrs Catchmore, the Guv's wife, told me that nobody knows where O'Flynn is, even his own wife, although I'd be sceptical of that because I understand she's a nasty piece of work.

'Of course, there could be all sorts of reasons for O'Flynn's absence – in hospital after an accident, a short holiday his wife forgot about, away on business, and so on, but it's too much of a co-incidence. I don't know if a licence is needed to trade in stun guns, but the police very much want to know why they were hidden in a building under his control, and what's his purpose.'

'Are you glad to be away from all of that?'

'Well, I met you, didn't I? And that's not so bad, so yes I am glad.'

'D'you know, Jon, I really can't decide if you have a way with words, or not. I think I ought to review all of the nice remarks you've made to me. Hmm, yes, I will.'

'Go on with you! You know I love you to bits.'

'Really? No, I didn't know that, you've never said.'

'Ah, sorry, just a figure of speech.'

'Jon, any minute now the situation back at your firm is going to be a piece of cake compared with what might happen here *very soon*!' Jon shook with suppressed laughter, holding his hands up in mock surrender. 'I give in, Olivia, I really give in!'

'Mmm. I don't entirely accept that, and I'll let you off just this once, but only because I want to know what you're going to do about the home office, so to speak.' They were now happily grinning at each other at how Jon's tactless remark had been overcome.

'Going back to your question, Olivia, I really couldn't do much to help back there. The two other directors are taking the pressure off Mrs Catchmore, and the only outstanding work that I know of is a quotation for a customer Roger and I visited. I couldn't do that as I don't have the details nor the experience needed. It will have to wait until the Guv and Roger are recovered, but

I'm sure that the customer will tolerate a short delay.'

'You said that I looked confident, and so I am. Suppose O'Flynn is arrested, and found guilty of some crime connected with these stun guns, then surely he'd lose his position on the Board? Even if he wasn't convicted, then equally he'd be deemed to be unfit to be a director, and I suppose could be voted off, but I don't know the individual shareholdings, or if that would make any difference. As a newcomer I admit that to an extent I was in dread of O'Flynn, but I'm not now. When he knew I'd joined TLC he was shouting and rude, perhaps the same as he was to Janice, but if he was quiet and sly by nature he could have moved his storage elsewhere. I wonder if his nephew feels safer in custody than on the outside with O'Flynn rampaging around looking for revenge because his nephew caused the discovery. When I took this job I was bursting with confidence, but that collapsed on learning about the firm's finances, or lack of them, and problems on the Board.'

However, after all that's happened in the last three weeks up to and especially including today's news, there is an interesting future ahead of all of us which is already happening as I speak. I'm so glad that you've been involved, Olivia, and hasn't this been a good way of getting acquainted? Much better than having met at a party or in an office, although do you realise how much we don't know about each other? I've no idea where you live, or with whom you live, if anyone, which I hope not, other than your parents, and you know nothing similar about me. Please could we spend some time together answering those questions?'

'Yes, but not now, you've ten minutes to get to Alan's office.'

'Oh, blast, will you be around later this morning? For lunch maybe?'

'Yes, but *go* Jon, there's a car outside for you.'

***

Alan Stone had assembled his team for the meeting, as expected, and again Jon felt quite at home with them all as 'good mornings' were exchanged. They took their seats in a small conference room.

'Did you sleep well, Jon?' Alan enquired politely, with a knowing grin lurking at the corners of his mouth. 'I did indeed, thank you, and I'm told that Olivia did also. Only hearsay, you understand.' Jon replied in similar vein to much laughter from the others.

'Seriously, Jon, were you two a team before you came here?'

'Not at all. I first spoke to her at the embassy weeks ago when I phoned for some background to the country when preparing to come here, then once again asking about accommodation. I met her for the first time as I met George Turbeville-Blyth, and his deputy William Spencer. Why do you ask?'

'We felt that you work well together as a team, and we were impressed last evening at dinner by the interest which she took in our potential business together.'

'I'd like to think that it is a personal interest – no, that's ridiculous – she does show a personal interest, but probably also because she works in an investment bank.'

'Not in the diplomatic service, then?'

'No, she's seconded to the embassy for a short spell, going back to the UK soon.'

Roy was his usual quiet self, and he asked a searching question. 'Jon, would or could the investment bank be useful to TLC in the matter of loan capital, and could Olivia decide that?'

'Part of her job is to look for lending opportunities, and I hope she'll think that our joint venture would qualify for loan capital, although I think that TLC's too small to talk to a an investment bank merchant bank, or an investment bank as they're called in the US, because the loan entry level is in millions. However, perhaps her bank could give an intro to a more suitable private bank in the UK.'

Roy's next question could be a killer if not handled carefully, striking a balance between avoiding the truth and not lying. Jon was ready for it. 'Couldn't your Finance Director liaise between our two companies, and between yours and that bank?'

'No, that would not be a good plan, if I may explain. He's very precise and focussed in his work, but tends to be a little humourless in company, given to upsetting people by too direct speech, and would not fit in with such circumstances as ours last evening. He doesn't understand the relevance of combining enjoyment and hard work to succeed in business.'

Pam Stone was no less shrewd than Janet Howell. 'Jon, is there something that you're not telling us?'

You bet there is, Jon thought. 'Yes, Pam, but it's really a problem within the company, such as could occur anywhere. Our FD couldn't see the need to come here to investigate the damaged conveyor belt, and couldn't understand the possible benefits that could accrue from such a visit, therefore he was in dispute with his Board colleagues, arguing that it would be money wasted. When he saw me and heard me presenting a case for coming here he was quite frustrated and angry.'

Along came another question which he had to answer, and had wanted to avoid. Alan and his colleagues were riveted by Jon's answers, hanging on his every word. 'So, Jon, we're all, I'm sure, wanting to know how is it that you've arrived here after all that opposition?'

'Between the five of us please,' he said, looking round at the others in turn. 'I think that TLC has a strong "family" bond, but the CEO is less active than he should be, and dithered about this trip, so from frustration and overconfidence, if you like, I offered to pay for it myself. And here I am.'

'*You* are paying all of the expenses for being here, Jon?' asked Alan, in surprise.

'Yes, and I don't think that I am mistaken, do you? In any case they'll be recoverable eventually but I just wanted to speed things up.'

There was a pensive silence in the room.'Jon, pardon me for asking, but if we do work for TLC, would you be paying our bill?'

'Not personally, Alan, no. When I approve a quotation I'm authorised to instruct a contractor up to a cash limit, while telling the office that I've done so. You'll then get a confirmation order by email. But if a repair was a simple ten-minute job I would pay, to keep matters simple.'

He then raised a laugh by insisting, 'While I am interested in developing co-operation between us, I draw the line at disclosing my cash limit. But could we return to the reason for this meeting, which is to agree your terms for repairing that conveyor as one subject, and to touch upon a possible future partnership as another subject?'

Janet Howell opened a thin folder on the table, and handed Jon their quotation.

'Thanks, Janet.' It was simple, straightforward, and short. The simplest he'd yet seen, causing him to turn it over to read what was written on page two, but there was no page three.

Jon looked up from it to see five smiling faces gazing at him. 'Is this it, Janet?'

'Yes'

With no hesitation, Jon took out a pen, signed the acceptance clause, and slid the document and the pen across the table back to Janet, who in equal silence also signed. Trying and failing to keep a straight face she leant across the table to shake hands with Jon, smiling broadly.

'I have two questions now,' he said. The room tensed a little, but then to uninhibited laughter, he asked, 'Firstly, please may I have a coffee, and secondly, may I use your loo?'

Someone offered, 'Down the corridor, second on the right.' On returning to the meeting he found another man standing in welcome, offering his hand. 'Hello, Jon, I'm Paddy Fenn, Chief Mechanical Engineer. I have been out on site, and it seemed from the laughter as I came back in here that I missed all the fun.'

'Hello to you also, Paddy,' Jon acknowledged. 'Not fun, but an enjoyable way of doing business together. We had just concluded an agreement for Stone Industries to repair a conveyor on behalf of my company.'

'Ah, yes,' Paddy said, 'between Roy and me we've located what spares we need, and leaving the doors aside we could start work in ten days. Agreed, Roy?'

'Correct,' Roy replied, 'but there's the matter of power being restored to the mine, which I discussed with the Minister earlier today. He sends his compliments, and asked "How's the squash?" hooting with laughter at his own joke. What was that all about?' So Jon had to explain the 'blazer stories' to them all, and when the laughter died down Alan Stone remarked, 'I still for the life of me wonder how you get on so well with Gavuzzi. It's amazing, Jon.'

Jon had done all that he could at that stage, and was becoming restless to arrange his return to the UK, so he postponed any in-depth discussion about the possible partnership until the TLC situation had been resolved. He decided to change the plan of the meeting.

'Ladies and gentlemen, if you please, I'd like to amend our plans for this meeting, and postpone any formal discussion about an agency in Zed until I've consulted our Board of Directors. I am absolutely not changing direction, but if you consider what I'm taking back with me by way of results and reports, it's quite a lot for them to absorb all at once, and if I initiated a discussion about an arrangement with you, they could think that I'm going too fast. However, having hinted about such an arrangement to our CEO's wife, who's also a director, she may remember and ask about it. If she does, that'll be different, and I'll seize my chance. What do you think, please?'

'Well, what do you all say?' asked Alan Stone. 'It seems a reasonable plan to me.' Unsurprisingly, they took their lead from their boss, murmuring agreement.

'So, Jon, are you leading up to saying "goodbye" for now?'

'Yes, but not so abruptly, Alan. Apart from the results of our business both done and planned, I am grateful to you all for your sociable company, particularly last evening, which augurs well for the future. I know I keep emphasising the overlap of business and pleasure, but it works, doesn't it? I really should leave you now to return to your work, and I relish the prospect of being in your company again.'

So to the accompaniment of good wishes, handshakes, and kissed cheeks with the ladies, he left them with a final wave as he was driven off.

CHAPTER EIGHTEEN

Despite George T-B's assurance that there'd be no charge for Jon's use of the embassy's facilities he felt to be in a moral debt, so he went straight to the embassy to make it all official. On arrival, he was waylaid by William, with his usual courtesy. 'Good morning, Jon, I trust that you are well. The Ambassador would like to meet you.'

'Oh, and good morning to you too, William. I have been wanting to meet him. What's he like?'

'He's the acme of our perception of diplomats. He's courteous and polite, of course, particularly with his staff, but he has a wicked sense of humour. You should get on well with him. Come with me, please.' A short walk down the corridor running through the embassy brought them to an inconspicuous door on which William knocked gently, resulting in a "come in, please" from a crisp and pleasant-sounding voice.

'Ah, Mr Jonathan Webb, good morning, I am pleased to meet you, I did not have the chance at the reception.' greeted the Ambassador as he stood. 'I am told that you are being successful in your purpose here. Please take a seat, and you also, William,' as he resumed his seat.

'Good morning, Ambassador,' said Jon. 'Well, I am certainly pleased with the results thus far, but it would have been impossible without the help from William here, and George Turbeville-

Blyth, and also Ms de St Croix. My company is indebted to you for all the facilities that I have used, so I wish to pay my way and settle my account with you.'

The Ambassador broke into a broad and pleasant smile and said, 'Mr Webb, Mr Gavuzzi has telephoned me. I have to admit that in the past when I've been forewarned of an incoming call from him, I've been in a degree of fear and dread in the expectation of difficulty with the gentleman, as usually proved to be the case. However, Mr Gavuzzi was pleasant and good humoured to the point where I became suspicious that he was after a concession of some sort, but I was quite mistaken. He offered his thanks for his invitation to George's reception which he and his Minister had enjoyed. It is customary for guests to write formally thanking for such invitations, but Mr Gavuzzi spoke of certain events of the day and the evening which led to their enjoyment. He indicated that I'd missed some fun that was at your expense, Mr Webb.'

'Yes, it was,' Jon admitted, 'but I didn't mind because the circumstances he's talking about were really amusing and couldn't have been contrived. I'm sure that they "broke the ice" with him and the Minister, and indeed with his minions at my meeting earlier in the day. I've seen him since to conclude some business, during which he was entirely pleasant and indeed friendly.'

'That is exactly the point that I'm coming to, Mr Webb. In normal circumstances we can't offer our help to businesses gratuitously, for that's not our role, but I am empowered to waive any usual charges if it is thought that a visitor has effectively acted on behalf of the United Kingdom. It is my opinion that you have been helpful to this embassy, Mr Webb, so you may continue to enjoy our facilities.'

'That is generous of you, sir, and on behalf of my company, I thank you.'

'Good, now if you'll both excuse me, there is some less interesting work that I have to attend to. Perhaps we shall meet again, Mr Webb,' and with his genuine smile he rose to shake hands with Jon, saying, 'Goodbye.'

'Thank you again, and I would like that. Goodbye, for now.'

Once out of the Ambassador's hearing, William asked, 'Well?'

'A very pleasant gentleman, William, and I liked his good manners to you. Taking him at his word, may I use your office, or the other half of it, please?

***

Jon phoned TLC, hoping to speak to the Guv. Alice MacInnes answered. 'Hi, Alice, it's Jon Webb here.'

'Oh, Jon, are you well? When are you coming back, you're needed here!'

'Probably the day after tomorrow, but I can't be sure. Is there another problem? And how's the Guv?'

'He and Roger are recovered physically, but strains still show. Your Mr Tindall's quite happy, but the directors are not. The Catchmores and Messrs Bryant and Phillips are with our lawyers now.' Jon wanted to shriek, 'What's the problem? Alice, get on with it!' and could hardly restrain his frustration, but calming himself with difficulty, asked again. 'What's wrong, Alice?'

'Jon, some years ago the firm had used up its overdraft facility at the bank, which wanted to close the account. It introduced Mr O'Flynn to TLC as a "Business Angel" and he made a substantial loan to TLC which was properly documented, covering all eventualities. Somehow, and they're all blaming each other for it, they missed a clause stating that the loan was on call in thirty days from notice given by the lender. Mr O'Flynn has now exercised that right, and there's no prospect of having the money within the thirty days, so the directors are worried about the firm being wound up.'

'What reason has he given, Alice? He knew TLC's cash position as of course he would as FD, so why call in the loan?'

'He's still not to be found by the police. His notice to us came from his lawyers, who, it seems, are intransigent and equally unpleasant as Mr O'Flynn. Which reminds me, Jon, Mr Catchmore asked me to warn you that Mr O'Flynn threatened you with violence because you had upset his plans, and referred to you as an "interfering bastard", I'm sorry to repeat.'

'None of this makes sense, Alice; he must be completely unhinged. He's deliberately acting against the interest of a company of which he's a director. Isn't that illegal?'

'I don't know, I really don't know, Jon, but wouldn't it be lovely to get back to normality? Mr Catchmore speculates that Mr O'Flynn is presuming that the contracts you've won in Zed could represent enough collateral to borrow against so that his loan can be repaid.'

'How does he know about those contracts?'

'Either he, or one of his friends, have hacked into our emails, Jon. He may also have read one sent addressed to you yesterday from a Mr Abbott about developments on this industrial estate. We don't know this Mr Abbott, but he reported that the housing developer is a company based in Belfast. He added that he and his wife drove to the building site to have a look out of curiosity, but work seemed to have stopped and there was nobody about. He adds that "your friend" is a director of the developer's firm. Is that relevant?'

'It could well be. If O'Flynn is funding the development but has no money, that may be why the work has stopped. Give me time to think please, Alice. Meanwhile, don't send me any emails, use the fax which I understand is difficult to be hacked into. I hesitate to ask, but is there anything else?'

'Oh, yes, I forgot to tell you. We have copies of your contracts as I told you, but they differ from the drafts which you sent earlier. Stone

Industries have stipulated that payment to them should be in sixty days from completion of works, and the Secretariat has changed their agreement to pay us in thirty days from completion.'

'That's incredible! People offering to pay us before we pay the contractor? But I haven't initialled the changes, so won't they be void?'

'Mr Catchmore thinks not, and says that for the moment he doesn't "give a damn!"'

'Fine. I must stop using this phone for now, Alice, but I'll call you again.'

***

He sat back in his chair, puffing out his cheeks in a huge sigh, and entirely disregarding where he was, let out an unrestrained expletive. 'Oh Jesus Christ! What next?'

'Something wrong, Jon?' said Olivia, appearing with a smile.

'Oh, hello, Olivia there you are. I'm sorry I didn't look for you after meeting the Ambassador but I was anxious to phone the office. I almost wish I hadn't.'

'Why?'

'I'll explain, but not necessarily in sequence. You remember O'Flynn? He has hacked into our emails and learnt about the contracts here. He has also invoked a clause in an old loan agreement he made to TLC, which led to him being on the Board, and disastrously the directors at the time didn't spot that the loan was on call at thirty days' notice.'

'Good God!'

'Precisely. I have only spoken to Alice, and the Board is closeted with our lawyers. There are questions: first, why call the loan in if it couldn't be paid, and when the firm's principle asset – its valuable lease on the factory – is illiquid. I think that O'Flynn is unhinged and desperate for cash. Why? Alice wonders if O'Flynn thinks that the new contracts could be offered as collateral for bank loans. What's your professional opinion?'

'No, they're too young, and have no cash value yet, although I haven't read their terms. If the directors failed to see that clause I think that they have a moral obligation to mortgage their houses and lend the cash to the company.' Then with a laugh she continued, 'You've put them on the spot in that regard by funding your business trip here yourself! What a classic precedent!'

Jon joined in with a mischievous chuckle. 'What a good idea, Olivia, but Sod's Law suggests to me that they all rent their houses, or have no equity in them.'

'What's going to happen now then?'

'If O'Flynn was expecting to make a heap of money from selling the guns on, he's got a problem because the police have them, so if he hadn't paid for them and is under pressure from his supplier for payment, he'll be desperate for cash from anywhere he can get it. Now that he can't deliver, perhaps he's also under pressure from his customer who'd been promised delivery. If he's dealing with crooks, he could be in personal danger. It's no wonder that he's missing.'

Olivia was puzzled. 'Jon, why are you so anxious about O'Flynn's problems?'

'I'm not, but I'm worried about their knock-on effect. I know nothing about O'Flynn's loan, but it must be significant if the directors are consulting the lawyers. Whatever its level, I don't see how re-mortgaging houses or selling the factory lease could be completed in the time remaining, and I'm sure that the directors' spouses would have an opinion about second mortgages just to satisfy O'Flynn.

'I told you that when I joined the firm I soon realised that it had stagnated, so my job became little to do with design and more to do with getting new business. Now that the directors are preoccupied and distracted by this money problem, the firm could become as static as it was before I came. The profit from the contracts that we have here added to the recent one back home, can't sustain the firm for long.'

'Jon, you told me of your confidence in TLC's future, have you changed your mind since this news about that loan?'

'No, I'm sure that I haven't, for if I had, I wouldn't be trying to work out how to get round these problems, and the more I talk to you, the more new ideas come to mind. Fantasies, if you like.'

'It seems that I have my uses.'

'Indeed you have, dear Olivia, and please consider this. Suppose that instead of running around in circles trying to meet O'Flynn's deadline, the directors just let him get on with pursuing repayment by legal means, then even presuming that TLC's lease has value, O'Flynn would have to wait for the forced asset sale. What do you think of all that? But remember that I'm not a lawyer so I can only use 'layman's speak'.'

'I need time to catch up with your way of thinking, Jon, but suppose the directors do actually re-mortgage and pay off Mr O'Flynn, what happens even if he's voted off the Board, or right out of the picture for any reason, how will TLC go forward?'

'I don't understand your question.'

'You said that TLC is short of cash, but even if things go to plan here there are only a few thousand pounds of net profit to be expected in the short term. I think you've done a brilliant job here, Jon, dealing with the present problems and setting up potential new business with Gavuzzi and Stone, but that doesn't pay tomorrow's wages back home. I know there's that order from your friend Mr Tindall, but you need more business, especially from the UK.'

'You're talking exactly like a clearing bank branch manager, Olivia.'

'I know, but it's true, isn't it? And you're the best TLC person to go and get new business, but that doesn't alter the fact that TLC needs capital as a float until more cash from sales arrives.'

Jon didn't argue with that, but was getting a little rattled with Olivia, who he thought was patronising him by stating the obvious. He'd made it clear to her that he wasn't involved with the firm's finances, so was unaware of its capital reserves, or its access to capital. He had funded the Zed business because of O'Flynn's presumed veto on spending the money, and the Guv's lack of confidence in the trip. He was not yet prepared to divulge to anyone, even Olivia whom he trusted, that his late father's estate would probably result in substantial funds coming to him as the only child. His father was probably – as the current cliché went – cash poor but asset rich, having a freehold house in The Bishop's Avenue, North London. Probably worth enough to solve TLC's immediate problem, which Jon was prepared to consider helping with, but absolutely not when O'Flynn was still a director or shareholder, or had any lien on the company, and anyway it would take months to complete the sale and wind up his father's estate.

Nevertheless, he had to answer Olivia's remark. 'I understand what you're driving at, Olivia, but I'm not worried about day-to-day working capital. That's not my problem to consider, still less to resolve. When I get back I'll follow up my earlier mailshot, and begin other projects.'

Jon was becoming increasingly confident in his attraction to Olivia. She appeared to approve of his enterprising nature and headlong attacks at business problems and when at the end of the encounter with the soldiers he had indicated that she was the sort of woman he'd like for a long-term relationship, she seemed to accept that it was not said in the excitement of an adventure. If they became partners, would she find his day-to-day work for TLC to be less stimulating, and might he become more conventional and less exciting? Would that be a difficult challenge? Not likely, he said to himself, smiling.

She noticed his expression. 'Jon, your time here has been stimulating to say the least, and I doubt if anyone's normal employment such as your previous job could match that, so do you think that you'd get frustrated without the challenges you've faced here?'

He was astonished. 'Olivia, not for the first time you have read my mind accurately. How do you do it? But it could worry me for the future.'

'Whatever do you mean?'

'Well, suppose we were to, erm, well erm, live together, I'd never get away with any mischief at all.' She grinned hugely. 'I do not remember you saying anything about living together, I think you spoke about a long-term partnership. Anyway, what sort of mischief?'

He quickly fudged that question by trying to reassure her. 'Yes, I think there could be frustrations, but the answer to that is to generate new openings, and believe me there will be plenty of those working with TLC, always providing, of course, that the firm agrees. A couple of days before he died my father was insistent that I should grab every opportunity that comes my way, and if they don't, then I should create my own. He confessed to having drifted through his life, and was determined that I shouldn't do the same. So I won't. I'm indebted to him. Anyway, Ms de St Croix, what about you? You work in a bank in the City, very successfully I'm sure, but will that satisfy you after your experiences here?'

'No, it's going to be difficult, I admit. A barnstorming exercise like yours here would be impossible within an investment bank, it would be inappropriate.' She thought for a few moments, and murmured, 'I suppose I could work alongside you in TLC, or in something else. That might be good. Then with a smile of obvious enjoyment, she asked, 'What do you say to that, Mr Jonathan Webb?'

CHAPTER NINETEEN

'I've thought the same once or twice, Olivia, wondering if we *could* work together. It doesn't matter doing what, although now if you'll forgive me, is it something we could talk about? It's an interesting idea with possibilities, and might be exciting. Don't tell me that the idea's only just come to you.'

'It was spontaneous just now, but the idea's been lurking. We've got to think about this seriously, Jon, not so much about the details, but we've been in unreal circumstances and have to ask ourselves if normally we would say what we've said to each other so soon after we'd met.'

Before she could finish, William rushed in. 'Sorry to interrupt, but there's a call from a Mrs MacInnes for Jon in George's office. It should have come through here.'

'Oh, I'm sorry, William, I shouldn't use George's room, please transfer it here.'

The instant the phone buzzed, Jon grabbed it. 'Hello, Alice, Jon here.'

'Hello, Jon. How are you?'

'Fine thanks … Yes, leaving hopefully the day after tomorrow, but I haven't yet checked flights. I will be late home so I could be in the office the day after that.' Then looking across at Olivia raising his eyebrows as a question and getting a nod, he added, 'I may have Ms de St Croix with me, she's been helping me … no, just seconded to the embassy. Do you have some news?'

Alice MacInnes spoke for several minutes, occasionally interrupted by Jon's "good God" or "bloody hell, Alice" then when she'd finished he said, 'Well that's an improvement, isn't it? But I'll phone Mrs Abbott to see if she's okay, and see you soon, Alice. Pass on my good wishes, please. Goodbye.'

He paused for a minute, thinking about the call. 'Olivia, there's a major upheaval at TLC, all to the good, with just one bit of bad news which I'll come to in a minute. The lawyers don't think the wording of O'Flynn's loan is legally enforceable, and wrote to his lawyers accordingly, who've washed their hands of him since learning of the stun guns, and no longer act for him. He's therefore stuffed for the time being, so the repayment pressure's off TLC for the time being at least.

'David Phillips, one of the directors, was prepared to raise money against his assets, and has successfully offered it to a new bank as collateral for an overdraft, so that pressure is also off the Guv. Alice says that Phillips was much influenced by TLC's sudden business progress, and wants to have a brainstorming meeting, over two days if necessary, to plan the future for us all. I have to prepare for that immediately I get back.'

'That's the good news, but what's the bad?'

'O'Flynn – well we assume it was O'Flynn – called at the house which has my flat and the one above owned by Eric and Sybil Abbott, my landlords and now my friends. He demanded rudely to see me, and tried to shove past Sybil, who to his astonishment punched his nose. When she threatened to phone the police the man turned and left in a hurry but strode on to an old patch of oil on the driveway, lost his footing, fell over landing on his right elbow causing him to scream in pain, and Sybil to laugh. He then swore at her and ran off. Sybil had no idea who he was.

'I absolutely must phone Sybil. By the way, you two will like each other. Oh, did you mind me suggesting that I'd have you with me when I returned to the office?'

'Of course not, silly, it's a good idea.'

He dialled Sybil's number, and wondered while waiting for an answer just how much he'd cost the embassy, but he really didn't need to care according to the Ambassador.

'Hello, Sybil Abbott speaking.'

'Sybil, it's Jon Webb, how are you? I've heard about that man attacking you.'

'*Jon*! It's good to hear your voice. When will we see you?'

'The evening of the day after tomorrow, depending upon flights but never mind that, have you recovered from the attack, and are your knuckles sore?'

'Knuckles? What do you mean?'

'Alice MacInnes told me that he'd tried to push past you and that you'd punched him on the nose.'

She laughed. 'Oh that! No, I came down to answer the door and to put a really stale crusty loaf in the wheelie-bin outside. It was as hard as a rock, and by chance was still in my hand, so I hit him with it, apparently on his nose because it bled profusely. When I threatened to call the police he left in a hurry but slipped on that patch of oil and hurt himself. Served him right.'

'Oh, Sybil, you're a heroine. And if you are capable of that sort of violence, please remind me to pay my rent on time! Tell me more when I'm home. Also I'm bringing a lady with me. Her name's Olivia, and she's been instrumental in helping me over here …'

'Ah, ha,' Sybil interrupted, 'a woman at last. Where's she going to sleep? But seriously, Jon, if it suits you both, we can put her up in the spare room.'

'Thanks, Sybil, that'd be kind of you. My flat's probably cold and damp after this time away, and not as nice I'd like it to be for a visitor. I'm looking forward to introducing Olivia to you. So I'll see you tomorrow evening, and thanks again for what you and Eric have done. Bye,' and he ended the call.

Then he realised he's got ahead of himself with regard to Olivia. 'Oh, bloody hell, Olivia, I've just been assuming that after we land at Gatwick you'd come back to my flat, but you may have gathered from my speaking to Sybil that I hadn't presumed you'd stay with me. I'm really sorry for not consulting you, or for even asking about your plans. I'm embarrassed. I haven't even

246

asked about your job, or when you're going back to work. I'm so sorry to be so full of myself.'

'Jon, believe me, it's not a problem. I could have interrupted you at any point in your conversations, and I'm quite happy. To be truthful, I think that the adventure continues, so I'm watching and listening with interest.'

Reassured, he sat gazing at her, saying nothing.

'What?' she asked.

Nothing,' he lied, 'just thinking. No, sorry, that wasn't truthful. I think that that flight tomorrow isn't going to be nearly half long enough to talk about our past, let alone the future. Can you spare a few days after we're back?'

She smiled. 'As long as you like, Jon.'

'Well, I just wondered if we could take a short break away after we get back, just to talk about life and what we like doing, and that sort of thing. I'm dreading you telling me that you'll be going to your firm's office in the States, but in the meantime, I must now speak to Gavuzzi, and the Minister, and Alan Stone, if you'll excuse me.'

'Good idea, Jon, and I'm staying here, to prompt you perhaps.'

So he rang Alan Stone to ensure that there would be nothing to delay his return to the UK, to be told that work on the conveyor belt would start in three days, and that Alan had already liaised with the Minister who was satisfied with that report. Jon's only difficulty was that in view of events back home he couldn't predict when he'd be back. He excused himself by explaining that as TLC was reorganising itself to speed up production, he was needed there for a short while. That was acceptable to his contacts, despite not being the whole truth. As a courtesy, he phoned Gavuzzi, and in his absence left an appropriate message.

'Can you think of anything else I need to do, Olivia?'

'I think that it would be an appropriate and very welcome gesture, Jon, if you entertained George and William to supper this evening.'

'Really? What about the Ambassador also?'

'No, that's OTT.'

'OTT or not Olivia, it would be tactless not to invite him. I'll ask George to do so, because I think it would be wrong coming from me, because if he declines he can tell George to fudge a reason. It's up to his judgement to come or not to come. I think that he may enjoy an evening with his senior staff.'

'Very well, but the others are free this evening.'

'How do you know?'

'I've suggested the invitation to them, and they've accepted.'

'Good grief! Brilliant! Where should we go?'

'The same place we went to with Alan Stone's party. It's not expensive, if you're worried about the bill. Another thing, Jon, William tells me that Mr Gavuzzi likes going there, but if we get there early at say, six, hopefully we'll miss him. Is that okay?'

'You bet, thank you, for two reasons. Firstly, I don't want to be accused of bribery for paying his bills, and secondly I'm getting nervous about my debit card's limit. There's money in the bank, but not much in my current account. Can you arrange transport, please?'

'It's done. Dave will drive us in a minibus, excluding the Ambassador who'd want to come separately, and if you're worried we can use my debit card. That should raise a laugh.'

'Olivia, I'm really taking advantage of you ...no! not that!...asking you to do all these tasks for me. Sorry, but while I'm on the subject, could you book UK flights for us, please? And if you need an upgrade to Business Class I'll pay the difference. I'll nip up to my room for the ticket.'

'Yes, sir, of course, sir, anything you say, sir, your wish is my command sir!'

'Anything? What a promising evening!'

***

The evening was remarkable. The Ambassador proved to be a man who cared for his staff, as William had told Jon. He was never aloof, but maintained a certain dignity while incorporating his humour into the others'. He admitted to Jon of his partial ignorance of how business worked, and became an avid listener acknowledging the benefits of Jon's explanations. The stories of the blazer incidents were retold to much laughter, as was the encounter with the soldiers and Olivia's dash for a pee when the Land Rover started. At the evening's end, when Jon and Olivia were delivered back to the house, there was definitely a sense of regret that it, and Jon's visit, had to end. Smiles and handshakes couldn't entirely mend that feeling.

As Jon and Olivia struggled upstairs to their rooms he said wearily, 'This has been a truly pleasant and thoroughly enjoyable evening, Olivia. Thank you so much for suggesting it and organising it, but for now, and don't take offence, I'm off to my bed!'

'Spoilsport!'

***

Their flight back was uneventful, pleasantly spent talking about each other's life and background. Jon learnt that Olivia was single, had no present partner, and lived in her flat in Barnes, south west of London, from where she commuted to the City.

They took a train from Gatwick airport to Eastbourne, then a taxi to Jon's flat. After opening the front door and letting them in, he called up to the Abbotts with, 'Hello, we're here.'

Sybil appeared on the upper floor, and invited them in. 'We left the door open so we could hear you return. Do come up, we're curious to know what sort of woman could possibly be associated with you.' When they met, she said, 'You must be Olivia. Eric and I are pleased to meet you because we know absolutely nothing about you, except that you must be oblivious to risk to be with Jon. Come in and meet my husband. Eric, this is Olivia, whose judgement is clearly in doubt.'

Left outside the flat and ignored, Jon was quite happy with all this nonsense which was typical of the Abbotts' sense of humour. Sybil reappeared, and grinning said, 'Oh, you're still here, well well.' Then she gave Jon a hug, saying, 'We're so happy you're back safely, Jon,' and in a whisper said, 'She's lovely, isn't she?'

'Come in, have a seat. What would you two like now? Dry sherry?' Eric asked. 'You must be tired after your journey, perhaps you'd like to freshen up, then we could organise a takeaway if you'd like. Olivia, our spare bedroom is free if you wish.'

Glancing at Jon, who gave an imperceptible nod, she said, 'Thank you that would be lovely.' Olivia complimented Sybil, saying, 'I hear that you're the lady who frightened off the intruder, believed to be Mr O'Flynn, I've been looking forward to meeting you.'

'Oh, that was nothing, Olivia, you'd have done the same, but as Jon had told me and Eric about a difficult man in the firm, I guessed who he was, and as Jon's proxy I hit him all the harder. Three cheers for stale bread, eh?'

Jon interrupted the ensuing laughter, looking serious. 'Sybil, did you actually phone the police?'

'No, because although I was sure that he was that O'Flynn, I didn't know exactly which police office to phone, and I was more worried about

Eric who'd heard the racket and was desperately trying to struggle down to help me. Bless him. Looking back now I suppose I could have asked the police to look out for a man with a bleeding nose, a patch of oil on his trousers, and maybe a broken arm.'

Ever the practical man, Jon said, 'But if you didn't, and nobody else has, that means the police don't know that O'Flynn's on the loose, if indeed it was O'Flynn. May I use your phone? This could be serious.'

'Go ahead, it's over there.'

He dialled Alice. Engaged. He tried the Catchmores. Also engaged. Back to Alice, it rang. 'Come on, come on, Alice, answer the phone!'

At last! She did. 'Good evening, Alice MacInnes here.'

'Alice, it's Jon.'

'Oh, how nice to hear from you, are you well …'

'Sorry to interrupt, Alice, this is important. Has anyone told the police that O'Flynn's been trying to get to my flat?'

'Sorry, Jon, I don't know.'

'It's got to be Sussex Police, but who's the officer dealing with the case?'

'Sorry again, ask Mrs Catchmore. Will we see you …'

He cut her off mid-sentence, and dialled the Catchmores at home. It rang. The Guv answered. 'Catchmore speaking.'

'Guv, it's Jon Webb. Sorry to be abrupt, but has anyone told the police that we think that O'Flynn's been to my flat, because they may want to know that.'

Quick off the mark, the Guv was heard to say, 'Millie, did you tell the police about O'Flynn going to Jon's flat?' There were background murmurs that Jon couldn't hear, then, 'No, she didn't, Jon. Good grief, we'll do so right now when you're off the phone. Good to hear your voice, see you soon.'

Jon sat down heavily in his chair, not realising that he'd stood for the phone calls causing concern among the others, who'd remained silent throughout. 'Christ!' he exploded. 'Look, everyone, sorry to spoil the evening, but I think we have a serious situation. Nobody's told the police about O'Flynn coming here, and there's no doubt in my mind that he's now a danger to me and a threat to any of my colleagues. We know he's hacked into TLC's emails, so he may know I'm back, and what's worse, he may have seen Olivia with me, and if so, I think she may also be in danger. If he's associated with criminals because of those bloody stun guns, we can't guess who his friends are.'

'Olivia, if it's okay with Eric and Sybil, please stay here tonight and tomorrow, and don't leave the house alone. I'll bring your bags up, and if you want to have a prowl round my flat use Sybil's key, but don't go in there alone, and don't answer the phone, or answer the front door. Please.'

'Aren't you being melodramatic, Jon?' Olivia challenged.

'No, and you've never seen me so worried. I don't care if people do think I'm panicking, but I've read enough in books, and seen enough in films, to know about hostage taking or threats to loved ones to make me take this situation seriously.'

'I agree with you, Jon,' Eric advised. 'Ladies,' he began, 'I think that we should take him seriously. Olivia, you are welcome and, I believe, safer here. Please accept our hospitality, and perhaps you could entertain us by telling us of your exploits with Jon, if you'll permit my sense of humour using "exploits".' So saying, he took the pressure off the tension in the room.

Olivia had obviously fallen for her hosts. 'Yes, I think you're wise, Jon, and I'd like to stay and I've seen you in enough unusual situations to rely on your common sense, which I won't argue with now. I've referred time and again to your business trip as an adventure, a sequence of events each leading unexpectedly to the next. Nothing could have been predicted, and if some author had written it all down as a novel in a book, the reviewers would have rejected it as implausible.'

'You flatter me, Olivia,' was Jon's response to those compliments, 'and I'm going down to my flat now to see if there's email traffic I haven't seen, and I'll bring your bags up, Olivia'

After ten minutes, he reappeared with Olivia's bags, clutching a printout. 'Here is a most pleasant emailed invitation for us all to a garden party. 'All of us?' queried Sybil.

'Yes,' Jon confirmed. 'Listen. I'll read it. It's from Mr David Phillips, a TLC director.'

TO Jon Webb
CC Henry and Millicent Catchmore, Alan and Jocelyn Bryant, Roger and Pamela Martin, Alice MacInnes

SUBJECT social event
ATTACHED travel directions

Jon, I have learnt from Mr Turbeville-Blyth at the embassy in Zed that you very sensibly recognised the help given to you by the Ambassador and his staff during your work there, by entertaining them all to dinner just before you left. He remarked upon a thoroughly pleasant evening, and rather mischievously or perhaps tongue-in-cheek looks forward to another similar event.

I recognise your contribution to the company's improved position, as do my Board colleagues, but without demeaning what you have done, we also appreciate the voluntary support and encouragement you have received from others who have no obligation to TLC or reward from it. In recognition of them the least that we can do is to offer them some modest hospitality, during which we will create the chance to meet and thank them.

Accordingly we have arranged a garden party at my residence the day after tomorrow starting at 3pm. The weather is, I'm told, but I don't promise, set fair. My grandchildren will have been here earlier, therefore the

*swimming pool will be heated if you wish to use it. Dress is
informal.*

*We most cordially invite Mr and Mrs Abbott, and Ms
Olivia de St Croix to join TLC staff, and will be pleased to
learn from you that they are coming.*

*Best wishes
David Phillips*

'I'll have to make sure that the Bryants, Alice,
and Roger and Pam have received this, but do I
accept this invitation on your behalf?' asked Jon.
There was a group murmur of assent and
pleasure. Eric said, 'That's thoughtful, Jon, he
sounds to be a good man. We look forward to
meeting him.'

Jon explained, 'There's been a great deal going
on in the company, much of which is due to him.
We don't have enough time now to explain
because it's a long, long, tale. I can tell you this,
though, I haven't enjoyed any previous business
efforts as much as this, and neither has Olivia,
have you?'

She made them all laugh by revealing, 'No, I
certainly haven't, but working with Jon hasn't
been entirely business, if you get my meaning!'

By degrees, the four of them began to relax. A
takeaway Chinese meal was ordered, delivered,
and enjoyed. Anecdotes from Olivia and Jon's
experiences began to emerge, and for the
remainder of the evening any concerns about
rampaging madmen were put aside.

Finally and with regret, Jon announced, 'If you'll all forgive me I really have to hit the sack. Thanks again, Eric and Sybil, and I'll see you tomorrow. Night, Olivia.'

'Just a minute,' said Sybil, 'are you two, er, that is, are you two, um, as they say, "an item"?'

For his answer, Jon took Olivia's hands in his, helping her to stand and unashamedly embraced and kissed her. 'I think so, don't you Olivia?' With her usual mischief she grinned and said, 'It's a possibility.'

CHAPTER TWENTY

The following day was a maelstrom of activity for them all. Jon was woken at seven by his mobile, showing 'number withheld' so he didn't answer it. Possibly O'Flynn trying to find him. Sybil knocked, offering breakfast at eight, and announcing that the ladies planned to go shopping for garden-party clothes – whatever that meant, thought Jon. He replied that he was going to deal with such outstanding matters as his late father's estate, his satellite phone bill, his bank account, utility bills, and other post and emails.

It later transpired that Olivia, taking him at him word, had visited Jon's flat when he went to his bank. As instructed by Jon she'd gone in there with Sybil, to whom Olivia said, 'I was impressed by its tidiness, quite unlike my previous partner's flat, and in a motherly sort of way, I'm proud of him. I could live with this man.' Sybil showed her typically mischievous expression and warned Olivia, 'really? shall I tell him?'

Finally, the end of the day arrived, at which point both she and Jon went contentedly for their separate nights' sleep, after realising how long it took to properly recover from all of their previous exertions and stress, and how important it was to 'recharge their batteries' for the next day's event. They each became aware that their relationship was building in a comfortable way to suit them both. The only black cloud over them was the unstable and threatening O'Flynn, which prevented complete relaxation, leaving Jon constantly on edge.

***

The afternoon of the garden party was warm, glorious and a sunny a blue sky. Just right for a swim, if you felt like it. Sybil drove them to the Phillips' home, where David and Rose, his wife, made them welcome. The pool was part of the back garden of the Phillips' house, behind a tall mature yew hedge acting as a wind break and to keep traffic sounds away. An attractive archway in the hedge led to a landscaped area surrounding the pool, decorated by stone flower containers and for evening events, cleverly sited lighting above and in the pool.

As other guests arrived, people were introduced and mingled, glasses were raised in mutual toasts and clinked, and good-natured threats of dunking in the pool were made. For Jon, Alice, the Phillips, and the Bryants, the highlight of the event would be the arrival of Henry Catchmore and Roger Martin, whose doctors had advised that the relaxation of the party would be good for them, although driving and returns to work were out of the question.

Their wives having at last driven them to the party, they were welcomed by applause, with Henry making a particular point of individual greetings to everyone in turn, but to the assembled guests he then announced to unanimous boos, 'If you don't enjoy yourselves, I shall make a speech.'

The Phillips' offspring served the simple but good food and wine, but nobody drank too much, nor was anyone interested in doing so, just for the first time in many weeks relaxing in sun loungers, or drifting from one group to another and enjoying the company of newcomers.

Sybil, Eric and Jon were chatting with Olivia who said 'The sun's rather bright. Sybil, I've left my sunglasses in your car, could I have the key, please?'

'Of course' Sybil said, fishing in her bag and giving them to Olivia, who went off through the arch in the hedge back to the front of the house.

Within minutes the gathering heard a desperate scream, '*Jon, Jon, help, please!*'

'What the hell? Where's Olivia?' he demanded of anyone. 'What's going on?'

As if for an answer, O'Flynn appeared from the front garden with his left arm round the neck of the desperately struggling Olivia as he half dragged her along, waving a closed shotgun unsteadily in his right hand, which was half supported by a surgical sling.

He was shouting, 'Stay where you are, you lot. Think you can get the better of me do you, Webb, you bastard? Do what I tell you, or she gets it, understand? Now, where's Catchmore?' From the other end of the pool surround Henry Catchmore shouted, 'Don't be stupid, Frank, put the gun down!'

O'Flynn screamed, 'Where's my fucking money, Catchmore? Get it, get it, now!'

Olivia was kicking, scratching and struggling against this demented man, and Jon was beside himself with desperate rage. He ran round the pool towards O'Flynn, who with an injured arm couldn't get a proper grip on the gun but, still not releasing Olivia, he aimlessly let fly both barrels at Jon but missed and partly hit Henry who fell. Jon completely lost his sense of reason, charging at O'Flynn who threw Olivia away from him and clumsily reloaded. As the gun swung towards him and without a second's delay, Jon dived as deep as possible into the water making a large splash as O'Flynn came to the edge of the pool firing both barrels towards Jon under the water.

Looking up through the distortion of the water above him, and just seeing O'Flynn fumbling to reload yet again, Jon placed his feet firmly on the bottom of the pool and with all his strength pushed upwards through the water, breaking the surface and quickly grabbing the ends of the barrels before the gun closed, pulling O'Flynn down towards the water. But he lost his grip as O'Flynn's feet slipped on the wet edge of the pool, falling back heavily, striking his head on a stone flower container, and immediately stopped moving.

Jon stayed standing in the water, looking aghast at O'Flynn, horrified at what he'd just done. There was a stunned silence. The only movement was a slowly spreading pool of blood emerging from the back of O'Flynn's head where it lay against the flower container.

For a few moments nobody spoke, then David Phillips called from the house where he'd gone for more ice, 'Is Henry okay?' Lying on the paving, Henry was clutching his right leg which had been hit. His wife gently rolled up his trousers to reveal a pattern of wounds, doing her best to reassure her husband that he was still alive. In a degree of his usual humour, he retorted, 'Of course I'm bloody okay.'

Rose called from the house reporting that she'd phoned for an ambulance and the police, then hurried to help Olivia, who'd crumpled on the ground. Her dress was torn, her new shoes badly scuffed, and she was shaking in shock and distress. People were evidently too stunned to talk again after an event beyond their experience. Someone asked, 'How did O'Flynn know we were here?'

Alice guessed and said, 'Because he'd hacked in to our emails and read Mr Phillips' invitation to us, and couldn't resist the opportunity of us all being together as targets.'

Jon climbed out of the water and uninhibitedly embraced a trembling Olivia, who protested, 'You're all wet, Jon!' In the relieved tension of the moment, Jon said, laughing, 'Of course I'm bloody wet! I've been in the effing pool, didn't you notice?'

'Sorry, Jon. I want to get out of this dress which O'Flynn was pulling and I won't wear it again, and I'm going to ask the Phillips if I can have a bath after that man's been touching me. He's ruined my shoes by dragging me about.' Rose Phillips overheard, and offered a change of clothes to Olivia and to Jon, who was about her husband's size. Jon was extremely glad that he'd left his sports jacket with his wallet in Sybil's car. David Phillips found some old sacking and covered O'Flynn's body with it, saying, 'He doesn't deserve anything better.' Then, to the remainder of the party, 'Would anyone like another drink?'

Jon sank into a sun lounger, answering Phillips' question, 'Yes, please David, may I have a brandy?' As it was given to Jon, his hand was shaking, and in a faltering voice he asked, 'Was that manslaughter? It wasn't premeditated, despite us cursing O'Flynn and at times wishing him dead. I just tried to get the gun away from him. Where is it?'

'At the bottom of the pool, Jon, we'll leave it there until the police tell us what to do. You're not to worry, Jon, it was self-defence, it was an accident. We all saw what happened. You're not to worry.'

***

The guests were impressed by the quick response of the police to Rose Phillips' phone call. A police Sergeant and a PC arrived, wasted no time in pleasantries, and took one look at O'Flynn. The Sergeant instructed, 'Ladies and gentlemen, will you all please remain where you are.' Jon reassured him, 'Don't worry, Sergeant, but if you'll excuse me, I'm just going to the pool changing room over there.'

When the ambulance arrived the medics also took one look at O'Flynn, said nothing, and dropped the sacking to cover him. They went to Henry Catchmore and decided to take him to hospital for X-rays to ensure that no pellets were deeply buried in his leg. His wife insisted on going with him, and both were warned by the Sergeant that their statements would be required later. Another vehicle was ordered to remove O'Flynn's remains.

Answering the Sergeant's questions, both Bryant and Phillips gave identical reports of events, which were written down by the Constable and corroborated by all of the other guests. The Sergeant was more interested in what Jon had to say.

'Would you tell me in your own words what happened please, sir?'

'My friend Olivia, who's just gone off to change and recover from shock, went to get her sunglasses from a car out at the front of the house. The next we heard was her screaming for help as O'Flynn – that's him lying over there – dragged her back here by her neck, as she kicked and scratched at him. He was holding that shotgun which is now at the bottom of the pool, as you can see. It was closed, so I presumed it was loaded but O'Flynn was waving it about dangerously. He was shouting, "Stay where you are, you lot. Think you can get the better of me,

Webb, you bastard? Do what I tell you, or she gets it, understand?"'

'He then shouted, "Now, where's Catchmore?" From the other end of the pool, Mr Catchmore shouted, "Don't be stupid Frank, put the gun down!"'

'O'Flynn screamed, "Where's my fucking money, Catchmore? Get it, get it, now!" Olivia was kicking, and struggling, and O'Flynn saw me trying to rush round the pool from the other side of the deep end towards him. He was waving the gun around because his right arm was injured and he couldn't hold it steady. He let fly both barrels towards me, but missed and hit Henry who fell.'

'I lost my self-control completely, and ran at O'Flynn who had kicked Olivia away and was reloading. He raised the gun to point at me, but just in time I dived into the pool as O'Flynn fired both barrels again at me while I was under water. I looked up through the distortion of the water above, saw O'Flynn trying to reload but I grabbed the gun, and pulled him towards the pool. As his feet got to the wet edge of the pool he fell back heavily and stopped moving. I didn't know why he did, because all I could see was the soles of his shoes.'

'Why did you go into the water, Mr Webb?'

'It was all instinctive, Sergeant, the splash hopefully confused the man, but I knew I'd be safer under water at point-blank range.'

'How do you mean?'

'Shotgun pellets vary in size and aren't very heavy, so I assumed that they don't travel far under water. Anyway, I don't think any of them hit me, so I'm okay apart from bumping my shoulder on the bottom of the pool'

'Why did you try to pull him towards the pool?'

'Oh, for heaven's sake, Sergeant, it's bloody obvious isn't it? Self-defence!' He was frustrated by the policeman's apparent lack of common sense. 'Now, if you'll excuse me, I want to go and see my friend.'

'Sorry, sir,' began the Sergeant, 'but I have to ask you to come with me to the station where we can take your statement formally,'

'Whatever for, Sergeant?' Jon protested. 'I've just told you what happened and everyone else has said much the same. I don't understand. Look here, there's been an accident, just an accident, so what the hell's the point of going over everything again?' Then in alarm and very much shaken he realised, 'I get it now, you don't believe me and are now suggesting that I killed the man deliberately. Am I right?'

'Sir, this may have been an accident as you said, but because a death has resulted the circumstances must be investigated. I understand from you that you grabbed the deceased's gun to pull it from him in an effort to prevent its use. Is that correct?'

'You know it is.'

'Mr Webb, I do not know if it is correct, I am asking you. Please appreciate that a person is deceased and that as you were the last person in effect to have contact with him the circumstances must be established.'

Jon was horrified. 'Christ! Are you are saying that someone may want to claim that his death was intentional?

'Yes, sir.'

Jon shuddered as he brought to mind the possibility of hundreds, or thousands, of accused innocent people who with their last breath before execution had insisted again, and again, "I didn't do it!" He changed his approach to the Sergeant. 'Sorry, Sergeant, I didn't understand your reasoning, but I do now. What can I do to help?'

'Just leave your friends here, please, and come with me in the car to the station. You are technically under arrest. Gather your personal effects because you'll be away for an hour or more, although we will bring you back here.'

A very dazed and anxious Jon found Olivia watching. He kissed her wet hair and asked, 'Feeling better?'

'Yes, Jon. Rose has been really kind and thoughtful. I've had a quick bath and washed my hair and am beginning to feel myself again. We're going to go clothes shopping together sometime. What about you?'

'I have to go in the police car to the nick to answer all manner of questions and make a formal statement, and anything else they think of. I'll be away for at least an hour. I'm a bit shaken to be honest. I had a shower in the pool's changing room, and David's lent me these clothes. The other guests are all recovering from shock, which I think is reasonable, but David wants to talk privately to you and me.'

'What about?

'I've no idea, but this party can't end abruptly because you'll all want to talk about what has happened and if you stay until I come back I'm sure to bring news that I'm "off the hook" so I'll just say bye for now, and see you later.'

He collected his coat from Sybil's car and left with the Sergeant, who had given his instructions to the Constable, who had already told the guests not to touch anything, and indeed asked them to move away from the area of the accident. He advised that he would stay until the sergeant's return, but yes, he would like a cup of tea, thank you.

***

A subdued Jon eventually reappeared through the arch in the yew hedge, to be greeted by embarrassing applause from the remaining guests, Eric and Sybil having already left. The PC then left to take the car which brought Jon.

David Phillips was the first to speak. 'Could you use a drink, Jon?'

'Yes, please. It wasn't the Sergeant who brought me back, so I didn't invite him in. I had to repeat and sign a statement, give my fingerprints, and agree to surrender my passport tomorrow. They had to adopt the full procedure as if I was a murder suspect, but from the way they were speaking to me, I think that they agreed upon an accident. Perhaps that's a sneaky

way to lull a guilty person to be off his guard.
Clever. There may be an inquest, I suppose. I
must say to you all that I believe that Sussex
Police couldn't be faulted in the manner in which
they dealt with me and this situation.' Then, with
a rueful smile, Jon added, 'Some other officers
pricked up their ears at O'Flynn's name as the
deceased person, but the Inspector interviewing
me didn't react.

'Now, if you don't mind, I'd rather change the
subject, and talk about work, if that's okay with
you all?'

The Bryants, the Martins, and Alice all looked
washed out by events. None of them spoke of the
demise of O'Flynn, but Phillips referred to it
obliquely by announcing a de-briefing meeting
as soon as possible. Alan Bryant slapped Jon on
his shoulder offering, 'well done, Jon! causing an
'ouch, bloody hell, Mr Bryant!'

The party gradually broke up as guests left in
sombre mood, but as he watched them go Jon
wondered how each of them was pondering the
benefit of the absence of O'Flynn. David Phillips
invited Olivia and Jon to join him and Rose in
the last of the evening sunlight on his terrace,
and they finished off the remainder of a couple
of opened bottles. He began his approach to his
subject.

'Jon, I haven't heard half of the stories of your
adventures thanks to events today, but I do know
that you two have been working together, having
teamed up spontaneously when Jon got to Zed. I
don't know which of you played the major part

in the success of your work, but it appears, Olivia, that you simply dropped into whatever was your adopted role regardless of any reward, which I find amazing.'

Neither of you will know that I am chairman of a modest group of companies, which albeit successful, suffers from internal politics and challenges. There is an atmosphere of distrust between companies in the group and I don't know why, but there's a rot which has to be excised. You two have worked well and successfully together, and give the appearance that you could do that again. Would you like to consider taking on the task of resolving this problem for me?'

The four of them were sitting along one side of an old wooden garden table that Jon thought could have witnessed all manner of events in the pool and around it, just as they were now, marvelling at the sunset beyond the distant South Downs and gradually recovering from the afternoon's events. The last thing that Jon wanted was to become involved with trouble, with a capital T.

He moved around the table to take a chair opposite Phillips.

'David,' he began, 'forgive my candour, but today of all days is not the time for me to make impulsive decisions.'

'Of course not!' Phillips protested, with some irritation. 'I only asked if you'd *consider* the task, I didn't ask if you'd do it. Come on!'

'Yes, sorry, but I'm not quite myself this evening, which isn't unreasonable. Okay, I'll start again. Thanks for the suggestion, and what do you think, Olivia?'

'It's a compliment in its way, Jon, so thank you, David, despite many questions. Are these companies only in the UK, and how do you know of this distrust? What's been done to resolve it already, may I ask?'

'Fair questions, Olivia, and yes they're all UK based. I first sensed an "atmosphere" between two of their CEOs in a meeting I had with them to resolve a distribution issue. Each blamed the other for difficult relationships with a shared transport company, which offers lower prices on a shared-load basis than it would to either firm for part loads. 'I've been itching to step in and "bang heads together", so to speak, but I don't want to get involved with details of operational issues. The situation within the group only manifested itself earlier this year, and by the time it became apparent, Jon had started to make an impact within TLC and I decided to wait to see if an outsider could solve the problem. Now is the time to see.'

Olivia spoke again. 'It could be interesting, David, but I may have to finish my secondment in Africa, and I work for a bank which has the habit of whisking staff off to its US office for short periods of work there. I couldn't commit myself to anything of a long term nature, but I'm not rejecting your enquiry out of hand today.'

Jon's face was a picture of dismay after that US job prediction. He had already guessed that at some time Olivia may go there for a spell, but now she'd made it sound imminent. 'Are you serious?' he asked quietly. 'When do you expect to leave the UK?'

'I don't know for certain, probably not for another three months, could be six. It's normal in international companies. Shifting staff around gives them more experience, and added value to the firm. It wouldn't be for long.'

She smiled at Jon, and said, 'Trusting in your sense of humour, it's partly your fault for having me tag along in your successful business venture. I have to report my activities here regularly to the bank and it thinks I should get a lot of credit for the result.'

Jon protested emphatically. 'What do you mean "tag along"? You do get credit, and anyway, we were a team, weren't we? Still could be.'

The conversation stopped while Olivia, Phillips, his wife, and even Jon, pondered upon his remark as they wondered if the two were an 'item'. Did 'still could be' mean as in work? Or in life, as partners?

After a few moments Jon broke the silence. 'Nothing can be decided today or even tomorrow, or next week. I also have unfinished business in Zed, and work in TLC that I'd started before I left for Zed. I want to suggest at the debriefing meeting some changes now that it's known that TLC has better business prospects, and I want to be involved with them if the Board agrees.'

Phillips raised an eyebrow. 'What changes, Jon? Sorry to interrupt.'

'Well, the whole fabric of the company needs a makeover, David, to say nothing of the building's appearance. We should implement all that, then re-launch the firm, with at the very least a web site. All that's for tomorrow, because at this moment I would very much like to take a short break, say a long week-end away, especially if Olivia would care to share it with me.'

She looked deliberately doubtful, trying hard not to grin. 'Was that a hint, or a question, or a suggestion, or an invitation? Whichever it was, it wasn't very romantic, if you had romance in mind. Did you?'

Jon uttered a blatant lie. 'Certainly not! It's just an opportunity to talk about David's suggestion. Purely business, that's all.'

'If you think I'm going away with you only to talk shop, forget it! But I would go if I choose where we'd go.'

'Agreed.'

'It's Rye, in Sussex. I've never been there, and there was a photo of Mermaid Street on my parents' lounge wall, and I'd like to stay at the Mermaid Inn. It's very old and friends tell me it's good. So we'll go there. Agreed?'

David Phillips took Jon and Olivia back to Eastbourne, dropping them off outside Jon's flat. Stepping out of the car, he offered the car keys to

Jon, saying, 'Here, use my car for the duration. Phone me when you return from your break, and enjoy yourselves. Don't hurry back.' He shook hands with Jon, and kissed Olivia's cheek. Watching all this with a smile was Rose Phillips, who'd followed in her own car to take her husband home.

***

Jon couldn't have been more grateful for the use of Phillips' car, which he couldn't have driven himself away from the party after at least two brandies and wine in him. He resolved that to have his own was now urgent. Favouring a Land Rover, he checked that he still had the contact number he'd been given by the man at that bus stop, and planned to phone it later.

Back in his flat, he realised that after his recent overseas work he was short of decent clothes for a few days presumably, so was Olivia, who'd gone upstairs to recover hers from the Abbotts' flat. He went up to check, to be greeted by Sybil.

'Hi, Jon,' she said, 'I must say that was an eventful afternoon, wasn't it? I can't say that we enjoyed it all, but at least that man O'Flynn got his comeuppance, didn't he? Eric and I liked the TLC people. What's happening now?'

Jon asked, 'has Olivia told you that we're off to Rye? She's wanted to visit there for years, and there's a lot to see and do in the town and round about. I came up to see if she needs to go shopping, because I'm going to and maybe she wants some things.' Olivia heard that, and appearing from the spare bedroom had a suggestion.

'Jon, I didn't have much to eat today, and at the end didn't have an appetite anyway. Why don't we take the Abbotts out for a late dinner now and in the morning kit ourselves out on the way to Rye? I can get everything that I need at the Sovereign Harbour shops that Sybil told me about, and it's on our way. Well?'

***

None of the four of them had much of an appetite and settled for 'pensioners portions' at a carvery, although they did manage to work their way unashamedly through two bottles of wine. The conversation swung from topic to topic in the middle of which Jon googled the Mermaid and phoned for a room reservation to get the last one on offer for their. welcome break

The following morning was a busy time, and a little difficult when coping with sore heads, and Jon whingeing that his own head was clear because he hadn't drunk much because he had to drive today. "The poor dear!" the unsympathetic women had said last evening as they took more wine for themselves.Over breakfast up at the Abbotts, Sybil had been watching Jon and finally asked, 'Are you okay, Jon, you're looking glum, when you should be happy. What's the matter?'

'You're right, and I feel gloomy because I foresee reality setting in. Consider all that's happened this year. The discovery of TLC's poor finances, then my naively taking the Board by storm, a new order with cash coming in, the so-called exploding conveyer belt, a venture into the unknown in Zed, involvement with an embassy, the distraction of O'Flynn behind everything, the assault on Roger, doing business with the Stones, tussles with Mr Gavuzzi et al., O'Flynn's death, and above all meeting Olivia.'

'You should be pleased!'

'I know, I know, and I am. But before long Olivia expects to go Stateside for a spell, and I have to admit before you all that that is a looming shadow. Call me a romantic if you wish, but after the adventures of the year there's coming towards me a crashing anti-climax.'

Olivia gave nothing of her own feelings away, but tried to brighten him up. 'Jon, if or when I do go, I'd be back soon.'

'Yes, but "soon" is a relative term, and can mean minutes, days, or months.'

She tried again, and from her expression it seemed to Jon that she shared his feelings, and he hoped so. 'Jon, the adventure isn't over. Look at what you've started, yet to be finished. You'll be popping back and forth to Zed, there's your flat move to cope with, there's more business in the UK to find, there's David's problems, and there's the TLC makeover that David liked the sound of. Maybe I can help. Postpone it till I come back!'

That did the trick. Olivia helping in TLC! Doing what, where or how didn't matter a damn. The prospect of working with her was the proverbial ray of sunshine.

'Right. Okay. I agree. Come on, Olivia, let's get up and go off to Rye! Thanks for breakfast, Sybil and Eric, we'll see you late on Monday.' Then as an afterthought, he said, 'Oh, bugger! I'm supposed to be at that debriefing meeting whenever it is!'

'Eric, do me a favour please, phone the office and tell whoever answers that I'm off for a few days and that I'll be back sometime next week. Perhaps!'